D1246936

## BY KIERSTEN WHITE

**The Paranormalcy Series**

*Paranormalcy*
*Supernaturally*
*Endlessly*

**The Mind Games Series**

*Mind Games*
*Perfect Lies*

*The Chaos of Stars*
*Illusions of Fate*

**The And I Darken Trilogy**

*And I Darken*
*Now I Rise*
*Bright We Burn*

*The Dark Descent of Elizabeth Frankenstein*

**The Slayer Series**

*Slayer*
*Chosen*

**The Camelot Rising Trilogy**

*The Guinevere Deception*
*The Camelot Betrayal*
*The Excalibur Curse*

*Beanstalker and Other Hilarious Scarytales*

**The Sinister Summer Series**

*Wretched Waterpark*
*Vampiric Vacation*
*Camp Creepy*
*Menacing Manor*

*Star Wars: Padawan*
*Hide*
*Mister Magic*

# MISTER MAGIC

# MISTER MAGIC

A NOVEL

KIERSTEN WHITE

NEW YORK

*Mister Magic* is a work of fiction. Names, places, and incidents either are products of the author's imagination or are used fictitiously. Any resemblance to actual events, locales, or persons, living or dead, is entirely coincidental.



Published in the United States by Del Rey, an imprint of Random House, a division of Penguin Random House LLC, New York.

Del Rey and the Circle colophon are registered trademarks of Penguin Random House LLC.

Hardback ISBN 978-0-593-35926-6
Ebook ISBN 978-0-593-35927-3

Printed in Canada on acid-free paper

randomhousebooks.com

2 4 6 8 9 7 5 3 1

FIRST EDITION

*Book design by Simon M. Sullivan*

To everyone who comes to me with hungry eyes
and furtive desperation, whispering,
"What's it like after you leave?"

# MISTER MAGIC

Your favorite childhood television program feels like a fever dream.

You don't remember it at all until I start humming the theme song and then—oh, I can see it in your eyes. That wash of images, ideas, feelings.

Because that's what you remember. Not the title of the show. (Was it *Mister Magic*? *The Magic Show*? *Magic Time*? Everyone will tell you something slightly different.) Not any of the plots or individual episodes. Not even the names of the six children who were as real to you as your own friends.

You only remember how it made you *feel*.

The excitement when those kids stood in a circle in that featureless black room, said the magic words, and then threw that ephemeral cape up into the air. The terrible, delicious tension as you watched it drift down, impossibly slow. Waiting. Hoping. Always with the strangest undercurrent of fear that maybe *this* time it would fall straight to the floor, nothing special or wonderful revealed, the magic lost. And then a release of breath and clapping as the cape elegantly defines the sudden figure of Mister Magic himself.

He's an impression more than he's a man. Top hat, looming presence. The black background coming to life with just a splash of red on the underside of his cape.

What did Mister Magic look like? He was tall and enormous. He was slight and lithe. He didn't have arms or legs. He was all arms and legs. He was a person. He was a puppet. One thing everyone agrees on is that we never saw his face. But don't you remember—you saw it once, didn't you?

*Did* you?

The one exception to our failing memories of the show: the theme song. You still know it all these years later.

Go on. It's right there. I'll start.

*Take my hand*
*Stand on your mark*
*Make a circle*
*In the dark*
*Close your eyes*
*And wish with me*
*Keep them closed*
*And now we see*
*Magic Man!*
*Magic Man!*
*Magic Man!*
*He's here for me!*

Doesn't it feel good to sing it, to have the magic back for a moment? The magic that was always there for you, that always worked.

Until the day it didn't.

Across the internet, you can find people who swear—and this isn't possible, because the show wasn't broadcast live—that they saw it. *Saw* the episode the cape fell and hit nothing. And then saw little Kitty, the smallest of the circle of friends, scream. (You didn't remember it was called the circle of friends until you read it just now, and it feels like a puzzle piece settling into place, doesn't it? That circle, those friends, *your* friends.)

Some swear they saw Mister Magic disappear on the spot. Some swear they saw the sets crumble to the ground. Some swear they saw the whole place catch on fire. (The fire took place later, after the show ended.)

Obviously, none of the people posting their vivid memories actually watched anything violent on their screens, but their spongy kid minds filled in that gaping darkness, that absence where Mister Magic had been. Where the magic, at last, failed.

But that's the thing about childhood memories. We can't trust them. And, in the case of *Mister Magic,* we can't verify them, either. Try to look up any version of the title on YouTube. It's not there. You can't find copies, bootleg or otherwise, anywhere. So, you remember the show, but you *don't.*

Absent recordings, or scripts, or literally any ephemera from when it aired, I've got the next best thing:

The circle of friends.

Back together, at last. Thirty years after tragedy shut down production and they were flung out of their loving magic circle and into the real world—whatever that meant for them.

Some were easy to find, excited to reminisce and reconnect. And some were deliberately impossible to track down. But I have a little magic up my sleeve.

It's the television reunion you didn't know you needed. And, now that you're humming that song, trying to figure out if you ever *did* see Mister Magic's face, thinking about how those kids felt like your best friends—now that you're remembering—you've never needed something quite this much, have you?

Me neither.

And so, dear friends, at long last . . . it's Magic Time.

# ONE

The thing is, the doors were open that morning.

Val knows—she knows, she *knows*—that waking up to find both doors of their sagging cabin opened wide to the world is probably only because Dad wasn't sleeping well, and that she should tie a bell to his foot before bed tonight. Just in case.

But.

*An open door is an invitation,* she whispers to herself. And she keeps the doors to their cabin firmly closed all the time. She'll have one of the ranch hands rig up some sort of lock system, up high, where Dad won't be able to reach it.

That'll fix it. She can stop worrying.

She doesn't, though. She worries through the morning riding lessons, worries through lunch with the camp full of awkwardly pubescing little delights, worries through the early-afternoon group activities, more riding, cleanup. All her favorite things—especially the cleanup, knowing parents are paying a small fortune so their daughters can spend the week doing the chores Val hates most—are eaten up by the worry.

By late afternoon she's mostly shaken it off, though. Sometimes an open door is just an open door. It doesn't have to mean anything.

One of the girls, Lola, freckled and sunburned and wonderful, raises her hand. "Miss Val?"

"You know where the bathroom is," Val answers. "You don't have to ask when you need to go." It's almost time for pickup, which means she needs to get Poppy from the goat pen. The other five dusty and happy and tired campers are here with Val, finishing up in the stables.

"No!" Lola giggles shyly. "It's not that. Do you have any kids?"

An image flashes in Val's mind. A girl, even younger than these, her brown hair forever fighting to escape messy pigtails, with eyes so blue they break her heart. Val smiles. "Not yet, but I know there's one in my future."

"How?" another camper, Hannah, asks, wrinkling her nose beneath smudged glasses. Val resists the impulse to clean them for her. Independence is part of what her camps promise, even if it means dirty glasses. Val's been running the summer programs for Gloria's Ranch since she was twenty, and they're the absolute highlight of her whole year.

Val shrugs. "I've always known."

"But aren't you getting too old?"

Val lifts an eyebrow. Lola scowls and elbows Hannah, but Val shakes her head. "No, it's okay to ask questions. Questions are how we get to know the world. And the answer is, I'm not too old. Not yet."

Her heart ticks like a clock, but she still has time. Val's belief in her blue-eyed girl is as solid as her belief in gravity. The when and the how are questions she doesn't let herself ask. It's easy not to ask questions. Take the question, put it behind a door. Close the door. Leave nothing open. She is aware of the hypocrisy of always encouraging her students to ask questions when she denies herself the same freedom, but there's a whole door in her head just for the cognitive dissonance of *Do what I say, not what I do*.

"Do you have a boyfriend?" Lola blurts out, and suddenly this interrogation makes sense. Lola's father finds excuses to linger at every drop-off and pickup.

"Only when I want to," Val answers. "Sometimes I have a girlfriend." Though *boyfriend* and *girlfriend* are generous terms for the relationships she allows herself to have.

Still, her answer has the desired effect of rapidly changing the subject as all the girls' eyes go wide. Val can see the follow-up questions bubbling, but they don't have time. She has to get to Poppy before—

"Damn it," Val whispers under her breath. Poppy's mother has already pulled up in a Mercedes SUV that has about as much functionality as the designer boots she sent Poppy in for the first day. And Poppy's still in the goat pen instead of the stables.

Val claps her hands. "Okay! Last one out of their barn clothes has to muck out Stormy's stall tomorrow!"

The girls shriek and dart away to remove the coveralls and boots Val gives them to protect the too-cute clothes their parents always have them wear. Val cuts across the dusty path to intercept Poppy's mom before Poppy hears what's about to happen.

"Hi," Val says. She can't recall the woman's name. She never can with other adults. It's hard to care.

The sunglasses come up, pushed onto carefully styled hair. "What's Poppy doing in the goat pen?"

"She's working with our baby goats, Luke and Leia, training them to—"

"I'm paying you for riding lessons!"

Parents always trot that out as leverage, but technically she isn't paying Val at all. Val doesn't get paid. She smiles politely. "You're paying for a week of day camp at Gloria's Ranch, which includes experiences with a variety of animals. And *can* include riding lessons, if the girls want that, which Poppy does not."

"It's not up to her! I want her to learn how to ride!"

Val resists the urge to smack the sunglasses off the woman's head. "Poppy is spending a week outside building confidence with friends and animals. Do you want me to force her into a saddle and watch her have a panic attack? Because that's not safe for Poppy or the horse."

"But I'm *paying*—"

"No." Val cuts her off. "Look at your daughter. Right now."

Poppy's perched on top of a bale of hay, expression intense with concentration as she balances next to a tiny baby goat. She gives a command, then jumps off and turns around expectantly. The goat follows. Poppy whoops in delighted triumph.

"But—" the mom says, her anger deflated in the face of Poppy's elation.

"She's afraid of horses. It's a perfectly rational fear. Horses are terrifying creatures. Barrel chests and pin legs and have you *seen* their teeth?"

The woman raises a perfect eyebrow. "It sounds like you're scared of them."

"Oh, absolutely I am. I ignore it because I have to. But there's no reason for Poppy to overcome this particular fear. No one *needs* to ride horses. She's a remarkable little girl, and when she grows into a remarkable adult, she'll remember how her mother listened to her and helped her find other things she was good at."

The woman sighs out the last of her anger. "She does look happy."

"And filthy." Val wrinkles her nose. She's not even pleased that she convinced this woman she was right. It was always going to go this way. When Val sets her mind to something, it happens.

The woman laughs, fully won over. "And filthy."

"Poppy! Into the barn!" Val points and Poppy hops across the pen like a little goat herself.

"I really wanted to buy her cute riding clothes," her mother says, wistful.

Sometimes Val forgets that adults are just children with both more and less autonomy. She smiles slyly and nudges the woman with her shoulder. "You know, we have riding classes for adults, too, and *you'd* look fabulous in a new riding outfit."

Val's rewarded with another laugh and a thoughtful glance toward the stables. The woman's already picking out which horse is prettiest, probably imagining owning one herself. Good for business if she stables it here.

*What would we do without you, Val?* Gloria asks in her mind, and Val thinks back what she always does: *You'll never have to find out.*

It tastes bitter today.

Putting her feelings aside, Val oversees pickup. She's careful to keep her distance from Lola's dad, who had definitely prepped his daughter to ask about Val's relationship status. She never dates people where attachments will form, which makes anyone with children off-limits. Val remembers every child she's taught over the last eighteen years; she knows *she'll* be the one to get attached. Fortunately, Poppy's mom monopolizes her time and Lola's dad leaves, disappointed, with the rest of the kids and parents.

Val does one last check of the stables, making sure the gates are latched and everything is put away. "Until tomorrow, you enormous nightmare beasts," she says, saluting the horses and flipping off Stormy for good measure. Near as she can tell from the ranch hands, every stable has a Stormy—a surprising number of which are also named Stormy. But knowing that Stormy isn't an anomaly doesn't make her like the rotten mare any more.

The goats are in great shape, thanks to Poppy, so Val sets off across the field, past the big house toward the cabin she shares with her dad, same as when they came here thirty years ago.

Thirty years. *That's* it. That's what's nagging at her, setting her off since this morning. It's August 1, which marks thirty years since they arrived at the ranch and never left again. She undoes her thick, dark braid where it coils down her back. It feels heavier than normal.

She'll take a long shower—assuming the water heater is working. It's almost as old as she is, but she works every day, so why can't it? Then she'll read to Dad and get him to bed, then find one of the hands to come help figure out a new lock system.

The sun's low and blinding behind the cabin, so she doesn't notice until she's nearly there that the front door is gaping open.

Val doesn't want to go in. Can't go in. The open door is a vulgar invitation. Whatever's waiting is as bad as anything—almost anything—that's come before. It takes all her tremendous will to put one foot in front of the other. She can't tell herself it's just an open door. She knows better.

Open doors swallow you whole.

She stops on the weathered front porch step, the silence inside the dim interior overwhelming. Words like an icy breath on the back of her neck come to her.

*And when you're in trouble and need a friend's hand, just reach out and whisper, you know that you can . . .*

It's like finding the deepest, darkest hole, and sticking her arm in. Knowing something will take her hand. Knowing it's been waiting for her to reach out and ask all this time. Knowing full well that when she does, she can't control what answers on the other side.

Val puts one trembling hand through the doorway into the beyond. "Please," she whispers. "Please." It's as close to praying as she's ever come. She holds her hand still and waits, but nothing takes it. Nothing answers her plea.

She steps inside and none of it mattered, anyway. It never mattered. The open doors were a warning, but she was wrong about the message. Nothing had gotten in. Something had gotten *out*. Escaped, and left her alone.

Dad's dead.

Subject: Reunion??

Hi, guys.

Yes, it's really me, and yes, it's really legitimate. We're going to have a reunion in honor of the thirtieth anniversary of the end of the show. I've vetted the podcast. I think they'll do a good job honoring the show's legacy.

The easiest thing would be to fly into the Salt Lake City airport and then take a commuter flight down to Saint George, rent a car, and drive from there. I'd pick you up but my schedule is a constant disaster. Who knew having six kids would be busy? Lol

But if you coordinate your travel schedules, you could drive in together. More efficient and cheaper. Don't worry about the cost, though. The podcast's sponsors will reimburse you. Within reason, obviously. I'm attaching directions to the house. I know it's late notice, but I think it's important. A lot of people never got closure. Including us. Especially us.

I hope you'll come. I really have missed my friends.

Yours,
Jenny

# TWO

"I still remember the first night he showed up, carrying you." Gloria stares out the window over the sink. Her hands are sunk into soapy water, but she's not really washing anything. The day outside is brilliantly sunny, a riot of green and gold life, not at all funereal. Gloria's eyes are misty behind blue-framed glasses, carefully matched to the blue eyeliner that, like her hairstyle, she committed to in the 1980s and never abandoned.

Ostensibly Gloria was taking care of all the arrangements, but that really just meant she directed while Val did all the work. That's how it's always been between them, and preparing the big house for mourners is no different.

Val doesn't mind. She doesn't know what she'd do without a task, without work. She doesn't know how to feel this . . . whatever *this* is. Is it grief? It vibrates closer to anger. If she were one of her campers, she'd tell herself to take her time, that she's allowed to feel how she feels. But she doesn't know how she feels, or even how she wants to feel.

Dad's dead, and she has no idea what that means for her. What it changes, if anything. He's been gone a lot longer than he's been dead. It felt so strange, seeing him lying there, peaceful. In nice clothes, and without his omnipresent work gloves. She never saw him without gloves on. His hands were so small without them, so frail. Puckered and pocked and terrible to look at. She wishes she hadn't seen them.

*Wait.* "Carrying me?" Val came here when she was eight. Why was he carrying her?

"We all worried about you, you know," Gloria says, lost in the memory. She pulls a glass from the soapy water as if puzzled by what it was doing in there. "You didn't speak, not a word. Not for that entire first year. I'd find you sometimes, standing in the middle of a field, eyes squeezed shut, left hand clutched in a fist with your right hand over it like you were holding it closed. Always that same pose. I wondered if you were maybe, well. You know." Gloria taps the side of her head like it explains the rest, leaving a cluster of soap bubbles on her temple.

"Dad never talked about—" Well, anything. What did they talk about, back when he could still talk? The day's tasks. A notable detail from whatever nonfiction he was reading. Nothing that mattered, nothing that had any real emotion attached to it. There were the rules, and the rules were unassailable. He only got mad at her when she tried to break them, like when she'd sneak here to watch television with Gloria's older children. *It's dangerous,* he'd shout, marching her back to their lifeless cabin.

Dad considered a lot of things dangerous, though. School. Friends. Doctors. Val rubs her wrist where there's an extra bump in the bone from a bad break at twelve that Dad set himself. She tugs the sleeves of her borrowed black dress lower, to cover the bump and the scars. People will be arriving soon, and she doesn't want questions. Guess she still has a lot in common with Dad that way.

Today at the cemetery was the first time she'd been off the ranch so far this year. Sometimes she forgets that the rest of the world is out there, big and bright and noisy. Dad made the ranch their whole life, and it really isn't a bad life, but.

But.

Dad's gone and it's not *their* life anymore. It's just hers. How does she feel? A ghost of the resolve she felt on her thirtieth birthday drifts past her. She was going to leave, and then Dad had his stroke. No doctors. Only her. And so she stayed, and she's still here, and the version of herself determined to set out is as dead as Dad is.

"We'll need more than that." Gloria is eyeing the stack of plates Val put on the counter.

"Why?" The graveside service was small, just Gloria and a couple of her children who could make it, plus three of the ranch hands that like Val. They didn't really know Dad, since he couldn't get around well the last few years. But they were there for her, which she appreciates.

Gloria dries her hands and reaches into the cupboard for more dishes, handing them to Val. "I put the reception details on my Facebook."

Plates shatter on the floor. Val stares down past her empty hands at the broken pieces. "What?"

Gloria delicately steps around the ceramic shards and takes Val's hands in her own, their calluses a matching set. Her voice is gentle, the same way she talks to Stormy when the horse is worked up over nothing. "He's at rest. Safe, now. No one is going to come for him."

Gloria pats her cheek and then goes to the closet for the broom. Gloria is old-school Idaho with a healthy distrust of the government, letting Val drive as soon as she could reach the pedals, never caring about licenses or employee taxes or anything official. That disdain for paperwork extended to the man who worked for her as a teen, then showed up a decade later with an eight-year-old. As far as Val could tell, Gloria didn't bat an eye about taking them on, didn't question why he couldn't be legally employed, or why he wouldn't enroll his daughter in school, or why they stayed put and stayed hidden. She probably assumed that he had done something illegal, which, in her opinion, wasn't the same thing as *wrong*. After losing a beloved brother to AIDS, Gloria stopped listening to other people's definitions of good and bad, trusting her own judgment that told her Val's dad was a good man.

But the thing Gloria doesn't get, the thing she's never thought to ask—

*Were they hiding for his sake, or for Val's?*

A fear coils in Val, locked behind the oldest, thickest door. It whispers that *she's* the reason they've been hiding for thirty years. Not her dad.

*What did you do?* her mind shouts, but it's not her voice that yells it. She doesn't know whose voice it is, but she knows whatever she did, it was bad.

*She's* bad.

Dad knew what she did. And he watched her so carefully, and he kept her here. *Safe,* he'd say at the end of the day. *Safe,* instead of good night, or I love you. She never knew if he meant they were safe, or the rest of the world was.

She asked, once. About where they came from. About whether she had a mother, more family.

He had looked so terrified that his fear had claimed her, too.

"Gone," he had whispered. "Don't ask again."

Val was afraid, so she never did. And as the years passed, the fear didn't fade but she grew into it. Grew around it. Grew stubborn and strong-willed, ignoring the shape of the fear at the core of her. And even though she wanted to know, *needed* to know, how her mother died, she wasn't going to ask. Not ever.

Now Dad's gone, too. It's a door she can't open again, and she has regrets. So many of them.

No matter. She takes the outstretched broom from Gloria and sweeps up the remains of the plates, then finishes preparing trays of food and pitchers of drink. What a funny custom, when someone dies, to feed other people. To nourish and comfort them when she's the one whose entire world is in a cemetery twenty minutes away.

Gloria was right about the plates, though. More people show up than Val had expected. So many of her summer camp and riding students, some still children, some fully grown adults, which makes her feel dizzy and vaguely panicked. If they're that old, how old is she? But it's lovely to see them, lovely to have this reminder that their summers together meant something to her students, too.

Local ranch hands from the last three decades appear as well, hats in hand, wearing their nicest jeans and cleanest boots to pay respects to her dad. They seem to have known a different man than she did. One who was friendly and funny. One they cared about, one they speak about with fond gratitude.

And now she knows, at last, that the feeling threatening to drag her breathless to the floor is sadness. Her father should have had this while he was alive. Friendship. Companionship. A sense of his place in the world.

Val should have had it, too. Gloria's shiny, slippery floral couches are full in the living room, the den is packed with milling people, the heirloom Turkish rug in the dining room shuffled over with dozens of pairs of feet. The big house is an old design, eschewing modern openness for modular separation. Traveling from one space to the next feels like a shock every time.

She'll have so much cleaning to do after, but it's worth it to see this evidence that Dad existed. That he mattered to more people than just her. And seeing so many of her past students gives her hope that maybe she matters, too.

It also eases her worry. No police have come knocking, no SWAT teams descending on the ranch with a decades-old warrant for her arrest. So far the only bad thing to come of Gloria breaking the rules and posting Dad's name on her Facebook is that Lola and her hopeful father are here.

Val sees Lola's father searching in the entrance to the dining room, so she ducks through the kitchen and back hallway, checking that the guest bathroom is still in good shape before returning to the main entry. Maybe she'll escape upstairs for a bit.

The front door is hanging wide open, though. Scowling to ignore the spike of fear it triggers, Val closes it. She's definitely going upstairs. At least until Lola and her father leave. She doesn't trust herself to be kind right now. *Smile, be sweet! To all that you meet! A girl who is good, does just as she should!* Val rolls her eyes at the old rhyme that always pops into her head in situations like that. Watching Gloria run her own ranch taught Val that she never had to defer to men or apologize for her existence.

Still, that rhyme lingers. Val doesn't owe anyone a smile. Not ever, but especially not today.

She turns and nearly bumps into someone. He's white, lanky or gawky depending on the generosity of the viewer, but Val tends to be generous with people. They're all interesting in their own ways. He has a beard in place of a jawline, thick and dark like his hair, and his rectangular glasses disorientingly magnify his hazel eyes. Their gazes meet.

Something claws free in her chest, a burrowing creature bursting to the surface.

He drops his glass with a thud, spilling water on both their shoes. He doesn't even look down. His eyes are a spotlight, pinning her in place. She knows him. How does she know him?

"Valentine," he says, so softly it sounds like a secret.

It takes her a moment to realize why it's so shocking: No one here knows her as Valentine. On the ranch, everyone assumed Val was short for Valerie, and Dad encouraged it.

So that means—

She remembers, now, that year she spent not talking. She had been *terrified*. So terrified she couldn't think, couldn't see, couldn't speak. She can't say what she was afraid of, but the fear—the fear, she remembers. That fear is back, a fist in her throat.

Once again, she can't speak, can't do anything but be pinned in place by those eyes.

She's too shocked to move as his fingers slip between hers. It feels like climbing into bed at the end of the longest day.

"I can't believe I finally found you," he says, and before she can catch her breath to ask how he knows her—how she knows him—he bursts into tears.

OMG did anyone else see there's a new podcast on Mister Magic? The first episode is up and there's going to be an actual reunion with the last cast!

@imreadyru Dude I haven't thought about that show in ages!! I used to hurry home from kindergarten every day so I wouldn't miss it! I'd always steal my dad's reading glasses and pretend to be what's-his-face! He was my favorite friend.

@imreadyru Link?

@imreadyru Really, all that's going on in the world right now and you're posting about a reunion of a children's show no one remembers

@imreadyru @chk234523 if no one remembers it then how do you know it was a children's show, lighten up

@imreadyru Do they say which cast members they have?? Wasn't Ronald Reagan on it???

@imreadyru @homeboy562 pretty sure Ronald Reagan is dead so I doubt he's going to pop up on a podcast, though the Reagans were into seances so who can say

# BUCKLE MY SHOE

"Oh my god." A new man takes in the entryway scene. Val's still holding hands with the stranger. She feels as though she's been caught doing something shameful. This new man has jet-black hair streaked with elegant silver at both temples, and his suit fits like it was made for him. His shoes are burnished to a shine that makes Gloria's carefully polished floors look dingy.

"Isaac, what did you do?" he asks.

*Isaac.* The name slots into a space in Val she didn't realize was empty. Isaac. The man with the glasses, holding her hand and crying.

Isaac releases her. But he's laughing as he wipes under his eyes. She has the oddest impulse to take his hand again, a spike of panic that she's lost something precious. "Sorry. Sorry, just—it's been so long, you know?"

Val doesn't know. She looks to the other man for help.

He raises an eyebrow. He's got dark-brown eyes, olive skin, and a smile that looks as expensive as his suit. He'd be at home on one of Gloria's soap operas that Val sometimes catches glimpses of.

Apparently, her confusion is obvious. His voice is soft, almost hurt, as he says, "You don't recognize me, do you?" He puts a hand over his heart like he's been shot, but then his tone becomes smooth and playful once more. "Well, I'd never forget you, Valentina. All that hair."

Val pulls her thick braid, thinking. "Valentina," she repeats, and then she laughs despite her confusion. There's a hint of a memory there, how pretty she felt to hear her name said that way. Who *are* these men?

"Miss Val?" Lola says from the doorway to the kitchen.

Val jerks to attention. Right. The funeral. "Lola, I need your help. Get all the camp kids and assign them tasks. Someone to gather empty plates and glasses. Someone to wash the dirty dishes. Someone to dry. And someone to transfer food from the kitchen to the dining room when the trays are low."

Lola's posture shifts from tentative to confident. "I won't let you down."

"I know you won't." Val gives her a smile, then points the men toward the front door. She knows exactly what Dad would tell her. What he told her over and over to do if anyone ever showed up looking for them. But he's gone, and she thought all her answers were gone with him. "You two, outside, now. I want explanations."

The handsome man laughs. "Bossy as ever, I see."

"There's a difference between—" Val starts, but Isaac finishes.

"—being bossy and being in charge, and you're in charge." He smiles at her, showing small teeth that are crooked in a friendly way. If the other man's smile is dazzling, Isaac's is welcoming.

"Javi?" Isaac shifts aside for the other man, gesturing for him to go first.

Javi opens the door and they follow him out. Isaac's wearing a button-up shirt tucked into slacks. The shirt and slacks are wrinkled, but he smells like a bar of soap, and Val prefers it to the sting of cologne left in Javi's wake. Neither of them appears to be a cop or PI. No cop could afford Javi's suit, and she doubts an investigator would burst into tears upon finding her. Besides, they don't just know who she is. They know *her.*

Val leads them around the corner of the wraparound porch to

the side of the house against the laundry room. The last thing she wants is Lola's dad peering out a window and deciding to join them. There's a swing here that she and Dad installed a few years ago. Javi perches on its edge and Isaac hovers, watching to see what she does. She leans against the white porch rail and folds her arms. Isaac sits next to Javi, jolting them so Javi is forced to sit back. It's mildly humorous, watching the two adult men accidentally swinging, unsure what to do with their legs and feet. Some of the tension loosens in Val's chest.

She holds up her fingers. "One: How do you know me? Two: Why are you here?"

Isaac's face falls, but Javi's offended. "How do *we* know *you*? You don't know us?"

Val shakes her head, but her eyes drift to Isaac. It's not quite honest, saying she doesn't know them. She knows Isaac, but in the same way she knows how to breathe. She just does, until she thinks about it, and then she can't remember how to do it normally anymore. If she accepts that Isaac simply is and always has been, it feels right. But trying to figure out how she knows him makes panic flare, like missing a stair in the dark.

A closed door. Nothing gets in, nothing gets out. Val takes a deep breath. She knows how to breathe. She's being silly. "I—"

"Oh my god, there she is!" A Black man throws his arms wide and embraces Val. She freezes. She's been hugged a lot today, more than she's used to, but at least everyone who hugged her was someone she could name. This man, a head taller and far broader than she is, envelops her in a familiar way that makes her certain they've hugged before.

She'd remember him if she knew him from her life here. He's strikingly handsome, with beautiful dark-brown eyes, a shaved head, and a beard much more carefully shaped than Isaac's.

"Marcus." Isaac stands, sending the swing careening.

"Are you coming to the reunion? Tell me you're coming. I couldn't believe it when Isaac told us he'd found you." At last Marcus releases her and holds her at arm's length. Something in her face clues him in and he winces. Everything exuberant retreats and his features soften. "God, right. I'm so sorry for your loss. Of course you aren't thinking about the reunion right now. I'm just so happy to see you. And it sucks that it's under these circumstances." He gestures weakly at the house behind them.

"She doesn't remember us." Javi's smile is wry, but there's a bitter undercurrent to his voice, like a mouthful of grapefruit.

"What?" Marcus's hands drop from her shoulders as though burned. "I'm—what?" She had thought the transition from exuberant to gentle had been drastic, but now his face shifts again and he's—god, he's sad, she's hurt him, this man she doesn't even know. It makes her stomach ache, seeing that hurt on his face, knowing she's hurt him again.

Again. How had she done it *again*? What was the first time?

None of this answers any of her questions. Except . . . Marcus asked about a reunion. They have her mixed up with someone. She's disappointed when she should be relieved. They really *don't* know her, but she wishes they did. "I never went to school, so, no reunion invites."

"For the show," Javi says flatly, eyes narrowed.

"The show?"

"You know, with—" Marcus cuts himself off, then changes tactics. "The children's program?" he prods, watching her carefully. "The television show we were all on together as kids?"

"What the actual fuck?" Laughter bubbles free from the torn-up landscape of Val's chest. She giggles, and then, somehow, she's crying. For the first time in years, actually. She can't remember the last time she cried, the last time she let herself just—

*Feel.*

Dad's dead, and she's still here, and these men, these three bright, interesting people, know her and she doesn't. Doesn't know them, and is suddenly sure that she doesn't know herself, either. Unless they're lying, unless this is some sort of terrible prank, unless—

Marcus pulls her close again and she rests her head against his shoulder. His hands on her back are huge and comforting and she knows *this* hug. She knows Marcus, and Javi, and Isaac, and they know her, and she doesn't understand how but whoever they are, they aren't liars. Which means there really are answers now, impossibly, after thirty years.

She takes a deep, shuddering breath and wipes her eyes. A jaunty tune plays in her head. *Smile! You're okay. Smile! That's the way.* Her mouth responds to the instructions. "I'm good. Now: Tell me about this show and how we all know each other. I really don't remember anything."

"How far back are we talking?" Javi asks.

Val reaches in her mind, but immediately recoils. It's like sticking her hand through the darkness of her front door the day Dad died. If there ever were any childhood memories, there's nothing she can get to now. She shut all those doors so tightly, they might as well never have existed.

She shrugs, ignoring how upsetting this is. That fucking *smile* tune keeps repeating in her head. "I don't remember anything before coming here."

"When was that?" Isaac studies her with those spotlight eyes, like he's afraid to look away. What does he think will happen if he does?

"When I was eight."

"That's when you left us," Javi says. "You've been here the whole time?" He glances around and she's suddenly glad he can't see the dilapidated, slumping cabin she shared with Dad. The way none of the cupboard doors sit at right angles. The way they have to go to the back porch to access the bathroom addition. The way she spent more time sleeping in a nest of blankets in her closet than in her own creaky twin bed, because the bed always felt too exposed. Too lonely.

She's thirty-eight years old, and this is all she has to show for her life: a funeral in a borrowed house, in a borrowed dress. A borrowed life. "The whole time, yeah."

Marcus rubs the back of his neck and looks over the way they came, like maybe he wants to leave and pretend none of this ever happened. Is he embarrassed for her?

Is she embarrassed for herself?

"Our timing couldn't have been worse." Javi flashes her that expensive smile. "Let's trade numbers and we'll talk when things have settled for you. Besides," he says, pulling out a sleek phone, "we need to get going if we want to be there on time after this detour."

Isaac runs his fingers through his hair. It falls nearly to his shoulders, shiny and brown and poorly trimmed, like he never meant to grow it that long, he just couldn't manage to get it cut. He doesn't take his gaze away from Val.

"Yeah," Marcus agrees. "We didn't think this through. We were all just so excited when Isaac found the post about your dad and we realized we could see you." His beautiful eyes are warm and sympathetic. "I'm sorry. Go back in. There will be time to talk after."

"After what?" Val's desperate to keep them here. She might not be able to pry open all the doors to her past that she's closed, but maybe they can. Borrowed memories to match her borrowed life. "You have to leave right now? For this reunion?"

"Don't worry about that," Marcus says. "No one expected you to come, because—well, no one knew where you were. Besides, it's sort of an oral history or podcast or whatever." He waves a hand dismissively, showing a ring-free finger with a telltale indent from a recently removed band. There's a story there, and Val wants it. She wants all their stories. She wants her own stories. "So if you don't remember anything, there's not really a reason for you to go." He cringes. "Besides to reconnect, of course! Which we will. When it's a better time."

Isaac's posture is tense, every line of his body rigid as though he's holding himself back from something. From leaving? From talking? From taking her hand again?

"We were really on a kids' show together?" She can't believe it. Watching television was absolutely off-limits. Dad never let her.

She glances back at the front of the porch. It leads to one of the only safe doors. Val sighs. She can't leave her father's funeral, and she can't ask them to stay. "Promise you'll call me. I don't have a phone, but I'll give you Gloria's number."

"Of course! We—" Marcus starts, but Isaac interrupts him.

"Does your mom know yet?"

"What?" Val turns to him sharply.

"That your dad died."

"My mom—" Val tugs her sleeves lower over the burn scars on her arms, wishing she could cover her hands, too. "My mom's dead."

Isaac frowns, confused, then his eyes widen and he glances at the others for a moment as though searching for reinforcements. "Who told you that?"

"My dad." But . . . *Gone,* he'd said. Gone was not the same as dead. Her heart beats faster.

Isaac offers her the truth gently, like placing a can of tuna near a feral cat. "I saw her a couple years ago. She actually lives close to where we're headed. I can get her address and phone number for you."

Dad lied.

Dad lied without lying, let her believe a lie for all this time. He knew—he *had* to have known—that she was convinced she'd somehow killed her mother. And he'd let her believe it, so she'd stay.

"I'm coming." Val declares it without thought, seized with a sudden fear that as soon as they go, they'll take her past and future with them. Her mom—her mom, god, she still has a *mom*?—will be gone once again. She'll walk back into that funeral, alone with people who didn't know her father, because no one actually did. With people who don't know her, because she doesn't know herself.

"What? Really?" Marcus asks.

"Sorry, I mean, can I come? I need to see her. And I don't want—" She pauses, taking in these men, this unexpected lifeline. Maybe when she reached into the darkness and asked—maybe this was what she was asking for, even if she didn't know it.

"I don't want to be here anymore," she says. She hadn't been sure before, but now she knows. She stayed here out of loyalty to her father and love for her camps and Gloria, true, but more than anything she had stayed out of fear for what would find her if she ever dared leave, convinced that she had somehow killed her mother. A woman still alive and well. And her father had known.

But Marcus's expression makes it clear what a big, weird ask this is. She didn't remember any of them, and now she's inviting herself along on their road trip. She flashes another tight smile. "Actually, sorry, you guys don't have to take me. Just give me her address."

She'll take one of the old trucks. She doesn't have a license, but Gloria won't care.

"You're part of the circle," Isaac says. "There's always a spot for you." He offers her the smallest hint of a smile. Her eyes glance off it like it's a blade she'll cut herself open on.

Isn't that what she wants, though? To be cut open so she can autopsy her past?

"But your father's funeral." Marcus gestures helplessly.

She can't believe her father let her live in a lie all these years. It makes her feel actively insane, like her brain is simultaneously fighting over whether to hold on to the foundation of her entire life or to reject it entirely.

Dad was never cruel. But he was also never warm. He couldn't quite look at her, his eyes always glancing off, just like hers had from Isaac's smile.

What did he see in her that was too painful to look at?

She needs to see her mother, to have undeniable proof that her dad lied to her. Or proof that she's falling for the strangest con ever. But, like Gloria, Val trusts her sense of people. None of these men are lying to her. Why would they?

Val tries to give Marcus an ironic grin but can't manage it. Her tone comes out as grim as she feels. "My dad's dead. My mom's not, apparently. That's got to take priority."

"Val wants to come," Javi says to Marcus. "And we all know that when Val makes up her mind about something, it's going to happen."

Marcus laughs, the sound a bright lure hooking Val through the chest. She wants to laugh with him. With all of them. She wishes she were going to the reunion. It sounds easier than what she's doing.

"Do you need help packing?" Isaac asks.

At least that's one kindness Dad left her. "Nope." She leads them off the porch to the line of trucks behind the house. On the end is a rusted hunk of junk that, for all appearances, will never run again. She wrenches the door open and reaches behind the cracked and flaking seat for her duffel bag. They have go bags stashed in several places on the property.

Not *they*. There is no more *they*, only Val.

She takes the cash from Dad's, then leaves his bag, ignoring the curious looks from her three new old friends. The lane where all the visitors' cars are lined up glistens like a chrome river, offering a current to lead her away from here at last.

"I feel weirdly compelled to warn you about stranger danger," Marcus says. "I'm such a dad, but . . . you're getting into a car with us to go to an unknown location. Without telling anyone where you'll be. And you don't actually remember any of us."

"I don't remember you," Val agrees, walking between Isaac and Javi, Marcus on Javi's other side. They fell into this order automatically, but Val has the strangest sensation it's slightly wrong. Like there are pieces missing. She's not supposed to be next to Javi.

"I don't remember you," she repeats. "But I *know* you, and Isaac knows where my mom is. That's enough for me, today. Besides, I've spent the last thirty years hauling bales, fixing fences, wrestling goats, and wrangling horses. I could kick any of your asses."

Javi laughs. "You always could."

"And on the way, you can tell me what I forgot?" She's hoping they'll play along and help her pretend this is normal.

"Where to start!" Marcus is still smiling, but his eyes are distant. Javi puts a hand on his shoulder, and at the same moment Val's fingers brush Isaac's. It feels like velvet darkness. The safety of being unseen and unseeing.

Isaac unlocks a silver sedan. "Are you sure you want to come?" he whispers, so softly Val thinks he's talking to himself for a moment. For once, he's not looking at her, but down the road. He shifts closer to her, and his movements contradict his words: fingers brushing hers, grasping, while his words push her back toward the house. "Your dad must have had his reasons for what he did, for what he told you about your mom. And you didn't ask for us to find you."

She did ask for that, though, in a way she can't explain. She's not sure she wants to go with them, but she is sure she *needs* to.

Besides, Isaac's right. Dad brought her here for a reason. It's time to find out what that reason was.

# Mister Magic

From Wikipedia, the free encyclopedia

*This article is about the children's television series. For other uses, see Mister Magic (disambiguation).*

This article is missing information about the studio that produced *Mister Magic,* the distributor, and the networks that broadcast it. Please expand the article to include this information.

This article does not cite enough sources. Please help improve this article by adding citations to reliable sources. Unsourced material may be challenged and removed. (January 2013) (Learn how and when to remove this template message)

*Mister Magic* was a serialized radio drama that transitioned into a children's television program with the advent of home television availability in the late 1930s. The show ran from the 1940s until 1991, which, combined with the unknown length of the radio drama—rumored to be one of the first such programs of its kind—makes it the longest continuous running broadcast in history. [citation needed]

After fifty years on television, production unceremoniously halted due to an on-set accident.

**Contents** [show]

## Show Description

*Mister Magic* centered around six children and their friend, Mister Magic, who could be called into existence whenever they needed help. No scripts or recordings of the show can be found, but recollections revolve around the children playing imaginative games and learning lessons from Mister Magic in the form of catchy rhymes. [citation needed]

*When we care about others*
*We share what we've got*
*But if you don't work for it*
*Nothing is your lot*

No cast lists exist, but over the decades many prominent figures had their start on the show.

[Section removed by editor for lack of sources. If you believe this was done in error, learn how to report it.]

## Broadcast History

[Section removed by editor for lack of sources. If you believe this was done in error, learn how to report it.]

## Cult Following

In the decades since it ended, *Mister Magic* has developed a strong cult following. [1] Several **Reddit** pages are devoted to the show [2] [3] [4] [5] and its impact, [6] as well as theories about how and why it ended. [7] [8] [9] [10] [11] Fandom is splintered into factions: those that insist Mister Magic was a **puppet**, [12] [13] [14] those that insist he was an actor in costume, [15] [16] and those that think later seasons of *Mister Magic* were the first convincing example of a CGI character. [17] Numerous pages are also devoted to matching adults with the child actors from various generations of the show. [18] [19] [20] [21] [22] [23] [24] [25] [26] The most famous of these is **Ronald Reagan**, who is rumored to have been one of the child voice actors on the radio play. Television and film star **Marcus Reed** was part of the final cast [citation needed] but has never confirmed involvement or spoken about it in interviews.

Several true crime and mystery podcasts have covered the show's abrupt ending, including **Murder, She Podcasted**, [27] **Dingoes Ate Her Baby**, [28] and **Where Are They Now**. [29] A *Mister Magic*–themed podcast, *Magic Time,* released several episodes investigating the history and impact of the show before it was pulled from apps. [citation needed]

A petition on **Change.org** to start a revival of *Mister Magic* currently has 350,000 signatures. [30] Because the rights to the property were held by a defunct production company, no one knows where to send the petition. [31]

Famous fans of the show include actor **Chet Pennington**, [32] **football** player **Tom Brady**, [33] **Supreme Court Justice Brent Harrell**, [34] talk show host **Candy Carlton**, [35] and **Vin Diesel**, who credits the show with his desire to become an actor because "I just wanted to be one of the friends so bad and live in that magic." [36]

According to urban legend, **Diane Sawyer** tried to do an investigative look into the history and mystery of the show, but the network refused to approve the segment. [37]

## References [show]

# THREE

"I have so many more questions than I did before." Val stares down at the cracked screen of Marcus's phone where the Wikipedia entry for the show is still open. Marcus leans between the driver's seat and the passenger's, watching.

"Is this you? Marcus Reed?" Her finger hovers over the link in the article.

Marcus snatches away his phone. "Oh no, don't click that. It's mortifying. Wikipedia always chooses the actual least flattering photos ever taken."

"You're a movie star?" Val can see it. He has such striking features, and there's something about his presence she reacted to immediately. Maybe he has that effect on everyone.

"Absolutely not. I did a few things after our show, child star nonsense. One sitcom in my teens. It was awful; no one watched it."

"I watched it." Javi's forehead is pressed against the glass. He's sitting in the back with her, but he's wearing sunglasses and has been mostly silent.

Marcus's eyes flash to Javi, touched and surprised. When Javi doesn't volunteer anything else, Marcus continues. "Anyway, I left all that behind for the glamorous world of middle management."

"And after the show, you've all kept in touch?" Val can't call it *our* show. Had she really been part of a group of child actors? How could she forget something like that?

Her question hangs in the air with an unexpected weight. At last Isaac clears his throat from the driver's seat. "We all scattered. Not much choice in the matter, since we were kids. You've been on the ranch this whole time? Never lived anywhere else?"

"Nowhere else." Val's gaze skims along the landscape. They've been driving an hour and this is the farthest she's been from the ranch since—when? After puberty her looks changed enough that Dad sometimes let her go out for supply runs with Gloria, but they were few and far between. When she hit her twenties, she did the occasional bar night with ranch hands, finding easy hookups. But after Dad's stroke, she almost never left. Never leaving made staying easier.

"You must be a good rider," Marcus says.

"Mmm. You know those people who are hardwired to love horses from birth? There's nothing they can do about it—it's an absolute need for them to have horses in their lives? Yeah, that's not me. I think they're terrifying."

"Horses, or horse people?" Javi asks.

"Horses. Horse people are lovely."

"Nice life, scared of horses and surrounded by them." Javi pinches the bridge of his nose under his sunglasses and takes several deep breaths. He's definitely carsick. Val wonders why he doesn't ask for the front seat. But Marcus is such a big guy, he'd be uncomfortable back here. Maybe they worked it out earlier.

"What do you do?" she asks Javi, trying to distract him.

"You know those people who are hardwired to be vicious lawyers from birth? There's nothing they can do about it—it's an absolute need for them to be vicious and lawyers. Yeah, that's me. I think we're terrifying."

"At least you have smaller teeth than horses," Val says, which earns her a laugh.

She looks expectantly in the rearview mirror to see if Isaac will chime in about what he does, but he doesn't volunteer any information.

She catches a glimpse of her own reflection. Dad's eyes were murky blue and round, downturned at the outer corners in a way that always made him look a little sad. Hers are dark brown and almond-shaped. Does she have her mother's eyes? When they meet, will she feel like a part of herself is looking back? What will Val say? What does she want her mother to say? When she tries to imagine that moment, she comes up blank.

"So, the show?" Val needs to keep them talking, make them fill in the silences so she doesn't have to think about what they're driving her toward. An exit sign declares their location to be Pocatello. She wants to say it out loud to play with how it feels, staccato and bouncy on her tongue. So many funny little places in the world, and she's seen so few of them. "How young was I when I was on the show?"

Javi lowers his sunglasses and searches her face. "You really don't remember anything, do you?"

She shakes her head and he lets out a puff of air. "Must be nice."

"Why? Was it bad?"

"No," Isaac says swiftly, signaling to exit the highway. "It wasn't bad. It was—"

"It was amazing, until it wasn't," Marcus says. "And it was hard to leave it so abruptly."

Javi nods grudgingly. "Yeah. Anyway, you were—what, eight?—when it all went down."

Her heart picks up, a warning. She shouldn't have gotten in this car. She was safe without this information. Maybe she should have stayed. Maybe she doesn't want to know what Dad hid her away from all these years. He couldn't look directly at her most days, but he took care of her, didn't he? He taught her to read and write and fix an engine and stitch a wound closed herself.

But he lied, too. She can't trust anything about their life together now.

"And then the show ended." Isaac pulls into a gas station and parks in front of a pump. "It couldn't go on, not after you left."

Val knew it. She did something, and that's why her dad took her and hid. Behind every closed door is an oozing sludge of shame: the knowledge she's always carried that she did something *bad*. She just can't remember what.

But they can.

"What—" She puts a hand against her throat, pushing against her own pulse. Trying to trap it in her fingers so it will slow. "What happened?"

Javi and Marcus burst free from the sedan as though they can't get out fast enough.

Javi strides toward the gas station store. Marcus stretches like it's been longer than an hour in the car, in a way that leaves Val sure he's avoiding her eyes.

Isaac gets out and opens her door. "We were all kids. It's hard to remember specifics, or to talk about it. And Jenny requested we not share information or memories. The podcaster doesn't want us to influence each other."

It's both a letdown and a relief. It's one thing to suspect you've done something unforgivable. It would be another to have it confirmed. But . . . she can't help feeling there's another reason they're avoiding talking about this. It can't just be to protect the purity of the podcast recollections.

"Anyway," Marcus says, a smile punctuating his dismissal of the grim topic. "We had, what, a couple of years together? So you probably started on the show when you were six?" He looks to Isaac for confirmation, but Isaac shrugs noncommittally.

"Hard to say." He stares down at the car keys in his hand like they're heavier than they should be. "Time passed different then."

"It really did." Marcus's gaze takes on that distant quality again. One hand drifts up to his own shoulder, arm crossing over his heart. "Like—like we'd been doing it forever, and would do it forever. Until it all stopped. And now here we are, and I'd say it's like no time has passed but really too much has. I think the reunion will be good for all of us. We can talk about everything that happened." He stares out at the thrumming green of an Idaho summer, and Val can't tell whether he likes what he sees. He refocuses, turning to her and dropping his hand. "You should stop by the reunion, after you see your mom. If you want to. I'm sure once we do our interviews it won't be a problem if we trade memories."

Val imagines their memories like shiny coins. She wants them in her own hands now, but apparently she has to wait. "Is it just the three of you?"

"Jenny helped organize it," Isaac says. "She's already there, with the podcaster."

There's the name Jenny again. It means nothing to Val, but she's worried it will somehow be hurtful if she admits that. "Where's *there*? Is it in Idaho? How much farther?"

Marcus gives her a chiding smile. "Ah, there's that information you should have gotten first and given to someone you trust. We're headed to southern Utah, in the desert where the studio was. We were all waiting for a connecting flight in Salt Lake City when Isaac told us he might have tracked you down. So, we rented a car and raced here."

"And *you* told someone you trust that you were driving into the middle of nowhere, Idaho, to meet a woman you hadn't spoken to in decades?" Val raises an eyebrow, and Marcus laughs, saluting her.

Val isn't the only impulsive one, then. They gave up seats on a plane to drive into Idaho on the hope that they'd find her. It makes her feel less foolish. They had no guarantees, either.

But Marcus is right about one thing. "Can I use a phone?" she asks. Isaac hands his over and she shoots off a quick text to the only phone number she knows, but also, more depressingly, the only person who will miss her. The text to Gloria is both an apology for leaving and a note that she'll be gone for a few days. She feels more than a little guilty about it. Gloria is in mourning, too. But Val knows if she tried to explain what she was doing, she would realize how stupid and absurd it is and talk herself out of it.

This whole trip is a bad idea. But that somehow makes it more appealing. Giving in to impulse instead of grief and anger, like a bar hookup to take the place of actual relationships or connections.

But—shit. "Are you still flying? Are we driving back to the airport?" Val has limited cash and no ID.

Isaac takes his phone back and starts to fill the tank. "No more flights until tomorrow. We'll get there sooner driving."

Standing still makes her too nervous, so she enters the gas station to use the bathroom and buy a bottle of water. The interior is tiny and old but well maintained, a maze of wire racks holding anything one might suddenly need at a pit stop in Pocatello. Javi passes her on his way out, clutching a bag she hopes contains Dramamine.

After agonizing over how much money to spend on snacks, Val takes her selection to the counter. The clerk there is a young person, mid-twenties, with short shaggy hair, enormous eyes, and a name tag that says BRANDON. Brandon barely makes eye contact, silently ringing up Val's purchases.

"Yo, Mack!" a woman shouts from the back storeroom. The change in the clerk is instantaneous, posture straightening and face lighting up. "Found a whole box of Hostess that expired last week! Date night's on me, baby!"

The clerk lets out a tiny, high bubble of laughter, and Val's aware she's witnessed something private and precious. She wishes she could transform someone that completely just by calling their name.

"Anything else?" The clerk gestures to a display of lotto tickets and gum. Big Red was Dad's favorite. He used to pull out a stick and rip it in half. Val would always take it, happy to share something with him, even though she hated the flavor and spat it out as soon as he wasn't looking.

Now she's spitting on him, on the only thing he ever asked of her: to stay safe and hidden. She's still in her funeral dress; that's how long it took her to abandon what he wanted.

This is insane. She'll call Gloria and ask for a ride. Go back to the ranch and the life she knows. Chalk up this detour to grief and work up the courage to just call her mom like a normal person. She doesn't know these men, doesn't remember *Mister Magic* or any of it, and—

"Ready?" Isaac asks. He's watching her, eyes magnified, like he can't see anyone else in the whole world. His hand brushes the small of her back with his long, slender fingers. There's a flutter of something, and this time it's not fear or recognition, it's—

Hope?

She's already been found. There's no going back, not really. She can't live in between anymore, suspecting but not knowing. It's cowardly, and Val isn't a coward. She pays, then spares one last glance at the clerk, now leaning against the counter and looking through an open door at whoever makes her so happy it changes everything.

"Ready," Val answers. She isn't, but she has to be. It's time for change.

To: Jenny.Poplar@zmail.com
From: mci@mci.biz

It was her. She's with us, but she doesn't remember anything. Thought her mom was dead, wants to meet her. Call me?

To: mci@mci.biz
From: Jenny.Poplar@zmail.com

Do not take her to that woman. She'll ruin everything. We don't need to talk. Just make sure Val doesn't disappear on us again. None of this works without her. You know what she cost us, and what's at stake. Get her here and I'll take care of the rest. Don't overthink it. We're almost there.

# FOUR

Javi has a migraine so no one talks much. It feels nice, flying down the highway, watching the landscape change. Maybe they'll just keep driving forever. Val wouldn't mind. It's less terrifying than what they're driving toward.

God, when did she become such a chickenshit? She should be happy to be reunited with her mom. Why would Dad lie to her about her mother, though? Was he the one who did something bad way back then, after all?

But if it was Dad, not Val, why does shame cling to her like burrs? Maybe her shame is a mistake, a lie, a misunderstanding. Maybe a reunion with her mother will at last free Val. She imagines walking up to a door. Knocking. Waiting for it to open.

The thought of a door opening into the unknown makes her feel sick to her stomach. Or maybe Javi's carsickness is contagious. Val swallows hard, trying to shake off the sensation. She'll walk up to a house and her mother will be outside, gardening. She'll look up and they'll have the same eyes and she'll know it's Val without Val having to say anything. And then—

She'll cry? Val will cry? Val doesn't want to cry. Maybe they'll hug. Her mom will explain everything in a way that absolves Dad, in a way that absolves Val, in a way that absolves everyone. Everyone will be innocent, the last thirty years a mistake.

No, that feels even worse. She has to think of some other way this will be okay.

Val runs scenarios in her head like breaking in a horse as they drive through northern Utah. Salt Lake Valley is so flat and brown that the looming mountains feel like gray parentheses containing the harsh sentence of the desert. Gloria visited Salt Lake a few times to shop with her daughters. Val always wanted to go, too, but she couldn't. Both because she couldn't go that far from Dad, and because she wasn't one of Gloria's daughters. Much as they were nice to her, Val wasn't family.

"Val?" Isaac's eyes are on her in the rearview mirror. "Are you okay?"

"I'm fine," she says, because it's what she always says. If she says it firmly enough, she believes it, too. Like *fine* is a blanket she can pull from the ether and wrap around herself.

"How about a dramatic reading?" Marcus offers. "There's a Reddit page where people talk about their moms thirsting over the man in the cape." He waggles his eyebrows lasciviously. Val assumes the man in the cape is the titular character from their show.

Javi lets out a groan of a laugh. "That's so creepy. Please read them all right now."

Marcus clears his throat. "*Was it something about him, my mom mused one night over too much box wine, or was it just because he entertained you kids for a few damn minutes so I could have some time to myself? The way that cape draped, hinting at what might be beneath . . .* "

Javi holds up a hand. "I changed my mind. I don't want to hear this."

"*How,*" Marcus says, shifting his voice to indicate a different writer now, "*can you justify sexualizing a classic children's character?*" His voice changes again. "*Calm down, it's not like she's planning on*—god, I can't read this part aloud, but let's just say it involves a graphic sex act with a resident of the Hundred Acre Wood."

"Tigger. Has to be Tigger." Javi's eyes are still closed, but this conversation has given him life once more.

*"No one actually remembers what Mi—what the man in the cape looked like or who he was, so we're not sexualizing a character, we're sexualizing a memory of a character."* Marcus pauses, scanning. "Someone brings up Bowie in *Labyrinth,* and then someone else chews him out for going off topic and it continues like that. I wonder if there's fanfic of the man in the cape."

Val wants clarification. "What's fanfic? And you're talking about Mister—"

Javi's hand slaps over Val's mouth. His eyes are bloodshot and narrowed as he shakes his head before freeing her. "We don't say that name outside the circle."

"What?" Val's baffled. She glances up front but Isaac is staring at the road and Marcus won't turn to look at her. "Is it like—what's that play that people won't say the name of?"

"*Macbeth,*" Marcus says. "Sort of, I guess. Maybe. I don't know. I thought it was just me, still following the rules."

"I don't say it, either," Isaac offers.

"But why?" Val asks.

"It was your rule." Javi leans back, apparently satisfied she won't try to say it again. "You tell us."

Val resists snapping that she can't tell them because she doesn't remember. And even if she could, it's not like *they're* telling *her* much.

But Marcus is tuned in to her annoyance. There's no venom in his answer. "It was a rule, like those ones you have as a kid that you can't ever get past. Superstition. Don't step on a crack or you'll break your mother's back sort of thing."

"So it's superstition?"

Marcus ignores her question, continuing. "Or sitting too close to the television will make you go blind."

Isaac nods. "Don't eat thirty minutes before swimming."

Javi's tone is moody, his chin tipped up at an odd angle. "We're all still trying to be good and follow the rules."

"*Know the rules, lay them straight.*" Val sings it without really thinking. It's something she tells the girls at every camp.

"*Mistakes and traps will lie in wait,*" Javi continues. "*But you'll skip home without a care, if you keep the rules and always beware.*"

"How do you know that?" Val's shocked. She thought she made it up, or got it from some long-forgotten children's book.

Javi lifts a dark eyebrow at her. "We must have sung it together a hundred times."

Val leans back, her head spinning. "I had no idea it was from something. It was just always in my head." She has a whole mental catalog of those silly rhyming songs. She might not remember anything about the show, but it's still inside her, somewhere. It has been all along, invisible seeds flowering in unexpected ways.

She searches for another one of her rhymey songs. "*Tidy and clean—*"

"*That's the way,*" Marcus continues. "*It'll keep the dark at bay.*"

"That's weird, now that I'm actually thinking about it. What dark are we keeping at bay?"

Javi shrugs. "Bad writing. Most of them are like that, going for an easy rhyme over actually making sense." He holds up his phone and wags it in a tsk-ing motion. "Jenny texted again to make sure we're not talking about the show. She's very insistent."

Val deflates. She doesn't have any memories of her own. She needs theirs. But surely she'll get to listen to their recordings. They'll stay in contact. After all, Isaac and the others went so far out of their way to reconnect with her. Already, she can't imagine going back to a life without them. There's something that feels right about being together. Right, but incomplete. Like there are still pieces missing. She wonders if Jenny is one of those pieces.

Regardless, Val already feels a little better, like whatever she locked away is closer to the surface. Maybe she really will be able to remember things if she tries. Maybe meeting her mother again will be easy and fun. Maybe she'll discover that her father fled with her in the middle of the night thirty years ago, lied about her mother's existence, and hid every moment of every day since for totally normal, easy reasons.

Right.

If they can't talk about the show, they can talk around it. "Why are they doing a reunion podcast?" she asks.

Marcus answers. "I guess it was one of the longest-running programs ever, which makes it important."

"Or just long." Javi scowls. "Having a lengthy history doesn't make something important or inherently valuable." His mood is once again like a storm system pressing down, stopping all conversation.

Val stares out the window as they leave the more inhabited parts of Utah and hit a long stretch of lonely highway. Without people forcing landscaping or agriculture, vegetation is sparse, scrubby green bushes in empty brown hills. When no great options for meals present themselves, they share snacks. Evening purples everything as twilight lingers well past nine. Their only stop is a lonely Chevron in a mountain pass, the wind whipping them so harshly it's impossible to talk once the car doors are open. It's a relief to seal themselves back into the protected quiet of the rental.

Isaac doesn't start the engine immediately. He stares down at his phone, frowning. "Bliss is a ways past our destination."

Val must look as confused as she feels, because Isaac smiles. "Bliss is the name of the town where your mom lives."

"That makes so much more sense than trying to figure out why you were being metaphorical."

Javi laughs. "Bliss exists beyond your destination. Sounds like one of those nonsense inspirational Facebook posts."

"My mom would repost that," Marcus says.

"Can we be dropped off first?" Javi asks Val. "I'm liable to get violently ill if we add any more hours to this obscenely long drive."

They've already gone out of their way for Val. Of course they should get priority. "Yeah, not a problem at all."

She regrets it, though, as they get back on the highway and night finally claims the infinite summer evening. Even if they're close to their first destination and make good time to Bliss after, it's late. Is she really going to surprise her mom in the middle of the night?

Maybe there will be motels in Bliss. Motels that don't ask for ID. She doesn't actually know how motels work, now that she thinks about it. Could she pay cash?

A sign warns them there are no services at this particular exit. Isaac takes it and they leave the highway behind, now on a two-lane road without any markings. The only things to be seen are scrubby bushes, illuminated by their headlights in shockingly quick bursts that startle Val every time, almost like the bushes are racing toward them and not the other way around. The darkness is a tunnel around them that makes it feel like they're the only things left in the whole world. After a long time—too long—something at last changes.

The road turns to dirt.

"This can't be right." Javi leans forward and grips the back of Isaac's chair as Isaac bumps them carefully along.

Marcus holds up his phone, but he has no reception. Grumbling in frustration, he pulls up a screenshot of the directions. "We took the right exit. The directions were clear. There haven't been any turnoffs or other roads or anything."

"But there's nothing out here. This is the middle of nowhere."

Val stares out the window. At the ranch, darkness always felt full. Trees rustling, the soft sounds of animals nearby, the tiny cabin shared with her father. Out here, it feels empty in a way that makes her want to take Javi's hand just so she knows she's not alone. She has the strangest urge to command Isaac to turn around. To take them back to the highway, back to the lights.

Isaac's patient voice is undermined by how tightly he's clutching the steering wheel. "We have plenty of gas. I'm giving it thirty more minutes. If we don't find the house, we'll turn around and find somewhere to stay for the night."

"A house?" Marcus asks, surprised. "I thought we were going where the show was filmed."

"We are." Isaac doesn't elaborate, so Javi nudges the back of his seat.

"It was filmed in a house?"

"Our families had to live somewhere during the show." Isaac shrugs, but it's more like a twitch. "None of you remember the house?"

At least Val isn't alone in that. Javi and Marcus both shake their heads. Then Javi speaks up again. "It's too late for Val to go surprise her mom."

Val hadn't wanted to admit it to herself, but he's right. She's already showing up out of nowhere after thirty years. She shouldn't do it in the middle of the night. Anyone would panic about a knock on the door that late. She doesn't want a spike of anxiety to restart her relationship with her mother.

"Stay with us tonight," Marcus says. "Wherever we end up. And then Isaac can take you in the morning. If that's okay?"

Val assumes Marcus is asking Isaac if it's okay, but they're waiting for her answer. She nods in a rush of relief. Both that she'll have somewhere to stay tonight, and that she gets to delay her meeting with her mom. It'll be better tomorrow, when she's had sleep.

But they're still driving, and there's still nothing out there. Val shifts, staring out the windshield with Javi. Marcus grips the armrest. Isaac leans forward like he's piloting a ship against a hurricane, though the night around them is as still as it is black.

The clock creeps forward with a terrible tension. If they don't find their destination tonight, that's it. Whatever spell got her in this car on this adventure will be broken. The others will realize they've brought a complete stranger along with them and regret their invitation. After all, how can a childhood connect them if her end of that connection is nothing but empty static? She doesn't have enough money for a motel, she doesn't know how to find her mother without Isaac, and she has no way home. Hell, she has no home, not really. Not without Dad.

Part of why she got in this car, what she's been running from, is the realization that she's been *waiting* for Dad to die. It makes her hate herself to acknowledge it, but Dad dying was the finish line. The end of her watch. And she had to decide whether to leave, or to keep staying. To continue on in the life her father gave her.

Running away was easier than making a decision. Though it was a decision in and of itself. She left. She loves Gloria, she loves the ranch, she loves her students. But it's not *her* life. There's nothing for her back there. There *has* to be something in front of them.

There has to be.

The car's tires hum against the dirt road, a constant noise. It's getting louder. Are the tires wearing down, or is the road changing?

Val extends her hand, an unconscious gesture, demanding what she wants: the house. Somewhere she can rest safely against the dark of the night and the dark of her mind. With Isaac, and Javi, and Marcus. Together, so they'll feel bonded to her. So they'll keep helping her. So they won't leave her.

And then, like magic, like holding an image in her head and falling asleep to find it made real in her dreams, a house looms out of the empty blackness.

"What the *fuck*?" Javi whispers.

The motion-triggered camera begins recording first, a few seconds of darkness with only the sound of soft footsteps.

Then light floods the image, whiting it out before the lens adjusts to reveal a woman standing in front of the screen wall.

She's short, with a body that hints it would like to be much rounder and softer were it not wrestled into brutal submission. She wears a flowing black shirt, collared and short-sleeved, with khaki slacks. No jewelry save a wedding ring, a dated solitaire that doesn't shine or sparkle so much as sit on her finger like a forgotten weight. Her hair, bleached blond with a line of brown and gray along the part, is pulled back into a low ponytail, neither luxuriously long nor stylishly short.

Practical. Plain. The only hint of her personality is in her shoes, bold purple flats.

Her gaze is fixed on the wall. She steps closer, cutting part of herself out of the camera frame. Her eyes are exhausted, concealer failing to hide the bags beneath them and the premature lines around them. She lifts a hand and puts it tentatively—even nervously—against the screen. Her eyes track back and forth, searching for something.

When she speaks, it's unclear if she's addressing the camera or the lifeless screen.

"They're almost here. We found her, and we'll fix it, at last."

Whatever her eyes are searching for, they don't find. She closes them, lowering her head so her forehead almost-but-not-quite rests against the screen. Her arms wrap around herself in a hug. "Can I—" Her voice drops to a whispered plea. "Can I see him? Please?"

There's a long pause as though she's listening, but the audio picks up nothing. At last, she takes a step back, eyes still closed. "I know. I know it doesn't work like that. I just—" For an exquisite moment her face is pure emotion, pain and anger and loss, and she's beautiful. And then, just as her hair has been brutally scraped back into a ponytail, her features scrape back into a bland mask of pleasantness. She fixes her posture, straightens her shoulders, smiles. "I have to make sure everything is ready. No one else is going to do it."

She strides from the room without a backward glance. The lights once again cut off seconds before the camera. There's a sound like a sigh in the darkness, and then the feed ends.

# LOCK THE DOOR

Isaac puts the car in park. No one makes a move to exit.

Javi jabs a finger toward the view out the windshield. "Again, I ask: What the fuck?"

The house stands alone in the middle of the night-dark desert.

*Stand* is the correct word. Val wonders if all houses have deep roots, whole sections of their bodies hidden beneath the ground. But this house, this inexplicable house, refused to stay buried and is rearing to its full height, ready to strike.

The exterior confuses the eye. There's a perfectly normal white stucco first story with white shutters and a white front door framed by geometric stained-glass windows. But instead of ending at a second story with a peaked roof, the windows go up and up and up, six stories high, with no variation, as if someone took six ramblers and stacked them one on top of another. A small balcony juts out from each floor, and the railings look like nothing so much as the exposed spine of whatever creature this house is.

"It should look like an apartment building, right? Like, this should make sense. But it looks like—" Marcus stops, unable to finish his sentence.

"It looks like someone put a regular house on a medieval rack and tortured the shit out of it," Javi says.

"Fun-house mirror version of a house," Marcus adds.

Val's never been in a fun house, but nothing about this house feels fun. It feels wrong, *off*. Not just the house itself, which could be chalked up to an epic architectural misjudgment. But also the location: The dirt road ends in a paved driveway, like this is a normal neighborhood. But there's nothing around them for miles. Miles and miles and miles.

Who would build a house like this, and why?

It's the *why* that nags at Val.

She doesn't want to be here. She knows it down to her bones. If her instincts told her she knew these men, she could trust them, those same instincts are telling her this house—apartment building—whatever the hell it is—is not her friend.

It's irrational, but she doesn't care. She left rationality behind when she got into the car. She leans back and folds her arms. "No. We aren't sleeping in that thing."

Marcus seems relieved that she declared it, nodding hurriedly in agreement.

Javi drums his fingers on the back of Isaac's seat, a nervous movement. "Why have a house in the middle of nowhere? It makes no sense. We couldn't have filmed inside. It's not big enough."

Isaac turns around, his eyebrows rising above the frames of his glasses. Val hasn't noticed them before now. They're elegant, dark swoops of emotion. "We didn't film here. This is where our parents lived while we did the show."

Javi laughs dubiously. "There's no way *my* mom, Vivienne Chanel Chase of the New York Chases, lived in that house."

It's not a house, though. It's a predator that assumed the shape of something familiar, something comforting, to lure them in. Val puts a hand over her forehead. She's losing it. The strain of Dad's death, the revelation that her mom is still alive. It's too much, and her brain is rebelling by assigning threat and meaning where there isn't any.

"I was older than you all." Isaac sounds wistful. Sad, even. "The oldest one. I remember coming here with my parents, before it started."

"Wait, so *all* our parents lived here? My mom lived here?" Val asks. "But she doesn't anymore?"

Isaac shakes his head. "They all left, after the show ended. She stayed in Bliss, same as a lot of the parents, including mine. That's why I know where she lives."

"Can you get her number from your mom?" Marcus asks. "That way Val can call before she shows up."

Apparently Val isn't the only one worrying about what her maternal reunion is going to be like. It's nice that Marcus has her back.

"They aren't friends." Isaac offers it simply, without explanation. Val senses there's a story there, but before she can ask, Javi interrupts.

"You said our *parents* lived here. Didn't we live here, too?" Lawyer Javi immediately noticed a detail Val hadn't picked up on.

"No. We were somewhere else."

"Like sleepaway camp?" Marcus asks, bemused. "But for a show? That's weird."

"Not many housing options all the way out here," Javi says. "Why would they film in the Utah desert, of all places?"

Val scans their dark surroundings, trying to see some other building.

There's nothing. But in that house, that impossible, unnerving house, her parents lived. Together. Back when Mom and Dad were a unit, before whatever happened, happened. Maybe there are clues inside. Or maybe just a sense, an idea. Maybe memories have taken root there and she can tug them out of the dirt, see what's wriggling beneath.

Maybe, if she can see what they were before, the after will make more sense. Maybe she'll feel ready to meet her mom again.

"Let's turn around, go find a motel," Marcus says, but he doesn't sound hopeful. "Val said we aren't staying here, and we all know she's in charge."

Val gives him a puzzled look. She's not even here for the reunion. Why would she be in charge? But despite her earlier declaration, there's something about the house that nags at her. She needs to figure out what it is. "Maybe we should take a look at it."

Marcus and Javi seem surprised, but Isaac lets out a resigned sigh. "There's nowhere else to stay, anyway. Not unless you want to drive another two hours."

"God, no," Javi says. He grabs his bag.

Val reluctantly takes up her duffel and opens her door, flinching from the onslaught of cold. Summer nights in Idaho are warm. But out here in the desert, the air greets her with a surprising bite.

There's a hum, like standing near a power line. Val looks up but sees nothing other than an infinite spill of stars. The car's engine must be overworked.

Isaac kills the lights and turns off the car. The humming doesn't go away, though. It sets her teeth on edge and makes it hard to focus. Maybe it's from a generator. How else would they power things way out here? The only illumination is from the house, standing sentinel. The others get out of the car, following her lead.

Javi waves his phone. "No reception. How are we supposed to talk to our kids?"

"There's a Wi-Fi signal," Marcus says. "Jenny will have the password, I'm sure."

"You all have kids?" Val asks idly, eyes on the house as though it will reveal something before she walks in.

"Seven-year-old boy." Marcus holds out his phone toward her. He gazes tenderly down at the screen, but there's also pain in the look. Val doesn't have to force a cooing noise. Marcus's son has his same gorgeous eyes, an absolutely adorable little boy.

"Five-year-old twin terrors." Javi extends his phone to show her two children dressed in nicer clothes than she's ever owned, hair perfectly styled, smiling at the camera. But they both have a glint in their eyes and a twist to their smiles that makes her suspect their perfect hair and pristine clothing didn't last long.

Isaac doesn't pull out his phone. "Charlotte," he says softly, looking back down the road in the direction they came from. Is he expecting someone else to arrive, or is he wondering if they should leave?

"How many kids is that?" Marcus asks.

Val gives him a confused look. The math isn't hard. "Four."

"No." Marcus laughs, pointing at the van parked on the driveway. It has one of those decals with stick figures for each member of a family. There's a dad, a mom, and then a veritable troop of stick figures with pigtails.

"Six?" Javi lets out a whistle of disbelief. "Six kids. And a dog."

"Do you hear that—" Marcus starts, but the front door opens.

A woman stands there, backlit so she's only a silhouette of impatience. "It's late and cold and none of you are wearing jackets. Come on." She steps aside to usher them in. It feels wrong to debate, so they all move as one toward the front door. As each person enters, the woman hands them a folder.

Val is last. She glances over her shoulder, into the darkness. She doesn't know what this door leads to. All she knows is the warning she felt in the car is back in full force, the sense that something here is wrong, has been wrong, will be wrong. But if her parents lived here, it's a good first step. And she has to stay somewhere tonight. Maybe tomorrow she'll be staying with her mom.

Besides, her wariness doesn't make any sense. The paranoia screaming through her is a remnant of her father's own fears. He kept her in one place for so long, of course going anywhere new would feel wrong and dangerous. Especially somewhere from their past, leading her to answers he didn't want her to have. He didn't even want her to have questions.

But he's gone, and she's here. She stubbornly takes the fear, the warning, and locks it up.

The woman holds out a folder for her. Val shakes her head. "No, I—"

"It's your schedule," the woman snaps. She must be the podcaster.

Val takes the folder, but tries to explain. "I'm not here for the reunion, I'm—"

"You don't remember me."

Val bites back a weary curse. Not the podcaster, then. So . . . "Jenny?"

Jenny eyes Val up and down once. "Valentine," she says, and it doesn't feel relieved or happy or romantic when she says it. It feels like a guilty verdict.

Then Jenny smiles and puts a hand on the small of Val's back to guide her all the way into the house. It's almost colder inside, and everything is so white it's hard to process. "I'm so glad they found you. Us girls, back together again. We're going to have the best time." Jenny shuts the door firmly behind them. There's a change in air pressure, like Val needs to clear her ears. She opens her jaws but there's no relief. Val had expected that hum to be cut off, but it's just as loud and all around them. She feels it in her teeth.

"What is that?" she asks.

"What?

"That noise."

Jenny shrugs. "The AC, I think."

Val's never heard one that loud, and the big house used a swamp cooler. But it's not worth pushing. She looks down at her folder. "I'm only tagging along to meet my mom. But it got too late to go there."

"We'll head out first thing in the morning," Isaac promises, eyes on the tile floor.

"Is it okay if I spend the night? Is there room?" It's a stupid question, given the size of this place. But it feels polite to ask.

"Absolutely," Jenny says, and her smile is still there but it feels like the stucco on the house, plastered on to hide something beneath. "Of course you can stay. You're one of us, aren't you?" She deadlocks the door, and the pressure releases in Val's ears with a low, trembling pop. "Right back where you belong."

hatandcape
@conspiraciesandtv

Okay listen I know this will disappear soon because they always do—they ALWAYS DO—but I have to say it: every site that talks about the specifics of that old show Mister Magic gets taken down. Every single one. Like you can talk around the show or about the show generally but anything substantial disappears. Last week I was reading a blog that was tracking down former cast members and today I went back to check something and the site was just gone. Disappeared. Like it never existed. And isn't it weird that not even YouTube has footage from the show? Its not like its that old—the last episode was in the early 90s. There should be something out there, but theres nothing. I've looked everywhere. And like there are no photos from set either, no one has any images of the kids or Mister Magic or anything. Which makes me feel like I made up the whole thing, like I hallucinated this show that I used to watch every single day?? So I asked my friend whos a librarian to check newspaper television listings from the late 80s and early 90s so we could at least find out what channels it aired on and maybe find the distributor or studio that way, and nothing. N O T H I N G. Not listed at all ever on any tv guides we could find. Which again makes me feel like I'm loosing my mind, but then I go on reddit and see people talking about their moms wanting to bone Mister Magic and how—how? Did we all collectively dream this show? How does everyone remember something that, for all intensive purposes, never existed??? I CAN STILL SING THE THEME SONG I STILL HUM THE MODESTY SONG WHEN I'M PICKING OUT CLOTHES WHY CAN I NOT FIND ANY EPISODE LISTINGS OR DESCRIPTIONS WHY DO I FEEL LIKE I MADE THE WHOLE THING UP

# FIVE

The house is like someone took a regular, perfectly banal and dated house, and bleached the whole thing. There's a small, L-shaped kitchen with white laminate counters, the corners chipped and one spot discolored as though someone left a hot pan where they shouldn't. An old white fridge, a white stove with coil burners, a white microwave taking up valuable counter real estate. A table for two, barely better than a folding card table, sits in the middle of the tile floor, which transitions without fanfare to alarmingly white carpet. There's a white satiny couch with white lace throw pillows. On a stand against the wall is the only non-white thing visible: a squat old television.

"Oh my god." Javi wriggles its two insectoid antennae. "Remember when channel surfing meant turning a knob to go through them one by one? My nanny had a set just like this in her room. We used to watch soaps on it. Sometimes I'd have to hold the antennae to get a clearer picture."

Marcus laughs. "Don't sit too close. You'll burn your eyes out, remember?"

Val has an insane urge to smash the television. It's leftover weirdness from Dad. She's not doing anything dangerous just being in the same room as one. It isn't even on. She doubts it works anymore. Everything in this place is old, a time capsule not unlike her cabin.

From the entryway where she's still hovering, Val can see stairs leading up, an open door into a small bathroom done in the same white as everything else, and a door across from the kitchen to what she assumes is a study or a library. For all its flaws, it's still nicer than what she lives in now. She's sure the house was classy when it was built, with its impossible-to-clean carpet, but it's never been updated. It doesn't seem abandoned, though. Like someone's been staying in it, or at least maintaining it, all this time.

Val stays where she is, keeping the kitchen between herself and the television. She wishes she could laugh about the weirdness of her fear, but it just makes her sad. She both misses and hates her dad. She's so tired.

"Do you want to go over the itineraries?" Jenny sounds exhausted, too. There are deep bags beneath her eyes, and some of her hair has made a break for it from her ponytail. She doesn't seem to be particularly excited to see any of them, a stark contrast with the warmth and emotion of the guys. No one's sure whether they can approach Jenny, either. Isaac is studying her, Javi has given up on the television but is still standing in the middle of the family room, and Marcus keeps setting down his bag and then picking it back up, like he doesn't want to settle here.

"Do we *need* to go over them tonight?" Isaac asks.

"Not necessarily. Anyway," Jenny continues, "the schedules are already inaccurate, since you all were supposed to arrive three hours ago."

"You printed one for Val," Marcus says. "So they can't be that inaccurate, right?"

"I'm efficient." Jenny's smile, there and then gone as soon as it has served its purpose, emphasizes the statement. "We'll go over them first thing tomorrow, then."

"I'm not going to be here tomorrow," Val reminds her, not sure if she should apologize for being here in the first place, or for being absent in the future. She's done something to piss Jenny off, but she doesn't know what.

Jenny's eyes flash to someone behind her, but before Val can turn and see who, Jenny shakes her head. "No, you're here anyway, you might as well stay. Do a few interviews. It'll make the podcast more complete."

"I can't."

"You *can't*?" Jenny's nostrils flare as she takes a sharp breath. "Typical."

"What do you mean, typical?" Val wants to explain that she can't because she doesn't remember anything. But more than that, she wants Jenny to explain *how* this is typical of Val.

"You can't even take a few hours to help us out, after what you did?"

Val's stomach clenches. "What did I do?" she asks.

"You left." Jenny's snarl transforms her. Then she lifts a hand and wipes it down her features, physically removing the expression. Her face becomes as blank as the kitchen she's still standing in. "Sorry, I'm exhausted. It's been a long day. Long year. Long decade." Jenny sighs. "I don't want to get into it now. Can we figure everything out in the morning?"

"Of course." Val's eager to smooth over whatever this was. But her readiness to agree seems to bother Jenny even more, who once again directs an alarmed expression over Val's shoulder.

"Where's our illustrious interviewer?" Javi glances around as though the open floor plan might contain a secret person. All their eyes move to the stairs; Val realizes they go down as well as up. The house has a basement.

"Tomorrow." Jenny waves dismissively. "Oh gosh, are you all hungry?" She asks like it's both expected and terrible. "I meant to text you to stop in Cedar City since you were running late." She steps toward the fridge.

Val puts out a hand to stop her. "Why don't you go to bed? We can take care of ourselves. We're all grown-ups here."

Jenny laughs dryly. "Right. Because grown-ups are so good at taking care of themselves."

Almost on cue, Jenny's phone rings. She glances at the screen and a flicker of rage crosses her face. But when she answers, her voice is even. "Yes? In the cupboard where we keep all the children's medications. Where we've always kept it. Yeah. The dosing is on the box. No, I don't know it off the top of my head. Just give her one, then. It's a placebo. She needs you to sit with her and rub her back so she can calm down enough to fall asleep. No, I know. Mmm-hmm. Okay. No, they just got here, I can't—" Jenny's jaw twitches, then her tone changes. "Hi, sweetheart. Your legs hurt? I'm sorry. Remember what we talked about?" Jenny opens the closed door across from the kitchen and reveals not a study, but a bedroom. She shuts the door behind herself, and the sound of her voice shifts to a song.

"Well, Jenny changed." Javi looks around the house as though it smells bad, but it only smells dry and cold. Sterile, even.

"Yeah," Marcus agrees, tugging on his ear. Val wonders if the change in air pressure bugged him, too. "She was the nicest one. Remember?"

Val's starting to hate that word. She looks in cupboards. Jenny wasn't kidding when she said she could feed them—they're well stocked. Val opens the itinerary, wondering if it lists meals. Instead, all she sees are names next to times. Her name is included in type, not added in pen. When did Jenny have a chance to do that?

Maybe Val can stop back after meeting her mom. Maybe having that plan to hold on to will make everything easier, make it feel like she's not scrambling around in the dark.

Then again, this house is terrible. She tugs on her ear, too, trying to shake loose the AC hum that seems lodged there somehow, like an insect has crawled inside and is buzzing right against her eardrum.

There's a package of granola bars in the cupboard. Jenny must shop at the same places Gloria does, where everything comes in boxes large enough to live in. Val takes a few bars and tosses them to the guys.

Javi snatches his out of the air. "So what, Jenny's different. We're all different. Val, for one. Can you imagine her ever agreeing to change her plans based on what Jenny wants?"

"None of us could be in charge with Val there," Marcus says, but his smile is fond.

Javi saunters to the stairs. "Mom's busy. Let's explore. Up, or down? Down, right? Gotta be down. That's where the bodies always are."

As Javi sets a foot on the top step, the bedroom door opens and Jenny commands, "Absolutely not."

Javi freezes, then laughs. "God, Jenny, your mom-voice is powerful. You could make a fortune bottling it up and selling it. Hit both the desperate-parent and mom-kink crowd."

Jenny rolls her eyes and cracks the first real smile Val's seen. "You haven't changed at all."

"Excuse me, I'm much handsomer."

"I don't know, I liked you without any front teeth."

"I've had a lot of offers to knock them back out. I'd have taken them up on it if I'd known you'd be into it."

Jenny shakes her head again, laughing. "Shut up, dork." She remembers herself and blushes, straightening her already straight shirt. "Downstairs is the interview area, so it's off-limits unless you're on the schedule. You might accidentally mess up the equipment. And anyway there's no point in exploring. All the floors are exactly the same." She waves a hand at the area around them.

Javi nods sagely. "Ah, yes, because the only thing that could improve this floor plan is to repeat it six times."

Jenny ignores him. "Javi, you're floor two. Marcus, three. Isaac, four. Val, five."

"Who's six?" Val asks.

"No one."

Val's pretty sure the Wikipedia article said there were six friends on the show, but no one has mentioned who the sixth was or if they're coming. As everyone picks up their bags and begins shuffling up to their assigned floor, Val spares a single glance downstairs. The stairs stretch longer and deeper than is possible, and—

A hand in hers, bigger than hers. Tugging her.

*Stop being so stubborn. I can't handle her anymore! You take her.*

*Come on, Vally-Wally. It'll be okay. I promise. And if you don't like it, you don't have to stay.*

*Don't promise her that! You're always spoiling her. It's your fault she's like this. The others are waiting. Stop embarrassing me, Valentine.*

Her hand is taken by a gentler one, and little footsteps patter behind them. The stairs, long, so long, the darkness at the bottom so bright it hurts her eyes, getting bigger and bigger like it's rushing toward her, like it's gaping open to swallow her, and the noise is everywhere, a hum so loud her teeth chatter, a hum *inside* her, and—

"Val!" Hands grab her shoulders and she stumbles back, falling hard onto her ass at the top of the basement stairs.

Isaac crouches next to her. "Are you okay?" He searches her face. "You looked like you were going to fall."

She shakes her head, closing her eyes. "Dizzy, I guess. Long day. Weird day."

"Pretty cold to talk about your father's funeral as a *weird day,*" Jenny says. "But then again, you have a bad track record with family."

"Jenny." Marcus's voice is a hushed warning. Jenny doesn't say anything else, just stomps up the stairs to show them their rooms.

Isaac extends a hand to help Val up. "Come on. You need some sleep." He guides her toward the second floor and she's careful not to look back over her shoulder at the darkness she's certain is pooling beneath them, waiting.

Hi, and welcome to my website! I'm Zoraida Romero, set designer. You might have seen my work on the YouTube series "Far From," the viral music video for Rash's "bluberry," and maybe even local storefronts (featured on my Pinterest page, **here**). Some of my inspirations are *Labyrinth*—see it on the big screen if you ever get the chance, the attention to detail was amazing—*Emma*—the 2020 version, I swear I could wear those sets, I want to devour them whole—*Stranger Things, Severance,* and *Beetlejuice.* I love sets that become characters in and of themselves and inform the narratives in dynamic or disturbing ways. This love began young, planted deep by my favorite show as a kid, *Mister Magic.* The way everything started on that blank black stage with no walls or floors or ceiling, and then as the kids played it was populated by their imaginations? Astonishing. Possibly the best example of dynamic set design that's ever existed, and I desperately wish I could link it here! I've tried everything to find copies of the episodes to study how they did it, but maybe it's better that I can't. It can exist in my memory as pure magic—the same magic I try to create in my own set designs. Check out my info page for contact information if you're interested in working together. Let me build a world of wonder for you!

# SIX

There's a door in the wall in front of Val. She can feel the movement in the air, the change in the atmosphere around her as it opens. But she's lying frozen, eyes closed, unable to do anything.

It smells cold. The kind of cold you can taste. The kind of cold that baptizes you with a promise of a perfect peace, if you'd only lie down and give yourself to it. Let the cold envelop you, hold you tight and whisper that you don't have to worry about anything ever again.

Someone sits on the edge of Val's bed and the mattress dips toward the weight, but still she can't move, can't open her eyes. She tries to tell herself she's fine, she's safe, but all she manages is a low whimper like an injured animal.

A single icy finger traces a circle in the center of Val's left palm, so light it tickles.

Val sits up, gasping. The world spins around her, everything off-kilter, before it settles into place: She's at the house in the middle of nowhere. There's no one in her room. And there's no door, open or otherwise, in front of her. Just a blank white wall. But that doesn't make her heart stop racing, because she's in bed . . . but she didn't go to sleep here.

It had felt too exposed. Not vulnerable to the people here, but to the place itself. Like the house is something to be wary of, something that needs to be watched. She could feel the basement beneath her, could see the stairs from the bed. When she tried to lie down, she couldn't manage to close her eyes, afraid that as soon as she did, the space between herself and those stairs, herself and that basement, would disappear.

Maybe that was why she dreamed of a door: wishful thinking. Whoever designed this place neglected to add bedroom doors. The only barriers she could put between herself and the stairs to the basement were the bathroom or the closet.

So, exhausted and unable to talk herself out of her fear, Val had dragged a pillow and blanket and curled up on the closet floor, the only place she felt safe enough to sleep.

How had she ended up in the bed, then? All the bedding has been neatly tucked around her, except a rumpled spot on the edge of the bed. As if someone had been sitting there to hold her hand.

She gets up, but nothing else in the room is disturbed. There's no hint that anyone moved her. But a shaking breath reveals something lingering: a hint of icy-cold air.

The window is sealed shut. Though that damn humming still vibrates around her, as far as she can tell there's no air conditioner running, no airflow. She's not imagining the cold, though. When she came in, the room smelled dusty and dry, tickling her nose and making her sneeze. Something changed, and she doesn't know how.

Val shoves on her boots and gingerly heads toward the stairs, her path lit only by the television.

The television? She pauses. It wasn't on when she went to bed. She didn't even look at it, definitely didn't touch it. But then again, the screen is dim, nearly black. It might have been that way all along, but she didn't notice when the lights were still on.

She reaches out to shut it off, but her fingers curl back. She doesn't want to touch it. As she hits the stairs and begins creeping down level by level, the televisions light her way, darkly glowing on each floor.

Val can't shake a clawingly insistent fear that she'll accidentally go too far and end up down in the basement. She stops mid-flight. How many floors has she gone down? She can't remember. Her heart picks up, her breath ragged. The urge to go back up, all the way to the top, just to be precise in her floor counting is almost overwhelming. She wishes she could laugh about it. Laugh at herself. But her hand trembles where she trails it along the wall.

She won't go back up. But she'll go down very, very slowly. Steeling herself, she continues. It takes longer than it should, like the stairs are stretching, taunting her. But she knows exactly when she's about to go too far. It was silly of her to think she'd go down to the basement on accident. She feels *sick* on that landing.

Val rushes out onto the first floor, putting as much distance between herself and the yawning descent as she can. She needs to be out of this house, somewhere without that icy scent lingering on her skin, creeping down her throat. The television down here is on, too, but its flickering light is stronger than the others. The thought of touching it is physically repulsive and she edges behind the couch, wanting something between them.

*Thanks, Dad,* she thinks. She latches greedily onto her annoyance, using it as a shield against the dread clinging to her.

The front door is unlocked—and it's open. Just a crack, enough to see the deeper darkness on the other side. She slips out into the normal chill of the middle of the night in the desert.

If only the house weren't so tall. She can't get somewhere it can't see her, somewhere she can't see it, somewhere she can't *hear* it. Val walks straight out along the road, past Jenny's van and Isaac's rental. If Val had the keys, she'd get in the car and leave. Drive back to the ranch, back to what she knows and has known.

She doesn't want to be here. Doesn't want to remember whatever her brain has worked so hard to forget. This was an awful idea. Maybe the reason she can't imagine a scenario in which meeting her mom is pleasant or happy is because no such scenario is possible. Not after this long.

Her left palm itches. She scratches it, cursing the dry air irritating her scarred skin, then takes a deep, calming breath. Explanations exist for everything. In the dream, someone touching her palm was her brain's way of processing that irritation flaring up. The cold air was the draft from the open front door somehow making its way up to the fifth floor. And she had been so tired and worn out from such a confusing, long day, she *had* actually fallen asleep in bed and only dreamed of getting into the closet.

She's fine. She's safe. She's—

She's not alone.

Someone's out here, directly ahead of her. A silhouette against the dark, a window into another night, somewhere else without any light at all. A black hole of a shape that she knows in her heart even if she doesn't know it in her head. That animal moan of fear and pain rises in her chest and then—

The person shifts. It's not a cape around his shoulders, it's a blanket. He turns, and a flash reflects off eyeglasses.

Isaac. It's Isaac.

Not—who had she thought it was, anyway?

Isaac raises a hand in quiet greeting. Crossing her arms over her chest, Val picks her way to him. Even though she's only in a large T-shirt and boots, it would be weird to ignore him. And there's no way in hell she's returning to her room. Not yet.

He's wearing the blanket from his bed around his shoulders. Val wonders if it would be warm enough to banish the memory of that icy smell. It lingers in her sinuses, caught at the back of her throat like mucus she can't clear.

Isaac nods upward at the Milky Way spilled wantonly across the darkness. "I can't remember the last time I saw this many stars."

"The ranch is almost as good. But I don't usually stay awake for it. Or wander around in the middle of the night."

"Bad dreams," Isaac says softly. Val's about to say yes when she realizes he wasn't asking her why she's out here, but rather telling her why he is.

"Yeah," she agrees. "Bad dreams."

He holds out a corner of the blanket, inviting her in. Val has the strangest sense of déjà vu: They've done this before. Not standing in the desert, but shivering in the darkness nonetheless. She's tipping, falling into a version of herself that she can't remember, but that somehow still exists.

*No*. She's not ready. The doors in her mind stay shut, and she doesn't move.

Isaac blinks, staring down at his offering. Like he hadn't consciously meant to do it. "I—sorry, do you want the blanket?"

"I'm fine." It's a lie, but maybe *I'm fine* is always a lie. A stubborn insistence to herself, forcing the world around her to conform to what she wants to feel. If she declares it's fine, then it will become fine.

"I feel like I'm losing my mind," Isaac says.

"You're not alone." Val gives him a smile she means to be wry, but worries is desperate.

"I just can't believe you're here. You're really here. I looked for you, after. I never stopped. I felt so guilty that I lost you, I shaped my whole life around the space where you were missing."

"*You* didn't lose me." Val stares up at him. "My dad took me."

"But it was my job to watch out for you, to help you. To make sure you were okay. And I couldn't do that anymore. I tried to keep you with us, but I wasn't strong enough." He looks down at his hands, then wraps the blanket around them as though unwilling to see them anymore.

Val takes a step closer. She wants to comfort him, but she doesn't know how. "I don't understand. What do you mean, you weren't strong enough?"

"It felt like it was my fault. One moment you were with us, on the show, and then the next, you were just . . . gone. And everything fell apart. No one knew where you were. But I was always the one who could find you back then, and I thought, maybe, if I could find you again, if I could know you were okay, if I could—" He stops, shrugging. "I thought it would fix things. It just took me so long to find you."

Val's head spins. She wishes there were somewhere to sit. She considers sitting right on the ground, in the dirt, trying to draw on gravity itself to stabilize her. Instead, she takes Isaac's arm. She's squeezing too tight, but she can't help it. "Wait. Are you saying my dad kidnapped me?"

It was stupid of her not to put it together when she found out her mother was still alive. But she couldn't imagine her father as kidnapper. He could barely look at her most days; hardly the attitude of a parent so desperate to keep their child they'd abduct them. Maybe it was about punishment? Some bitter vendetta against her mother. He'd never been cruel, though. It didn't make sense.

Isaac is surprised. He scrambles for words, upset and worried. "Oh, Val. I'm sorry. I assumed you knew, but that you stayed with him out of loyalty. Or that you chose to go with him in the first place."

*Stop embarrassing me, Valentine*. Val shudders at the memory. Was it her mother's voice? "Has my mom been looking for me? Will she be happy to see me?" The words hurt coming out. The fear in them, yes, but also the hope. Hope has far more hooks than fear, far more capacity to tear her apart from the inside.

When he finally answers, Isaac's words are careful again. "She's had a rough time, since it all happened. I haven't seen her in a while."

Val nods. Of course her mother's had a rough time. "I hate not remembering, but it's safe, in a weird way. I'm terrified of what could be there, you know? Inside me. Like I'm walking on the edge of a precipice, and if I fall in, I might not ever get out again. Or whatever climbs back out won't be me anymore."

Isaac extends the blanket once more, and Val steps in, lets herself be enveloped in his little cocoon of warmth. It's so familiar she wonders how she's survived all these years without this feeling. Without him.

She lets out a little laugh so she doesn't cry. "Is it crazy that I feel closer to you than anyone else in my life?"

"We were inseparable. Part of you knows it, still." Isaac states it as fact, and it makes her feel better.

They're quiet for a while. He tilts his head upward, his arm the lightest touch around her. Not so much holding her as offering support if she needs it. His tone is dreamy when he speaks again. "Maybe you're lucky. When we were kids together, that was the happiest time in our lives. I can see it in the others, too. It haunts us. Knowing what we had, and that we can never get it back. The trauma of losing you and then losing the show completely fucked me up. Maybe forgetting was your way of letting yourself move on."

"Move on to what?" Her throat is tight, her voice harsh and strained. "I never moved on. I never moved at all." She had loved her dad, despite everything. She even loved the ranch sometimes, the surprise of spring and the hot sticky expanse of summer, the peaceful inertia of winter. And she loved Gloria and the camp kids. Val had liked her life there when she didn't think too hard about it. But it wasn't *her* life, was it? She didn't choose it. None of it.

Val stares up at the stars, wishing she was anywhere else. But still with Isaac. That's the only part she doesn't want to change. "I didn't ever suspect my dad kidnapped me, because I thought it was my fault we were hiding. I thought I was—I thought I was bad, so I accepted it. All of it."

Isaac's voice is even softer than the starry light above. His arm circles her tighter, contradicting his next words. "Maybe you shouldn't stay. Write your mom a letter or something, instead. Take it slow, on your own terms, and leave everything else buried. The rest of us, we're not—we're not whole. I don't know how to explain better than that. You can still keep it down in the darkness, where you left it."

"What's *it*?"

Isaac shrugs. "Our childhood. The magic. The ending of it all."

She hates this house, hates this place, but she wants to know what she lost. What she did, if she did anything, because she still can't leave behind that sludge of shame at the core of her soul.

Surely that shame hadn't *all* been suggestion from her dad. Maybe if she can understand why she feels this way, she can be free of it.

"I want to know everything. Besides, it's too late to leave. It was too late the moment I saw you. Something burst free, and I can't bury it again."

"So you did recognize me," he says, wistful.

"In a way, yeah. Just like you recognized me."

"I'd recognize you anywhere. I was always going to find you, for better or for worse." Isaac's sigh shifts them closer together, and together they're safe against the dark and the cold.

*Inevitable,* Val thinks. But the word yanks her back to those stairs, to the basement waiting at the bottom of them. *Inevitable,* her mind repeats, but it doesn't quite sound like her own voice that says it.

**The Last Time the Circle Formed** by **Suffocating in the Dark**

*Mister Magic*

Mister Magic: Children's Television Show, Mister Magic, Chaos, Horror, Violence Against Children, Child Death

Author's Note: I saw the last episode of Mister Magic. I was only six but that shit has haunted me ever since. And don't tell me it wasn't broadcast live—I know, which makes it even more fucked up that they aired it. I've talked with my therapist about it so many times and she says that I created the memory to try to process a loss in my life at the time, but I don't think that's right. I really don't. Because I remember sitting on the worn brown carpet in front of the TV, so close I could feel its static. So close I could hear the hum of electricity. I'd reach out and put my hand on theirs sometimes, pretend like I was part of the circle. I knew something was wrong the second the last episode started, because the circle wasn't right. I felt sick watching it, my stomach hurt like it always did when I was anxious or scared. Why would I create that memory? Why would I create what happened next? Anyway, that's why I wrote this fic, trying to describe what I saw but in a story. You know. They even had a song about it: *Tell yourself a story, make it just like mine, live inside that story, everything is fine.*

But everything isn't fine on the last episode of Mister Magic, and if I had to live inside it all these years, so do you.

Language: English   Words: 3,500   Comments: 6   Kudos: 0   Hits: 298

# PICK UP STICKS

Val and Isaac stay out until the sunrise banishes night from the desert. Val's reluctant to return, and, judging by his slow steps, Isaac is, too.

Val doesn't know whether the house is more or less viscerally upsetting in the daylight. It's certainly more absurd, standing all alone. There's not a sound to be heard over that low hum. Maybe it's a desert insect, like cicadas. Too tiny to notice, too loud to ignore.

She wonders how many miles they are from the highway. Even though it's already heating up, it's baffling to Val that it's summer. There's no life here. The land is frozen, without hope for change. The dirt and rocks around them have a reddish tinge, a meager contribution of loveliness to the bleak landscape. Not enough to give her eyes anything to linger on. And the house looms over it all, watching. Ready.

*Ready for what?* Val wonders.

Val and Isaac walk shoulder to shoulder, their pace slowing the closer they get to their destination. "I'll shower and then we can go?" Val only feels dread, not excitement, at the prospect of meeting her mother. But that makes it all the more urgent to do it as soon as possible, before she can convince herself not to. She knows how good she is at deciding not to do something and sticking with it forever.

Isaac nods. The soft dawn paints him in undertones of blue, making him look nearly translucent. She wishes she could paint. The only way to capture the colors of his face would be in watercolor.

"I'll clear it with Jenny," he says, "but I'm sure the schedule is flexible."

Val is sure nothing with Jenny is flexible, but she doesn't want to be mean about someone she's only just met. And then they're back on the front step of the house. They both hesitate a few seconds longer than they should. The door flies open.

"Typical," Jenny says, rolling her eyes. She's got a bowl in one arm, vigorously stirring with her free hand. "Well, come inside, we don't want flies to get in."

There are no flies. Actually, there are no animals at all. Val follows Isaac in and leans against the counter near Jenny. She's delaying facing the stairs again. "You keep saying *typical*. What do you mean by it this time?"

Jenny pauses her stirring. "You two used to do that all the time. You'd disappear, and then Isaac would go after you, and it would be ages before he'd get you to come back. We never could figure out where you went. Only Isaac could find you."

"On the set?" There were probably lots of hiding places on sets. But why was another kid the one finding her, and not an adult? And why was she always running off?

Jenny narrows her eyes. Val knows the expression; she sees mothers give it to their kids all the time at the camps, trying to get them to admit to lying without outright accusing them. "You *really* don't remember it?"

Val shakes her head. "No. Sorry."

Jenny lets out a strange braying gasp of a laugh. Then she shakes her head and puts her regular smile back on, like pulling an apron over her clothes to protect them. Does Jenny pull that smile on the same way Val says *I'm fine*? Is it a conscious choice, or a reflex?

But Jenny evidently believes her, or at least accepts that Val's story isn't going to change under the pressure of a mom-glare. "Wow. Lucky you. Well, breakfast is almost ready, so sit down. Marcus has the first interview, anyway."

Val sits. Isaac has slipped away upstairs, leaving her alone with Jenny for the time being. Which is fine. She wants to chat with the other woman, find some common ground. She connected with the guys so easily, it makes her feel guilty that there's this brittle distance between her and Jenny. "You have six kids?"

"Mm. All girls. Oldest is twelve, youngest is three."

"Wow. That must be busy."

"It is." Jenny doesn't expound. She pours batter onto a griddle and hovers, laser-focused on watching the pancakes slowly brown. Or using it as an excuse to avoid conversing in-depth with Val.

Val knows the interviewer asked them not to talk about the show, but she doesn't care about cross-contamination with other people's memories. She'll take any information she can get. "When you say that I used to hide, what do you—"

"Do you have something nice to wear?" Jenny interrupts.

"To meet my mom?" Val hadn't even thought about it. She has jeans, some tees, and two flannel shirts in her duffel.

"No, for the gala tonight." Jenny flips a pancake so aggressively it slides right off the griddle. "Gosh *darn it,*" she mutters, scooping it up and throwing it in the trash. "You didn't read the itinerary, did you?"

"A gala? Isn't that like a fancy party? I thought this was a reunion to record a podcast."

"It's all in the itinerary," Jenny says through gritted teeth. "Why do I type these things up if no one is going to read them?"

"But I'm not here for the reunion." Val says it patiently, though she made it clear last night.

"Well, you're going to Bliss anyway, aren't you? That's where the gala is. The least you could do is make an appearance. Let people know you're okay. A lot of good people were hurt when you left."

"The gala is in Bliss? Where my mom lives?"

Jenny waves the spatula dismissively. "Everyone involved in—" There's a slight pause, as though Jenny is changing what she was about to say, then she continues faster to compensate. Does Jenny keep the rule against saying *Mister Magic,* too? "Involved in the show lived in Bliss."

A local town where the crew stayed makes sense. "Did the show really film all the way out here?" she asks. Isaac rejoins them, sitting next to Val.

"Yeah, this is hardly Hollywood." Marcus steps free from the stairs. He's freshly showered and looks great in a lavender button-up shirt tucked into gray slacks. He's not wearing shoes, and his rainbow socks slide along the tile floor. "Where's the studio?"

"Burned down. You know that."

Val's fingers clench around her scarred palms. "When was the fire?"

"At the end," Jenny says as though it's a complete explanation. Then she continues answering Marcus. "Besides, it's not unreasonable that it was located here. Hollywood hasn't always been Hollywood, and *Mister*—"

Marcus and Isaac hiss in unison. Apparently Jenny doesn't keep that rule. She gives them a flat look and continues, ignoring the way they flinch when she finishes saying it. "*Mister Magic* predates television. It's always been located here."

"*Here,* here? As in this house?" Val doesn't understand that. "Or as in Bliss? And the studio? It was here, too? By the house? Or also in Bliss?" She wants Jenny to give more details. When was the fire? It feels crucial to know, but also dangerous.

"Which question do you want me to answer?" Jenny gives her a flat look.

"All of them." Val grins sheepishly at her, and Jenny cracks a little.

"*Mister Magic* has always been anchored *here*-here. The house obviously isn't that old, only forty or fifty years, I think. There was a different building before that. And yeah, the studio was here, too." She waves dismissively as though that detail is less important.

"But there's nothing but desert around us." Marcus holds out his hand in a broad gesture. "Where did we live during filming? Why did our parents stay in this house if we didn't?"

Jenny shoves a plate in front of him. The pancake on top has a smiley face made of chocolate chips.

Marcus looks down at it, his expression not mirroring the pancake's. "I don't remember living anywhere in the desert. Actually, during the show, I don't remember my parents being there at all."

"They were watching." Jenny hands plates to Val and Isaac.

"Thank you," Val says, even though she's the only one who doesn't get a smiley face. "I can't remember the last time someone made breakfast for me. This was really nice of you."

"Oh," Jenny says, frowning in surprise. "You're welcome. Anyway, we're not supposed to talk about the show outside of the interviews. I already told you all that."

"How did the fire happen? Could we see where the studio was?" Val asks. "Technically it happened after the show, so we can talk about that, right?"

"You can't get inside," Jenny snaps, slamming down a pitcher of orange juice. She takes a deep breath, rubbing her temples. "I'm sorry. I didn't sleep well last night. This is—it's a lot. I thought I was ready to see you all again, but . . . you're different, and I don't—I need this to work. It's got to work." She shakes her head. "Marcus, you're first. Just go downstairs when you're ready."

"The interviewer is here? But we haven't—" Marcus starts.

Jenny holds up a hand. "Just go downstairs. I'm going back to my room." She leaves them, closing the door.

"Why does she get a door?" Marcus frowns.

"What did I do to her?" Val asks, gesturing at her plain pancake and then at their cheery ones. "Do either of you know?"

Isaac and Marcus share a look. Marcus shoves a huge bite into his mouth. "I gotta get down to my interview thing." He stands and hurries away, but pauses at the top of the stairs. He puts a hand against the wall and Val wonders if he feels it, too. That vertigo. Maybe there's something wrong with the house. Some sort of gas leak. But then Marcus disappears downstairs.

"You didn't do anything to her, specifically." Isaac pours a glass of juice for Val. "Being pulled off the show really upset her. It's all more personal because her family stayed in the area. We've talked about it a little, over the years."

"She feels left behind?" Val asks.

"Stuck, more like."

Val gets it. More than Jenny could ever know. She wants a chance to really talk with her, but it's clear Jenny's not interested in connecting. Isaac and Val eat in silence, each lost to their thoughts.

"I'm not going to that gala," Val says as she finishes. "I want to meet my mom, get some answers, and then decide what's next. If you can get me to where she lives, I'll figure things out from there. You shouldn't have to stick around and miss reunion things."

Isaac is staring at the front door, his expression determined. "That's a good plan. Actually, you should take my car, that way—" His head turns toward Val. The motion is stiff, unnatural. Almost like an invisible hand has taken him under the chin. Like he can't help but look at her. His magnified eyes are frozen on her face and something shifts. His determined expression melts away into a sad smile. "I don't want you to go through this alone. I'll stick with you, if you'll have me."

The relief Val feels is instantaneous. She doesn't want him to feel obligated, but he makes this all feel more doable. She leaves him before he can change his mind. After a quick shower and some fresh clothes, Val heads back downstairs.

On the second floor a hand shoots out and grabs her arm. Val lets out a shriek before she realizes it's just Javi. She glares at him, not sure if he was trying to be funny or what. He can't know how much these stairs bother her, but she's still flustered and angry when she says, "You scared me! I could have fallen."

Javi's expression is intense. "Don't leave," he says, keeping his voice low.

"What?"

"After you meet your mom. Don't leave. There's something else going on here. I don't trust this podcast story. I think they're trying to pin it on one of us. We need to—"

"Ready?" Isaac says, on the stairs below them.

Javi stumbles past her, suddenly artfully sleepy and disheveled instead of intense. "Coffee," he croaks, going ahead of them straight to the counter where a pot is waiting. Val follows, confused and alarmed. Javi won't look at her.

What is going on in this house? And what would someone be trying to pin on one of them? The fire. It has to be the fire.

"You two heading out?" Javi asks. "You should stay here with us again tonight, Val. Save you money on a motel." He raises an eyebrow at her.

Val makes a noncommittal noise. "Maybe."

Javi gives her a sharp glance, but then returns to a sleepy frown. He's not going to tell her anything else right now. Not in front of Isaac. "Also, who was creeping around in the middle of the night? And how do we fix that damn AC? It's freezing and so loud I could barely sleep. And why doesn't this place have any doors? Six floors and no doors between them. Were our parents swingers or something? Oh god, I shouldn't have said that. We're sleeping in those beds." He grimaces, selecting a mug and grabbing the coffeepot.

"That reminds me," Val says, thinking of the six floors, and the Wikipedia page mentioning there were always six friends.

"What does our parents being swingers remind you of?" Javi widens his eyes dramatically. "Do tell!"

Val shakes her head. "Not that. Who is the sixth cast member? Are they coming, or did they disappear like me?"

Javi freezes, staring at her with an expression close to horror. Coffee spills over the edge of the mug and he swears, pulling his hand back from where it was burned. "Are you fucking kidding me right now?" he whispers, but he's talking to her, not commenting on his accident.

"Val," Isaac says. When she turns, she's afraid of what she sees in his face. Pity, but also the same horror as Javi. "You don't remember Kitty? I thought we just weren't talking about her, but . . ."

Val folds her arms, tired and cranky. "How many times do I have to repeat that I don't remember anything?"

Isaac holds up a hand to pause whatever Javi is about to say. "Let's go for a walk."

He has that tone in his voice. The one Gloria used when Val was searching for her favorite ranch dog and Gloria had to tell her he'd been hit by a car. The one Val's dad *never* used, because if there were any hard truths to tell, he kept them to himself.

Val's heart races. It's the bad truth she's been waiting for her whole life. It's finally here. "Tell me who Kitty is and why you're all acting like this."

Jenny's voice comes from behind them. She's in her bedroom doorway, eyes hooded, tone even. "Kitty was the youngest member of the circle. And she was your sister."

The camera activates a few seconds before the lights. There's a sharp intake of breath, like someone inhaling deeply to relish a scent. Then the lights flicker on to reveal Marcus, standing at the bottom of the stairs. His shoulders are braced inward as his eyes search the room.

"Hello?" he asks. There's no one else, just a chair in front of the wall where the camera is mounted. But on the wall . . .

"Oh." He sits gingerly, his posture stiff and awkward. His smile is tentative, like a wave to someone you aren't sure recognizes you. "Hey. I didn't know this was going to be virtual."

A woman's voice answers. There's a slight distortion, like several voices speaking at once in almost perfect unison. "I can't be there in person."

"Weird setup." Marcus looks up and down. "They have the monitor or TV screen or whatever turned vertically, so it's like—I don't know, like a giant phone? And it's super thin. I can't see—" He starts to lean forward.

"Please don't touch."

"Right." He sits back. "Well, what do we do now?"

"I'm going to introduce you, like a real podcast."

Marcus smiles again, but there's more confusion than anything else in his face. "Isn't this going to *be* a real podcast?"

"Oh, absolutely. Okay. Here we go." Her voice switches tones, going higher, more lilting and practiced.

*Sitting across from me is everyone's favorite buddy, Marcus. Of all the friends, Marcus had the best imagination. He could pretend so well, he created entirely new worlds for us.*

*His big brown eyes are still as kind and gentle as ever, his curly hair now shaved. If you were here, too, seeing him in front of you, you'd be struck by how much you missed playing with him. Maybe even a little angry at how long he's been gone from your life. Being with him again makes you realize how much it hurt you when he left.*

*Marcus was an artist. He'd call out colors and images to splash the walls and bring that blank black space to life. Sometimes he did too much, too brightly. Sometimes he got lost in his characters, and Mister Magic had to pull him back. Do you remember that? The hand resting on Marcus's shoulder, the head bent to his ear? Marcus was so good at listening, so good at following instructions. When he was part of the circle, he fit in perfectly.*

*You probably have a lot of questions for Marcus. Is he an artist now? Did he bring that magic into the real world? Has he ever fit in as well as he did back then? Has he ever been as happy?*

Marcus's smile is frozen, his eyes wide.

"I'm open to notes," she says. "It's only an introduction."

"Oh, are we—we're just talking now? Is this recorded for the podcast?" He looks around, searching. He doesn't see the camera.

"Yes, all recorded. But everything can be edited. We can make it sound exactly how we want it to. How we need it to. So don't be afraid."

Marcus nods, bemused. "I guess I didn't expect you to go that hard. Not the format I was anticipating, either. I thought we'd be, like, in a circle? Sharing memories? I mean, it's a podcast about a silly kids' show that aired thirty years ago. Maybe you're taking it too seriously."

"Don't you?"

"Take it seriously? I loved being on it, but it was a long time ago. It all sort of blurs together. I hadn't thought about the room painting, about becoming characters, in a long time. God, that used to make me feel . . ."

Marcus trails off into silence.

Her narration voice comes back.

*His smile is very slight, as subtle as the paisley pattern on his shirt. There's no hint of the brilliant smile that viewers were rewarded with once upon a time. If Mister Magic sometimes made Marcus dim the radiance of his creations, it appears life has almost entirely dimmed Marcus.*

"Hey now," Marcus says, frowning. "That's not fair. Is this an interview, or what?"

"Right!" she chirps. "Like I said, we'll change everything we don't like. Do you remember painting the world around the friends? Creating that wonder out of nothingness for them?"

Marcus nods, looking at his hands. "I have all these memories of making backgrounds for whatever we were playing. But not 2-D. Actually *making* rooms and forests and everything in them. Was I painting sets or something? It took so little time, though. I can't—I can't quite figure out how it makes sense. I was on some shows, after, and there were scripts and stages and cameras. Directors. Lights. But I don't remember any of that from our show. Maybe it was just because I was older then and I noticed more things."

"So your other shows weren't magic?"

Marcus lets out a dry laugh, rubbing his hand along his shaved head. "Magic? Hardly. I was on one other kids' show, and then a couple of tween sitcoms. One feature film. But that's an awkward age to be on camera, and as soon as I got tall, they were worried I was going to be too *intimidating*." Marcus's face flashes with anger. "Anyway. I never managed the transition past child actor. Didn't even get a *look, I'm not a kid anymore* sexy breakout moment. I didn't release any albums wearing pleather and writhing around on an ice cream truck. Not a single one. And now I've aged out of writhing and pleather and breakout opportunities." He smiles, and then his smile fades, as though he's self-conscious. "Acting wasn't fun anymore. Not like on our show. I guess I grew up, you know? It turned into reality, instead of play."

"Was the show all play?"

"Yeah. Play, and the rules, and the lessons." Marcus's hand drifts to his shoulder, hovers just above like it's resting on top of someone else's hand. "*Dim it, that's it, lower the light. Dim it, that's it, don't shine so bright.* That's what I sang when I went too far, to remind myself to fit in better. I still hum it all the time. And the one about cleaning. I sing that to my son. He hates it." This time Marcus's smile is genuine. "I wish he had something like the circle of friends. I worry about him. He's a good kid. A great kid. But I worry about how my choices, my own damage, might be affecting him."

"What do you mean, your damage?" The voice is almost singsong, lulling Marcus even as it guides him forward. Deeper. He doesn't take his eyes off the screen and the impossibly deep darkness behind the interviewer. His pupils are slowly dilating, like a mirror to that blackness.

"Sometimes I think everything would be better if we had actually finished the show. If I'd had closure. Maybe I wish the show had never ended at all. It was easier back then. Simpler. After the show, I was always afraid of my directors, my agents, my mom." He grimaces, as though he didn't mean to include her. "I didn't want to stand out, or get in trouble, or disappoint anyone. And it's hard not to disappoint adults. Almost impossible."

"But you weren't afraid on the show?"

Marcus's eyebrows lift in surprise, as if the question is absurd. His pupils are so big now there's almost no visible iris. "I was never scared then. And he was never disappointed in me, not like that. He helped me. I actually—"

Marcus pauses, his hand returning to his shoulder. This time he squeezes himself in a strangely paternal gesture. He speaks with a hint of wonder.

"I guess he taught me how to survive. How to act, how to pull back, how to not reveal so much. I was always putting it all out there on display, splashing my heart across entire walls, entire landscapes, entire worlds. But that's how you get hurt. How you get seen, and destroyed. He made it easier for me. Easier to control myself, to be what I needed to be. It was a lot harder knowing when and what to hide once he was gone."

Marcus's hand twitches, his fingers digging into his shoulder like claws, before releasing.

"I felt safe with him in a way I never did after. I always figured my mom suspected who I really was, but I could keep her from *knowing*. With him, I knew he knew. Everything. Every part of me. And he was still there with me. And so were my friends. Javi. Isaac. Jenny. Val. Kitty." Each name is counted almost ritually, like beads on a rosary. Marcus's expression gets a little clearer, the brown of his irises fighting to reclaim their territory. "They loved me in a way I needed to be loved. They were always there. After a while, they were the most important part of everything, you know? He faded into the background, but their hands were always in mine. I *needed* them. I started the show right after my dad died; maybe it filled that void. Or maybe it was too soon, and that's why it takes up so much of my brain." Marcus shakes his head. "What was my mom thinking, taking me on auditions then?"

"Oh, but you were a lucky one—chosen from thousands of letters written by parents all across the country. No auditions."

"Really?" Marcus is surprised.

"Only special children, chosen. Mister—"

"We don't say his name," Marcus interrupts quickly. He passes a hand over his eyes, and his pupils shrink again, stop swallowing everything the screen is offering him. "That's a rule."

Her voice is playful. "A rule from the show? Like keeping things neat and tidy, smiling, listening to adults?"

"No, it was our own rule. The circle's rule. We only said his name when we had to."

"Val made that rule. So, it wasn't a *real* rule."

"If you had known stubborn little Val, you'd know that what she said went." Marcus's smile is affectionate. "She was in charge. Everything started and ended with her."

"Tell me more about him. The name you won't say."

Marcus shifts in his seat, hand once again resting on his own shoulder. "He didn't—I don't remember him ever talking. Did he talk?"

"Are you asking me?"

"You're the interviewer. I assume you've done your research."

"This is about helping you remember. Helping you return to who you were, then."

Marcus leans back, finally noticing how close he'd drifted to the screen. His arms cross in front of his chest, putting up a barrier. It's clear from his expression he's realizing how much he's said, how deep he's gone without meaning to. "I don't remember his voice, just his presence, and his hand on my shoulder when I needed to be pulled back. We got the lessons from . . ." Marcus squints. "I'm not sure. The scripts? I forget. But the lessons were important to the show. Regular moralizing stuff for kids. Doing what you're told. Being happy. Keeping your end of deals. Are you humming?" He looks around as though searching for the source of some sound. "Do you hear that?"

"Keeping your end of deals. That's an interesting lesson. Do you remember that one?"

Marcus laughs awkwardly. "Actually, now that I've said it out loud, it's kind of weird. One of those things you take at face value as a kid, but that feels absurd when you try to explain it."

"Try anyway."

Marcus tilts his head, distracted, searching for the source of the humming. "You know. How if you stick your hand out and ask for something, you have to accept whatever grabs ahold of you. That doesn't make sense. You don't hear that? Anyway, I'm not explaining it well. It's probably like—well, maybe it's a little like *you get what you get and you don't throw a fit*? I use that one on my son. He hates it. But keeping your end of a bargain is more complicated. Heavier. Because it's not just receiving, it's agreeing to give something in order to receive." Marcus shakes his head, losing his train of thought. "Maybe it's feedback. You really don't hear that? Is something playing on your end? It's driving me crazy. I can almost make sense of it, but . . ."

"Do you remember the song you opened with? Go on. I'll start: *Take my hand*—"

Marcus stands abruptly. "I don't want to sing it." He seems shocked by his own reaction but doesn't sit back down.

"That's fine," she chirps. "Would you like to watch it, though?"

Marcus sits slowly. "You have recordings of our show?"

"I have the show. We'll make a deal. I'll let you see later, if you sing the song with me then. You have to agree to give something in order to receive, right?"

He nods, a desperate hunger on his face. "Okay. Okay, it's a deal. I want to see it again. I need to, I think."

The voice lowers, practically purring. "You loved him. Even if you won't say his name, you loved him. Think about him. Practice the song. Hold on to it in your heart until it's time. And then, when we sing, you'll remember."

Marcus's smile is a little wary, a lot confused. He's said so much more than he'd meant to, and maybe doesn't even remember all of it. There's a dazed quality, as though he's waking up from an accidental nap. He stands again, but hesitates, something else boiling up in his chest like heartburn. Several emotions flit across his face before he leans forward, frowning. Either he feels more intense about this part, or he's angry, or he's upset. It's hard to tell. Marcus has worked for so long not to show his feelings, sometimes they get confused on their way to the surface.

"What if he really was just some *guy,* some actor, and he has no idea we're all still here, talking about him, thinking about him, trying to figure out whether he was a person or a puppet or an empty cape on a wire being danced around a stage? He's this looming, overwhelming figure in my childhood, and he's just some guy. Sitting in a living room, watching TV, drinking a beer. Never thinks about that weird job he had thirty years ago. I'll bet he doesn't even remember us."

There's that high giggle that doesn't quite fit the interviewer's voice. "Oh, he'd never forget you. I promise. Magic never forgets the taste of your friendship."

# SEVEN

Val stumbles out of the house, unseeing, unfeeling.

Kitty. A sister. A sister her dad—*their* dad—had never once mentioned. Is that who he saw when he looked at Val? Why he couldn't stand to talk to her, could barely make eye contact?

Why would he take Val and leave Kitty? Or was bringing Kitty never an option? Was she already dead? Was it . . . was it Val's fault?

And how could Val just *forget* about her? Had she gotten so good at putting things behind doors and shutting them away that she shut away an entire person?

Maybe this is the reason for her shame. She did something, and her sister died. When Dad said *safe,* he wasn't talking about keeping her that way. He was talking about keeping everyone else that way.

Val's a monster. She's always known, but now she *knows*. Regardless of what she actually did, Val forgot her own sister afterward. Erased her from existence. Who does that?

A hand squeezes her shoulder, soft but insistent.

"I'm so sorry," Isaac says. "I thought you understandably didn't want to talk about her. If I had known—"

"How could you have?" Val rubs her eyes. It feels like the grit of the desert has somehow gotten in them even though the air is heavy and lifeless.

"You've been through a lot." Isaac drops his hands to his pockets but doesn't move, content to simply stand beside her. To make sure she's not alone. *You were always hiding, and he could always find you.*

"How did she die?" Val's hands clench into fists and her scarred skin puckers over her itching palm. *A fire,* Val thinks. Kitty died in the fire. The one Val can't picture, but has worn on her skin ever since.

"I can't really say." Isaac shrugs helplessly.

"Were you there when it happened?"

"It's . . . it's confusing. Jumbled. I don't know what was real and what was nightmares after." He looks sorry not to have more to offer her. But who is she to get mad at someone's lack of clear memories?

"It was an accident," Val says bleakly, quoting the Wikipedia page.

"An accident," Isaac agrees.

"And I was there?" Her throat is tight, aching. Whether with the need to scream or cry, she can't say.

"No."

Val's eyebrows draw low in dubious surprise. "What? Are you sure?"

"That's the only thing I'm sure about. It happened after your dad took you."

She wishes she could latch onto that. But Val wouldn't have had to be on set to start a fire, would she? She could have started it outside, where none of the rest of the cast could see her. Maybe her dad caught her. Maybe that's when they left.

She can picture it. A little version of herself, lighting a match. Crouching down. But it's like telling herself a lifeless story. There's no emotion, no heat, nothing real to the images.

Isaac kicks at the hard-packed dirt. "So, what should we do now?" he asks, and she feels a pang of gratitude that he's still including himself. Being with Isaac is easier than being alone. She's never had that with a person before.

"Let's go talk to my mom and hope she knows more than we do."

He lets out a long breath. "Okay. But I feel like I didn't really prepare you. Especially now that I know you didn't know about—well, a lot." Isaac pulls off his glasses and rubs them on his shirt. His face looks oddly incomplete without them, like he's out of focus. "She's had a hard life."

"Yeah, I'd think so. One of her daughters died, and the other one—" Val wraps her arms around herself, wishing she could hug Isaac without it being weird. Her palm still itches, and she wonders: If she took his hand, would it make it all bearable?

Isaac puts his glasses back on and his face once again resolves into itself. His head does that strange slow turn, and his gaze settles on the house.

What did Javi want to talk to her about? Probably Kitty. Maybe he knows what happened. She should go in and ask him. Or maybe she's trying to put off what needs to be done. Talking to Javi feels easier, but her mom is the priority. She has to be. That poor woman.

"We should get going, then." Isaac tears his eyes away from the house. He twitches, almost a shudder. His discomfort with this place makes her feel justified in her hatred of it. They walk to his car and he opens the passenger's door for Val.

"Wait!" Jenny shouts from the house. "Where are you going?" She rushes toward them, panic on her face.

"To talk to my mom," Val answers from the passenger's seat.

"Are you sure that's a good idea?" Jenny looks at Isaac as she asks it. "If she leaves again—" She wrings her hands. "It won't be enough."

"I won't be good at interviewing," Val says. She's not going to talk on the record about any of this. Not until she knows more about what actually happened. And maybe not even then. That's probably what Javi was trying to warn her about—not to say anything official. Not like she could even if she wanted to. "You don't need me for the podcast."

Jenny glares at her. "I *needed* you thirty years ago, and you left. You were our friend, and you disappeared, and we all paid for it."

Val's surprised to see tears in Jenny's eyes. Maybe her anger is really just hurt. But before Val can answer, Isaac puts a hand on Jenny's shoulder, turning her back toward the house. He says something too low for Val to hear, but some of the tension leaves Jenny's posture. She nods brusquely.

"Don't be late for the gala!" she yells as Isaac gets into the car.

Sealed inside, Val expects more relief from the omnipresent hum. She turns on the radio to drown it out, but there's no signal and the static seems to only amplify the hum.

It's almost an hour before they hit the paved road and Isaac can go faster. By the time they merge onto the highway, it's nearly noon. At least it's actually quiet now, and Isaac doesn't try to fill the silence in the car with conversation. He seems content with whatever she offers, never pushing for more. But she's not content. Not at all. She needs something to think about other than obsessing over what she doesn't know.

"How old is your daughter?" she asks as Isaac passes a solitary semi truck.

"Six." He keeps his eyes on the road.

"What's she like?"

He sighs. "I haven't seen her in a year. It's a little ironic, actually, that I can't find a way to see my own kid. Did I tell you I'm a PI?"

Val lets out a dry laugh. "At the funeral, I wondered if you and Javi were detectives or PIs, but you didn't seem like the type."

One corner of Isaac's mouth curls up. "Was it the crying?"

"A little bit, yeah."

"All those years of imagining exactly what I'd say when I found you, and instead I dropped a glass and started crying." Isaac shakes his head, but his smile grows into something real. "To be fair, no one ever thinks I'm a PI, which can come in handy. I specialize in parental kidnappings."

He had said he looked for her, that he never stopped. Before she can ask, Isaac says, "Yeah, you're the reason why. Losing you when we were kids had a big impact on me. On all of us, obviously. Anyway. My one PI stereotype is I'm also an alcoholic. Both my parents are. My mom got it under control when I was in my twenties, but my dad never did. Kaylee—that's my ex—was fine with me when I was drinking, because I didn't care what she was doing or how hard she was partying. It was when I got sober that she didn't want to be with me anymore. Kaylee looked better on paper than I did, though, so she got custody. I got sober for my daughter, and I lost her because of it. I've been working to get her back ever since."

"I'm so sorry."

"Charlotte deserves better. Than Kaylee, and than me. She deserves so much more. I just—" His knuckles are white against the steering wheel again, his jaw clenched. "I'm working on it. I can make a deal."

Val puts her hand on Isaac's forearm. It's rigid, every tendon and muscle flexed. But he relaxes under her touch. "It'll work out. I know it will. And if I can help in any way . . ." She trails off. It's a stupid thing to offer. What could she do?

But he nods quickly. "Thanks. That means a lot."

She doesn't regret asking about Charlotte, though it was hardly the easy conversation topic she had hoped for. No wonder Isaac talked last night about their time as children being the best their lives would be. She's wasted all her years up until now hiding, and he's had the best part of his life taken from him. What pain are Marcus, Javi, and Jenny carrying?

The land around them is still the same up-and-down hills and mountains, with hardy green dots and that orange-tinted rock. It feels less threatening here on the road than it does at the isolated house. "I wonder what that color of orange would taste like," she muses.

"You remember that one?" Isaac asks.

"What one?"

He glances at her, eyes wrinkled in a smile. It's a relief to see it. "Color rain. From the show. We'd call out a color and it would rain what we asked for. They were all different flavors."

Val shakes her head, but there *is* a hint of something. A taste on the back of her tongue. "That's so weird. I've always looked at colors and imagined how they'd taste. I once told Gloria's kids I knew what the color green tasted like. They teased me for a year. Actually, they still tease me about it."

"You picked green every time." Isaac's eyes wrinkle even more. "Jenny liked pink. Marcus knew more colors than any of the rest of us; I still don't know some of the colors he'd pick. And Javi would always choose the weirdest colors he could think of, trying to find something gross to play a prank on us."

Val can *almost* remember. It's like a draft under a door, hinting at what's behind. But it's not lost on her that Isaac's leaving out Kitty. What color would she pick? "Sparkles," Val whispers, which doesn't make sense because it isn't even a color.

Isaac's smile fades. "Yeah. Sparkles. Anyway, Jenny would be mad we're talking about the show. We're not supposed to outside of the interviews."

"But I can't influence your memories if I don't have any real ones." Val shifts to look out her window. "How did they do that? The color rain? Seems like an expensive gimmick for a kids' show, dyeing water and pouring it down on the stage." She wants to know the trick behind it. Because now she can't get the strange sense memory of that taste off her tongue. Green wasn't green apple or mint or lime, it was *springtime*. A riot of life bursting free after a long winter.

"I don't know," Isaac says. "I remember it as actual rain. We pretended so well, it felt real."

"Yeah. We were all acting prodigies, and that was our one shining chance to show the world our chops, and then—"

"And then," Isaac finishes, "the magic ended, and nothing has ever tasted green again."

Val stares out at the infinitely repeating landscape. Maybe it's a set, a rolling one that scrolls the same scene forever. Hasn't her whole life been a single set, one repeating cycle of seasons with no actual change?

"What if you were right?" she asks.

"I probably wasn't." He tries to sound teasing, but doesn't quite manage it. "Right about anything, I mean. But what specifically are you referring to?"

"That the reason I forgot about the show is because I had to. Because otherwise I'd know I was truly happy then, and I'll never have that again."

Isaac taps his fingers on the steering wheel. They're long, slender fingers, ending in neatly trimmed nails. She likes the shape of his hands. She likes everything about Isaac, really, his angular body, the way his face is less than the sum of its parts, the way he pauses before talking to make sure he's careful with his words.

"But if things really were ideal, then Kitty wouldn't have— You should know, Val. You should know that—" He looks at her, his words catching, and then he moves his head straight forward again. "Well, you should know whatever you want to know. I think this is good, going to see your mom."

"I hope so." Val turns back to the endless road, watching desperately for any sign of change.

When the basement lights flicker on to reveal Javi, his fists are raised, as though expecting a fight. It takes him only half a second to slip back into his cool, calm self. He saunters forward and takes the chair in front of the screen.

"Hello, Javi," the voice says, lower than it had been for Marcus.

"If this was always going to be virtual, couldn't we have done it from somewhere more comfortable?" Javi crosses his legs, posture effortless and confident. "Or from home?"

"This place is important."

"Yet you didn't bother to make the trek out here, because you know it's unreasonable. You look familiar, though. Have we met?" His voice is puzzled, with none of the flirtation that usually lines his tone.

"Have we? Let me do your introduction. *To you, sitting on the rug in front of—*"

"Wait, is this it? The podcast? You're recording it right now?"

"Yes. Please don't interrupt. We have to focus."

Javi gestures for her to go on.

*To you, sitting on the rug in front of the television, Javi was exciting—and dangerous. As dangerous as a child on children's pro-*

*gramming could be, anyway. Javi alone challenged the narratives, questioned what they were doing, introduced an element of chaos.*

*Were they building a fort? Javi would try to build it so high he could climb into the sky. Were they drawing? Javi drew on himself, tattoos and scales and naughty words, and tried to get the others to join him. Were they putting all the toys they summoned back where they belonged in the empty darkness? Javi tried to sneak one under his shirt, to keep it for later.*

*It never worked, of course. Mister—*

"Hsst." Javi holds up a hand. "We don't say his name. It's a rule."

"It's not my rule. It's a made-up rule."

He tries for an easy smile, but there's an edge to it. "All rules are made up."

"Not in here. In here, the rules matter more than anything. You know that. Besides, I said not to interrupt." Her voice is sharper before it shifts back to a lilt.

*Mister Magic would always appear in front of Javi, blocking his way. And then you realized Javi was small—so small! Not nearly as big as he had seemed when he was bravely declaring he was going to climb right out of there, or as bold as he had acted when he graffitied his own skin, or as sneaky as he had been when he tried to hold on to something he wasn't allowed to own.*

*Javi would hang his head and apologize, and Mister Magic would put one long, long finger under Javi's chin and tip it back up. You would let out a sigh of relief, because Javi had been mischievous, and then he had been disciplined, and then he had been forgiven. He could rejoin the others, still be a part of the circle.*

*Javi was the adorable, mop-topped, impish embodiment of actions having consequences. He acted out so you didn't have to. He modeled misbehavior and then correction so you could do what you were supposed to, having already seen your impulses played out on the screen.*

*Aren't you curious to find out what actions the man now sitting before me—handsome, polished, perhaps with a bit of mischief in him yet—has accomplished, and whether there have been any consequences?*

Javi has a glint in his eyes as he folds his arms. "Well, that was something."

"Thank you. We worked hard on it." She laughs, the sound ringing through the room.

Javi softens a bit. "You have a nice laugh."

"Thank you. We also worked hard on it. Do you remember how you used to laugh? It made everyone who heard it feel like laughing, too. Made them wish they were laughing with you."

Javi tilts his head. "No one remembers their own laugh, only the laughs they get from other people. So, what now? Are we recording?" Javi looks around and he *does* see the camera, narrowing in on it. He raises an eyebrow. "A hidden camera? Really?"

"Not hidden, just unnoticed. There's a difference. Don't worry about the camera. We've built in fail-safes, is all. Redundancies." She pronounces the word with delicious emphasis, as though bouncing along each syllable. "It's terrible to be let down by something you depend on. Isn't that a funny phrase, though: *fail-safe*. Safely failing. Is there a certain safety in failure?"

"Are you actually asking me? Is this the interview? Have you ever listened to a podcast, because I'm pretty sure this isn't how they work."

"It's all the interview. It's all the podcast. Why don't you introduce yourself as you are now? It'll be nice to have things in your own words."

Javi flashes his teeth. "Okay. Sure. Hello, gentle listeners. My name is Javier Chase, but you can call me Javi. After all, we're already friends, right? We have been for a long time, if you're interested in a children's show that aired thirty years ago. I'd say get a life, but I'm here talking to you about it, so I can't really criticize."

"Have you?"

"Have I what?"

"Gotten a life?"

"As much as anyone does. I'm an attorney. Supreme Court clerkship thanks to nepotism. Went on to my family's firm, also thanks to nepotism. Easy to make partner when your name is on the building. Married a Kennedy. It was that or a Bush, and Kennedys throw better parties. Had two kids. Currently divorcing a Kennedy. Kennedy cast-offs are also a distinguished group, to be fair. We throw good parties, too. I'm trying to think what else I shouldn't say about myself."

"What do you mean, shouldn't?"

"Everything's supposed to go through our well-trained family publicist. Maybe a couple focus groups to test how well the information is received. I'm going to be in trouble."

"Trouble with who?"

"Don't worry about it. They won't be mad at you, and they'll be mad at me no matter what I say. I figure, why poke a sleeping bear when you can kick it in the balls instead? It's like my grandfather always says: *Commit to something for once, you useless sack of shit*." Something dangerous in Javi's eyes contradicts his lazy smile.

"Is that why you agreed to come to the reunion, then? To make your family angry?"

"My rebellious-teen phase was cut short; maybe I'm trying to recapture my youth. Were you a rebellious teen?"

"Neither of those things."

"Neither rebellious nor a teen? That sounds like either a very interesting story, or a very boring one." Javi laughs, running his fingers through his hair. "But lucky you. I gave both teenagerhood and rebellion a shot and it didn't end well. They made sure I learned my lesson. Trust me when I say they were not as gentle as our friend in the cape." He tilts his head up like an imaginary finger is beneath it. Then he twitches, lowers his chin.

"You have kids now. Are they learning those same lessons?"

Javi glares. "What do you mean?"

"I mean, who is teaching them? Do they have the gentleness of your friend in the cape, or are they learning the way your family taught you? You want to recapture your teen rebellion; what about your childhood happiness? What about *their* childhood happiness? Do you wish you had something like the circle of friends for them, where you know they'd be safe?"

"But it wasn't safe. Not in the end."

There's a static burst of noise, the background hum flaring to a barrage. Javi flinches and covers his ears. He looks smaller, a frightened cast to his usually confident face.

"We aren't talking about the end yet," the voice says, continuing on as though nothing happened. "We're talking about the middle. The infinite middle, no beginning remembered, no ending in sight. Wasn't it magical, six special friends just right for the circle, just right for Mister Magic to help, just right to help each other, and just right to help everyone out there watching, too? Learning and growing and being taught alongside them? Don't you wish you could give that to your own kids?"

His posture has shifted to defensiveness, no ease he can pretend at. He keeps glancing around the room. It's clear he feels observed in a way that is no longer performance for a camera. "I'm doing a good job. My kids are okay, I think."

"You think? Or you hope? Or you pretend not to see that they aren't?"

"I—"

"People think children's lives are simple, easy, but it's the opposite. *Everything* that happens around them affects them, and they don't have the power to affect any of it back. But in there, with him, you had all the power. You got to affect everything around you, literally change it with your imaginations, with your dreams. You got exactly what you needed. All you had to do was summon Mister Magic, and then follow the rules."

Javi flinches at the name, coming back to himself. His eyes narrow, and he leans forward, lowering his voice. "You seem really intense about a show that ended thirty years ago."

"Aren't you? Hasn't it influenced every decision you've made since?"

Javi pushes on, not answering the question. "Why are you really doing this podcast? What's the angle?"

"We're doing this because the circle broke, and when it broke, it broke the magic. It broke your childhoods. It broke *you*. You got pulled out too soon, and it wasn't fair. Not to anyone. We lost all those children watching, and all the children who should have been watching ever since. We want to close the circle again, for all of you, and for all of them."

Javi twists his mouth, like there's a bad taste. "Don't pretend like it was magical. If it was, Kitty wouldn't be dead. Have you found anything out about that? Was there some sort of abuse happening on set? You should loop me in if you're hoping to be Ronan Farrow or something."

"I don't know what a Ronan Farrow is. Do you remember any abuse?"

His jaw clenches. Unclenches. Clenches. Chin tips up again, then is deliberately lowered. "No. I remember getting in trouble. That was my role. But it was never—not then, no. No abuse then."

"*Then* is an interesting word to use. Was there abuse later?"

"Are you asking if the illustrious, respected, fabulously wealthy Chase family would ever abuse one of their own? Would ever show the child just a few shades too brown exactly what he meant to them, exactly how far they'd go to break him and keep him from embarrassing them?" Javi's smile is absolutely devastating. "Not in any way you can prove."

"So, on the show . . ." She hums a note to prompt him to answer, and Javi stares past her. There's something about the way the black of the screen, the absolute absence of anything around the interviewer, reflects in his eyes. Pulls something out of him, as if he can't help but want to fill that void.

"He let us know what he expected, and then we did it. Even me. It was easy. Maybe if I had stayed on the show longer, I could have learned that lesson well enough to avoid what came later." Javi's shoulders drop. He looks too tired to be wary anymore, his pupils at last expanding to swallow up the color. "You know what, yeah.

I do wish I had something like the show for my kids. To watch, or even for them to be on. I don't know how to get them out of what I brought them into, how to give them something gentler. Some way to shape them that doesn't break them in the process. I'm a grown man and I'm still afraid of my own family. Too cowardly to save my kids from them. Maybe Val's dad had it right. Snatch your kid and run, never look back."

The interviewer's voice is sharper, lower. "Does Val seem happy? Do you think he saved her from something?"

Javi shakes his head. "No. He didn't save her. She's nothing like what she was. Who she was. That Val would never have—she would never have left us, you know? Never. She's like a ghost now. Everything that made her special is gone. She didn't even—she didn't even remember Kitty. Can you believe that?"

Another burst of static so loud Javi cries out, covering his ears. "Can you make that stop? It feels like something's crawling into my brain."

The voice is smooth and silky. "Everything made sense when you were in the circle, and nothing made sense after. You felt loved, you felt safe, you felt whole."

Javi cautiously uncovers his ears, as though unsure it's safe. "Yes. And that's the most fucked-up— Sorry, language. I know. *Clean mouth, clean mind, happiness is what you'll find.* What I meant was, that's the worst part, isn't it? Even knowing what happened to Kitty, I still look back on that time and wish it hadn't ended. Wish I could be that kid, playing pranks, causing mischief when the stakes were impossibly low, when the correction was so gentle. When we all had each other. So maybe the idea is to take your kids and find your own Mister—"

Javi's jaw snaps shut. His hand comes up, covering his eyes. Blocking them from view. When he lowers it, his eyes are back to normal, and his expensive smile comes back. "Well, find your own magic, I suppose. The magic way to give your kids the perfect childhood that will turn them into better adults than you could ever have been. The magic way to undo whatever damage your parents did to you, to keep your kids happy and safe and protected forever. Maybe that's why *you're* still obsessed with the show, why we came here like moths to a flame."

"You miss the magic."

Javi waves his fingers sarcastically through the air. "The magic of childhood." But as his fingers fall, his face grows wistful. He repeats his phrase, this time whispered with longing. "*The magic of childhood*. You're good at this," he says, frowning. "I wasn't going to talk about anything real. How'd you manage what decades of therapists haven't?"

"Exactly what you said. *The magic of childhood*. Would you like to see it again, Javi?"

"See what?"

"The magic."

"The show? You have episodes?" He sits forward eagerly, hunger in his expression.

"I have it all. But you have to do something for me, first." The interviewer's voice becomes playful, a hint of mischief. The same mischief that was always Javi's role in the circle, inviting him to play along. "We'll make a deal."

Javi's eyes narrow warily. But he hasn't leaned back to put more space between himself and the screen. Because no matter what he tells himself, no matter how smart or cynical he is, Javi wants that magic back.

"What deal?" he asks, and this time the burst of static isn't painful. It's a welcoming purr.

# EIGHT

"Your hand okay?" Isaac asks as he exits the highway.

"What? Oh. Yeah. Something's irritating my palm." Val's skin is red and streaky, the scar tissue swelling like she has hives. "Is this Bliss? Can we stop for a bathroom break?" She doesn't want to have to use her mother's. It feels too intimate, which is absurd, considering this woman gave birth to her.

"We can stop. But this isn't Bliss. It's called Harmony, I think." Harmony is just a bunch of houses scattered on lots around the highway. Probably people looking for somewhere cheap to retire. Val wishes it were Bliss so she wouldn't have more time to think and worry.

Isaac stops at a gas station. Val lets herself daydream for a moment that they're on a road trip. They'll grab snacks and continue on to Zion, or the Grand Canyon. Val's always wanted to see the Grand Canyon. Now she wants to see it with Isaac. She can imagine more clearly what it would feel like to stand on the edge of the world with him than what it will feel like to meet her mother.

Guilt stabs her. She just found out her mom isn't dead *and* she has a dead sister, and she's already trying to forget it again.

When Val gets out of the car, the air is oppressively warm, like standing in front of an open oven. But at least the humming is totally gone. The insects must not live here. She hurries into the gas station, which is as warm as outside but also stuffy. It's cramped, shelves too close together with that strange small-town convenience store hodgepodge of anything someone might find themselves looking for. Condoms next to chargers next to children's toys next to a wide assortment of hats advertising Second Amendment rights. Isaac pauses in front of a throw blanket with an image of the *Mona Lisa*.

"Did you need this?" He gestures at it as though presenting a prize on Gloria's favorite game show, *The Price Is Right*. Val can't imagine any price is right for that blanket.

"I've never needed anything more in my entire life." Val laughs, then slips past him and uses the restroom. On her way out, she grabs a Coke. She doesn't want to spend what little money she has, but she needs the comfort of sugar and caffeine. At the counter, an older woman with black hair and a gorgeous magenta lip stain is reading a worn paperback.

Val puts the Coke on the counter. Isaac's already outside again, so it's just the two of them. "Hi," she says.

"Mm-hmm." The woman glances up. "Heading to Saint George?"

"No. We're going to Bliss."

The woman frowns, looking at her closely for the first time. "You're not from there. What are you going to Bliss for?"

"I—" *I'm going to ask my assumed-dead mother what happened to my forgotten actually-dead sister so I can confirm whether or not I'm responsible for every bad thing that's ever happened in my life?*

"I'm looking at real estate," Val says, instead.

The woman snorts a laugh. "Look elsewhere, sweetie. Trust me. You don't want anything out there."

Val feels like she needs to justify her lie. "I like the desert, though."

"The desert does have a way of wriggling into your soul. It's the only landscape that tells you the truth about yourself: You're small, and you're alone, and you don't matter. And that's okay." She pauses, pulling out a napkin and wiping the condensation off the Coke bottle before passing it back to Val. "But not Bliss. You don't want anything Bliss tells you about yourself. Go anywhere else. Okay?" She fixes her eyes on Val and waits until Val nods. "Okay. Good girl. Two fifty."

"Two fifty?"

"For the Coke."

"Oh. Right." Val hands over the money and takes her change, then hurries outside.

The woman has her spooked. Not because of her insistence that Val shouldn't go to Bliss, but because of Val's instinct to lie. If Val can't even say out loud why she's going, how can she handle talking to her mother?

"I can do this," Val says to herself. Dad turned her stubbornness against her, using it to keep her firmly in place at the ranch. She won't let anyone or anything stop her from finding out why they ended up there. She can do this, and she will.

She climbs into the car. Isaac already has it started, blasting the AC so it's comfortable inside. Sealed in against the heat, against the world.

"It'll be okay," he says. Apparently, she's not good at hiding her emotions.

Val holds his gaze like it's a lifeline. "Yeah. This doesn't have to change anything."

Isaac wrinkles his nose. "Well . . ."

Val lets out a shaky laugh. "Okay, it changes things. Everything. But that's what I want. Change. It's what I asked for."

"You asked for it?"

The day Dad died. The open door. When she put her hand through and asked, she didn't ask for Dad to be okay. She asked for something else—anything else—to be happening. And that's what she got, in the end, didn't she?

"*And when you're in trouble,*" she starts, lifting a hand.

Isaac grabs her hand fast. Too fast. She looks at him, surprised, but he smiles and squeezes her fingers. "We're not in trouble." He lets go and pulls back onto the frontage road. "You should know," he says, "there are a lot of frogs. At your mother's place."

"Frogs?"

"You'll see what I mean."

"Okay?" Val laughs at his attempt at mystery. They don't get back on the highway, instead heading east into the hills. The road is long and empty, but at least it's paved. After nearly an hour, without preamble or warning, they hit a small city.

"This is . . . adorable?" Maybe that's why the woman at the gas station hates Bliss. It puts shambling, sparse Harmony to shame. The neighborhoods are laid out in a perfect grid. The roads gleam black, the sidewalks white, the lawns green. Towering trees provide relief from the sun, placed evenly along every walkway, protecting every home. It's like a board game all laid out—one she wants to play. One she wants to be part of. There's a main street up ahead, lined with stately redbrick buildings trimmed in dark blue. Isaac doesn't slow, but she wishes he would. They pass a market, a school, a church, a city hall, and a building that looks like a hotel, with a white wraparound balcony and beautifully arched doors. Why couldn't they have stayed *here*?

"Yeah," Isaac says, "it's cute." He doesn't look to either side, driving straight and speeding up a bit.

Val wonders what it might have been like to grow up here. To go to school, to walk home to a normal house on a normal street. To attend that church, even. She wonders what denomination it is, with a soaring spire but no cross on top. Does her mom worship there? Would Val have?

Would living here have been actual bliss?

Isaac doesn't turn into any of the neighborhoods, though. He drives straight through town and around a hill. There's no green grass, no soaring trees. They're back in the desert, the mirage of Bliss evaporated behind them. Val deflates as their destination becomes clear.

The Blissful Springs RV Park grows from the ground like something found underneath a rotting piece of wood. The trailers are squat and chaotic, scattered around a central hub. She half expects them to sprout legs and scurry away as the car approaches. Now that she wants him to speed up, Isaac slows, easing into the park as though anticipating children playing. From the looks of things, no children have ever played here. Everything is sun-faded and cracked, tinted orange from the rust-colored dirt. A line of forgotten wash hangs limply, splattered with dust.

"Oh god," Val breathes out, seeing their destination ahead of them. "The frogs." Isaac wasn't kidding. If the park looks like fungal growth, her mom's place is the heart of the infestation. Heaps of stone and ceramic and plaster and plastic frogs form mounds around the lot of a trailer the color of bleached bones, complete with yellowed cracks and blackened rot climbing up from the ground. "It's deranged."

"Cheerful? Maybe?" It's no use, and Isaac gives up. "It's a little deranged. I should have given you a better warning."

Val feels besieged by frog eyes. But worse are the frogs that, due to weather or time, have no eyes at all. Isaac puts the car in park, cracks the windows, and turns off the engine.

"Don't come in with me," Val blurts. "I need to go alone. But don't leave!" She had planned on releasing him from his burden. But she can't stay here. And from the looks of it, her mom doesn't have a car. At least not one that works. She'd be stranded.

He takes her hand. Val was right about one thing, at least. When he's holding it, her palm doesn't itch nearly as much. "I'd never leave you," he says.

Someone else might make it playful, but Isaac says it with absolute sincerity, which is exactly what she needs right now. He feels like her only friend. More than that. Her only person. Her anchor. And yesterday she hadn't even remembered his name.

Oh god. *Names*. Val has no idea what her mom's name is. "I don't know her," she starts, but, as always, Isaac is there for her.

"Debra."

"Debra." It doesn't spark anything in Val. Or she's already so filled with jangling nerves she wouldn't know if it did.

Isaac hesitates, then talks fast. "Debra's not well. I don't know how else to explain it. She's not crazy or dangerous or anything, she's just . . . a little vacant."

Val steels herself. But she pauses opening the door. "If you hear sirens or see police coming—"

"Why would that happen?"

Val shrugs sheepishly, smiling to play it off as a joke. But it's not. Is there a statute of limitations on arson? On murder? On whatever she did that was so bad she closed the door on her childhood and locked it up tight?

Isaac smiles back, playing along. "If the cops come, we can Thelma and Louise it out of here."

"Didn't they drive off a cliff?" Val hasn't seen any movies, but she's read summaries of a lot of them online using Gloria's computer. She hates not understanding references.

Isaac makes a *yikes* face. "Right. Bonnie and Clyde, also dead. Butch Cassidy and the Sundance Kid, also dead. Running from the police in barren locations doesn't turn out well. So, let's hope it doesn't come to that." His smile drops and his magnified eyes seem to hold her as tightly as if he were hugging her. "Val, you didn't do anything bad. You were just a kid."

How does he always know what she's actually feeling? She wants to cling to his reassurance, but he's wrong. She *did* do something bad. That's why she never tried to change her life on the ranch. Because she deserved it.

Val climbs out of the car. The humming bugs are back, but it's not as loud. Maybe the plague of fake frogs scares them off. She picks her way carefully to the missing front porch. A screen door hangs askew a foot and a half above the dirt ground. Two stacked cinder blocks serve as a step up. She nudges the screen aside, raises a fist, and holds it in the air.

This is a door that can never be closed again. It's only ajar now.

If she reaches out, she doesn't know what will take her hand. She'll have to accept it, because she's asking. That's the deal. She's going to find out what she did, and maybe she'll have to pay for it, too.

Val knocks on the door.

After an agonizing wait, it creaks open to reveal a dim and dusty interior and an even dimmer and dustier woman. She's shorter than Val, her harsh gray hair cut close to the scalp. But her eyebrows are still a bold, dark mirror to Val's own, her eyes the same pixie shape ringed by the same thick, black lashes.

Val's hit by a wall of memories. The smell cuts through everything, though. Floral and stinging and musty. Her mother's perfume.

*Val's standing behind a door, chest heaving, jaw clenched, fists so tight her little hands ache. She can hear them talking about her, can smell her mother's sharp perfume lingering on the clothes in the closet where she's hiding.*

*"What else are we going to do with her?" Her mother's voice. "I'm done, Steve. I'm done. I can't keep going into the school, trying to sort out her messes. It's your fault she's this way, your fault she's so stubborn and defiant. We're lucky they're willing to take her at all. If you don't agree to this, then—"*

*"Okay." Dad sounds exhausted, stretched so thin he's ready to snap. "Okay, we'll try it."*

*"I'm not going!" Val screams, throwing open the door.*

*"Goddamn it!" her mother shouts back. "What are you doing in there?"*

*"You can't make me! I'm not going without Kitty!"*

*"You'll do what we tell you!"*

*But Val won't. They both know it. No one can make Val do what she doesn't want to. Val's going to win this argument, no matter what it takes.*

*She won't leave Kitty behind, not with* her. *Not in this house, not at that school without Val to protect her. She doesn't trust anyone else to do it. Not even Dad. He's not strong enough. Only Val is. Val doesn't care about leaving. She might even be glad. But she'll never, ever abandon Kitty.*

Val blinks, coming back to herself, back to right now. Back to the mother she hasn't seen in thirty years, standing in front of her with narrowed eyes.

Val raises her hand awkwardly, then lowers it. "Hi. It's me. Val. Valentine. Your daughter." She keeps tagging on descriptors, waiting to see the moment her mother recognizes her. Wondering if it will be tears, or joy, or anger. Bracing herself for anything.

Instead, her mother lets out a small huff of air. Her expression holds all the interest of someone flipping aimlessly through channels, resigned to finding nothing they actually want to see.

Val's long-lost mother shuffles to the side. "Well, come in, I guess."

When the lights flicker on a few seconds after the camera, Jenny is already walking for the chair, no hesitation. She doesn't sit in it, though. Instead, she stands close to the screen, searching. The fine lines around her eyes pinch.

She sighs with disappointment and shifts back. "They left. Isaac and Val. We'll have to push Isaac's time in here."

"We don't have to worry about Isaac. He's always where he's supposed to be."

"Yeah, except I literally just said he left with Val." Jenny rubs her forehead like she has a headache. "He'll come back, though. He will. And he'll bring her. Same as when Val would somehow crawl away. I remember the first time she disappeared. We were all frantic. It was time to clean up—we had made things chaotic, as usual, and, as usual, we had to put everything away before we ended it."

"Why?"

"You know why. He was there but he wasn't always *there,* especially not after Val took charge. But things like messes and misbehaving and crying called him to come teach us."

"No, I'm asking: Why did you need to end it? Couldn't you keep playing? Keep dreaming?"

Jenny's face darkens. "That was always Val's idea. She said we needed to rest, and we couldn't do that while he was there."

"Why not?"

"I'm just telling you what she said. *I* never knew why. Anyway, we were ready for rest time, but Val had managed to get herself lost. Not in the way that Marcus used to, where he'd pretend too hard and Mister Magic would have to pull him back. But, like, *actually* lost. Gone. The others were panicking, saying we had to have her with us before he came, before he saw. Otherwise we couldn't put him back, otherwise his cape would get too big and cold and—" She stops, a little frown deepening the crease between her eyebrows. "So, we were all yelling her name. Kitty was crying, of course. Javi was annoyed, probably that he hadn't figured out how to do this before Val did. But Isaac crawled around the darkest edges, pushing. Then at last he found the weak spot where she had slipped through. He put Javi in charge, which was the only real way to ever make him behave, and then Isaac disappeared, too. They were in there for so long. We cleaned and then we made messes and then we cleaned and then we made messes, anything to stall, so tired we could hardly even pretend to be having fun. Marcus was halfway through painting us a boring old playground by the time they finally came out, Val's hand in Isaac's. He was so relieved, and she—" Jenny's lips twisted to one side. Derision, but also confusion on her face. "She looked like she had woken up into a bad dream."

"*From* a bad dream, you mean. I know that phrase."

"No, that's not what I meant. Anyway. Isaac found her then, he found her now. He'll get her where she needs to be." Jenny bites her lip, like she's not quite sure. "She's so different. I'm afraid it's not going to be enough. She needs to remember, but she's—it's like she got left behind there, too, and this new Val is a poor copy." Her gaze goes blank, fixed on some unseen point in the black of the screen. "Did any of us actually make it out?" she whispers.

The interviewer's bright, high voice pulls Jenny back. "Isaac will find the Val we need. And you'll help. You're such a good helper. We can do your interview now, if you want."

Jenny lets out a laugh like bags under her eyes and stretch marks on her stomach and not a full night's sleep in more than a decade. "I'm not doing an interview. I don't want to talk about him. I want to talk *to* him."

"Well, that's not possible, silly! If you could call him, none of us would be here, would we?" The voice lowers, sharpens, grows more teeth. "*Would we?*"

"No." Jenny hangs her head.

"Exactly! But we'll stay on schedule. It's important to follow a schedule. You know that." The interviewer slips into her lilting podcast voice.

*Even if you loved the show, even if you watched devotedly until the last episode, you forgot about Jenny.*

*That's okay. Jenny would forgive you. She was the sidekick, the best friend, the one who was always there, ready to support you in whatever you wanted to do. Did she ever pick the games? Did she ever call out what they wanted to pull from the darkness around them? Did she ever lead, or rebel, or shepherd, or create, or demand? No. She was just Jenny. Right there, at your side. Ready to play. And that was all she wanted: to be included, to be approved of.*

*To be part of the circle.*

"Stop it," Jenny says.

*You might not remember Jenny, but she was important. Crucial to the magic, to the fun. And here's a secret: Mister Magic was with her more than anyone else. She was the only friend Mister Magic ever hugged, wrapping her tightly in his arms, encircling her in that cloaked embrace.*

"Stop," Jenny whispers, tears in her eyes.

*Jenny was the quiet, loyal heart of the circle of friends. She always listened. She knew every rule and followed them exactly. Jenny was the stone that keeps an arch in place, the link in the middle of a chain that never breaks. No matter what, Jenny didn't break.*

*Jenny isn't the little girl she once was, with her curls and crinkle-nosed smile and adorable dimples. The woman she is doesn't look like our friend. Not at all. Her hair is cut harshly, a line she thinks makes her look classy but really makes her look old. She's all angles and cold lines, and everything about her feels like a lie. She hasn't been able to fix anything since then, no matter how hard she tries to follow all the rules, and she's so alone and so sad and so pathetic. We can't remember why we were friends with her. Why we loved her. Why Mister Magic loved her. Maybe, if anyone could hug her like that again, we'd remember if she was worth loving.*

"Why are you doing this?" Jenny wraps her arms around herself, head down.

*Jenny was always the most loving, the most eager to be loved. Maybe that's why you forgot her. She didn't ask anything of you except approval. Maybe she's still asking for that. Maybe her whole life after leaving the circle has been looking at the world around her and asking, hoping, begging to be loved as completely as she was then. Maybe she's built an entire life, an entire family, an entire purpose around trying to recapture that.*

*And, from the looks of her, it hasn't worked.*

*How about a hug, Jenny?*

"You sound like a fucking psycho." Jenny glares through her tears as she looks up.

"*Clean hearts and clean minds, cleanliness at all times! Nothing dirty, nothing bad, always happy, never sad!*" The interviewer's voice drops suddenly, deeper, broader. "Language, Jenny. You learned that lesson."

"Don't," she hisses. "Don't you dare try to sound like him. I didn't think you were cruel."

A laugh, layered so it's somehow high and low at the same time, echoes through the room, surrounding Jenny. "It's a children's show. And what's crueler than children?" But as suddenly as it changed, the voice shifts again, back to the high, sweet pitch. "I'm sorry. Don't cry. Listen, I'll tell you more of the podcast! You can tell me if I did a good job, if people will like it."

"I don't want to—"

*Things fall apart; the center cannot hold. Did they feel it? Did they feel the rough beast, slouching toward them? Did you, watching the show? Could you sense the building tension, the coiling of doom, ready to strike?*

*Or was it the same as it ever was, right up until the moment it wasn't?*

Jenny slumps to the floor, holding her head in her hand. "I don't see the point of these podcasts. We don't need to build an audience beforehand. They'll come when it's ready. They always did."

"Things have changed, though. We can reach so many more people now! So many more little minds and hearts. The men promised, standing where you are. Promised and begged. If we could do this for them, they could fix it. We made a deal, so we're doing what we're told. You understand that." There's no teasing or accusation in her tone; it's a statement of fact.

Jenny nods, sitting back to rest against the legs of the chair. "We do what we're told," she repeats. "Keep going. You're doing great."

*If there were recordings of the show, if, say, I could send a link to a phone, what would you see?*

*Would you see a dated, silly program? Or would you see six ideal children, living in an ideal world, surrounded by magic they made for themselves, sealed away in that wondrous space where nothing can hurt them, where they make all the right choices, where they're exactly who any parent would hope their kids could be?*

*There's a reason parents loved Mister Magic. Why they felt safe leaving their children in his care. Both in front of the television, and in that perfect black wonderland. Where children could simply exist, free of the past, untroubled by the future.*

*What parent wouldn't want that for their child?*

Jenny's expression is flat. "Sure," she says. "Sounds good. You're nailing it."

Her phone chimes and she looks down before letting it fall to the floor. "No one tells you what it's like, being a mom. I want to be able to sing a rhyme and teach my kids exactly how to be. But it didn't work for me. I did *everything* I was supposed to, followed all the rules. I never stopped, even after, and I'm so sad. I'm so sad, all the time, and I don't know how not to be sad. I kept having babies thinking I wouldn't feel alone, that I would have my own circle, that I would be the center of it. But there's no circle. It's a chain, and you're right—I'm the link holding everything together and it's all just weight. It's weight, and it never lets up, and no one else ever holds it. No one else even notices it. I don't understand how I can be there every moment of every single day and somehow not exist at the same time. Most days I think I'm not even a person. Not to them, not to myself. I look at my girls and this *pit,* this yawning pit of despair opens in me, because they're so sweet and they're so new and they're going to go through everything I did, they're going to do everything I'm teaching them and telling them to do to be happy, and I'm *not* happy, and I don't know how to be happy. I haven't been happy since." She looks up at last, tears trailing down her face as she searches the screen. "I want the rules to matter. I want the rules to *help*. And I want my dad," she whispers.

The interviewer has no response to this.

Jenny doesn't wipe away her tears. "I want this part to be over."

"We've been in this part for so long, haven't we? *Have* we?" There's confusion in the tone.

"We have," Jenny says with a sigh.

"Come on, Jenny. We didn't mean to make you cry. You're everyone's friend, the best friend. The truest friend. Sing it. You'll feel better. *Take my hand . . .* "

Jenny looks so young, sitting there on the floor, eyes wide as she searches one more time for something beyond the screen. And then that yearning disappears, vulnerability and weakness and even hope set aside with ruthless efficiency. Jenny stands with a popping of joints. "I have to go get ready for the stupid gala. You already have my hand, you've always had it. You don't need me to sing anything with you."

Jenny walks out and the lights click off.

"But I *want* you to," a small, sad voice says, unheard.

# BAR THE GATE

Val's mother doesn't wait for her to sit down. She takes her own seat in a recliner so similar to the one Dad died in that Val can't catch her breath.

In fact, there aren't many differences between this cramped living space and the tiny cabin Val and Dad shared. A kitchen so small it's essentially useless. A yellowed overhead light fixture that leaches the life out of everything, making Val's mom look sallow and half dead. A door to a bedroom that's nearly all bed with a rumpled, pilling brown quilt. Next to the recliner is an upholstered chair. That would be where Val's love seat in the cabin was.

She can see it: Instead of sitting next to Dad, quietly reading, no one talking, she'd be sitting on that chair, next to Mom, quietly reading, no one talking. There was never going to be an idyllic childhood in a dreamy patchwork town. Not for Val.

But the comparison between the cabin and the trailer isn't quite right. At least the cabin came with the barn, the stables, the big house and Gloria, and as much outdoors as Val could explore. Here, she'd be trapped by the heat and the desert. And there's something that never would have been allowed with Dad: Debra has a television. It's a boxy old set, like at the other house, complete with an antenna. Nothing like the sleek flatscreen Gloria's kids bought for her a few years ago. Right now Debra's TV is playing black-and-white static, but that doesn't stop her from leaning back in her recliner and fixing her eyes on the screen.

The smell, too, is different. The cabin was musty but clean, thanks to Val. Here, beneath the overwhelming punch of perfume, there's sourness. Unwashed clothes, hair, body. Dad took care of her and then she took care of Dad. No one has done that for Debra.

It's easier to think of her as Debra, as a woman Val's meeting for the first time, rather than as her mother. Standing there on the patch of mottled brown carpet, Val doesn't know where to start. She had assumed she'd be assaulted with questions. Demands to know where she'd been all this time. How she'd been. Who she'd become.

"I like your frogs," Val says, because how else can she start this conversation?

"Toads," Debra corrects, scowling at Val's ignorance. "Toads are much better than frogs. Some toads can bury themselves in the mud, dormant, practically dead, for years. Maybe even decades. Until it rains again and the conditions are right for them."

"I didn't know that." Val hovers where she is, but the room is so small she's nearly bumping into her mother's knees. They're knobby beneath her faded floral housedress. Thick, ugly gray socks hide her feet.

Debra gestures irritably for Val to move. "You're blocking the television." She jerks a hand at the empty chair. "This time of day is when you girls used to be on. I always hope for a rerun."

*You girls.* Two of them. Debra lost both of her daughters, but one of them is back, and it barely seems to register. Val sits gingerly on the edge of the free chair. "Do you have any questions for me?" It's probably better to let Debra go first, and then Val can ask what she needs to know.

At last, Debra glances at her, a flick up and down with her brown eyes. "You're taller."

"Than when I was eight? Yeah, I grew." Val laughs, a tiny, incredulous sound. Isaac had tried to warn her about her mother, but he hadn't done a good enough job.

As though overhearing her thoughts, Debra jerks her chin toward the front door. "I saw that boy you're here with."

Val hardly thinks Isaac, nearing forty, is best described as a boy. But before she can say anything, Debra continues.

"He's been by a few times. Pestering me with questions about your dad, where we lived, things he did before we were married. Asking for photos. Harassing me. I'm glad he didn't come in." Debra narrows her eyes. The lines across her face, tracing the map of her life, are suspicious and unpleasant.

Val's heart picks up. "Isaac was looking for me. Didn't you want him to? Didn't you wonder where Dad took me?"

"Your *father,*" Debra says, and at last she seems emotionally invested in the conversation. Her tone is pungently acidic, all the bitter dregs left in the bottom of a bottle of expired vinegar. "He ruined everything. We got lucky, applying and being accepted to the show. We watched every day, and we could tell it was working. You were so *good.* He could see the changes, too. He agreed, we both agreed, you were getting better. We were doing what was best for you. I was so happy that Mister Magic was fixing you."

Val hadn't been aware she needed to be fixed. "And Kitty?"

Debra flinches, then practically spits the next part. "She didn't need it. *You* did. But you always got your way. Such a difficult little girl. And they wanted you—who knows why—so they were willing to take Kitty, too. She was happy, though. We watched every day. I always knew when my little girl was happy."

"Then why did Dad take me away?" Val knows only Dad could have answered that. Whatever Debra says will be her own side of the story. But that's the only side left.

"Because he's an idiot, that's why. A bad, selfish, spoiling father. He didn't care that giving you to the show was fixing you." She jabs a bony finger toward the television.

"Giving me to it?" That phrasing makes no sense, but Debra herself makes no sense, either. Living out here in a dirty trailer, with no friends or family except a collection of demented toads, watching static on an old television.

Debra continues as though she didn't hear Val's question. "You were going to be—" Debra shakes her head, clicking her jaw shut. Her eyes close and her face relaxes into something dreamy, an echo of long-lost hope and youth. "You were going to be so good. You were going to be sweet and happy, exactly the oldest daughter anyone would wish for. And I was going to be so proud to be your mother." Her eyes open again, and she doesn't look at Val. "And then he ruined it. He ruined you, and I lost Kitty."

"What happened to her?" Val asks, bracing herself.

A twitch runs across Debra's shoulders. "I didn't see," she snaps. "They called me in, yelled at me like what your father did was my fault, so I wasn't watching. It was the only one I missed. The *only* one. I watched every episode. All of them." She looks at Val fiercely, as though daring Val to question her integrity and devotion as a mother. "And they dared to blame me, to question whether I wanted you on the show. Of *course* I did. It was all I wanted for you. Even now, they blame me. Won't let me live in town. Never invite me to meetings. Don't let me back in the house. After everything I gave them! It's not fair!"

Val is at a loss. It sounds like Debra doesn't know how Kitty died . . . but also like it doesn't matter to her. Like that loss pales in comparison with losing the show. She hasn't even asked about Dad, or where Val's been.

Debra doesn't care.

Val scrapes her fingernails over her palm, the agonizing itch crawling up her arm toward her heart. All those years, hiding. Maybe Dad was hiding her from Debra. From being punished for failing to be the daughter Debra felt she deserved. From being punished for being the one who was still here.

A terrible last question burns Val's throat on its way out. "Did you look for me?"

Debra settles back into her chair, staring at the screen, waiting. "I couldn't handle you without him."

"Without Dad?"

"No. Without *him*." Debra holds out a hand, but instead of pointing at the television, she keeps her palm flat, fingers stretched, reaching toward the screen like she's waiting for someone to take it. "I lost both my daughters the day *Mister Magic* ended."

Val stands. The swirling static of the screen infects her with white noise and chaos and meaninglessness. Her entire life tips into a void of cruel absurdity.

Val's mother never looked for them.

*She never looked for them.*

Her father kidnapped her and no one cared. No one except Isaac. The part of her brain still functioning notes that Val should say goodbye, say she's sorry, say anything. But Debra's not looking at her. She's staring at the television with her hand extended, ready to receive whatever scripted prettiness it offers her in place of the living daughter standing right here.

Val can't leave with nothing. This can't be it. What had Isaac asked for when he was here? Information, and . . . "The photos," Val demands. "Where are they?"

Debra gestures in annoyance toward the TV stand. Val tugs open a stiff drawer. There's a stack of photos held together with a flaking rubber band. She wants to go through them quickly and then leave. But the top photo stops her dead.

Val recognizes herself. The same thick, dark hair, the same bold eyebrows and brown eyes, staring defiantly at the camera. Her arm is protectively around a smaller girl.

Brown pigtails, freckles, the clearest blue eyes. She's the little girl Val's always dreamed of. The one she knew in her heart was out there. The one she assumed she'd someday give birth to. She thought she didn't remember Kitty, but Val's been holding on to her this whole time.

Val never had a dream of a future. She only had a nightmare of what she'd already lost.

Hey Academic Reddit, want to see my thesis proposal that got utterly and completely rejected? Thanks for sending me down the Mister Magic rabbit hole and encouraging me all this time. Apparently no one with any sense goes near that show and all the rumors and legends around it. It's basically toxic. Now I have to come up with an entirely different way to finish my PhD in Media Studies, you assholes.

Hi, Professor Perkins,
For my thesis, I'd like to explore archetypes in children's shows of the 80s and 90s and how that influenced elder Millennial culture and attitudes. Specifically, I'll focus on three programs:

Teenage Mutant Ninja Turtles, breaking every personality into The Leader, The Fun One, The Smart One, and The Angry One / Rebel, with a note that obviously women were left out entirely to be the hypercompetent support system for all the men, aka The April O'Neal Problem. My main analysis will focus on the original animated series because that was what was in homes regularly, but will include looks at the first live action movie.

The Smurfs, delving deeper into the problems with Millennial childhood influences about gender roles, namely that every Smurf is defined by what he does with the exception of Smurfette, who is defined solely by her gender (to say nothing of the anti-Semitism and wildly offensive creation story of Smurfette, so I understand I will have to limit the scope of my analysis on this one).

Finally, Mister Magic. This is the most exciting challenge because primary sources are nonexistent. But it also differs from the others in that it featured actual children and their play, which, according to what I experienced personally and I've read online, was hugely influential for those watching. The last cast on the show fell into an interesting set of archetypes: The Mischief Maker, The Creative, The Friend, The Watchful Older Brother, and The Leader. (The youngest child on the show didn't seem to fall into any specific archetypes, though arguments could be made for The Innocent.) The kids were all guided and instructed by a shadowy, nondescript adult male figure, which has all sorts of symbolic possibilities. What is fascinating to me about this show is that The Leader was not a white boy, but a (still white) girl. The evolution of the narrative as The Leader exerted more control and Mister Magic began disappearing from episodes is particularly interesting. Before that, the structure of Mister Magic hadn't changed in its decades-long run, and a lot of viewers point to a girl taking the leadership role as what "ruined" the show.

I'd love to set up a meeting to discuss my direction and refine the idea.

Best,
Carrie Jakubowski

# NINE

The sun assaults Val's eyes as she stumbles off the missing front step, knocking over one of the cinder blocks. She nearly falls among the toads. Would she be buried here, sleeping like the dead until conditions change? Is that how her mother lives her life?

If so, Val is obviously not the hoped-for change. Debra remains in her trailer, content to watch static on the television.

Isaac's not in the car. Val looks frantically around and sees him hurrying toward her from the other end of the park. A woman behind him is shouting something, but Val can't hear what it is. Everyone here is crazy. Everyone here is lost.

Including her.

"Hey," Isaac says, "how did it—" He stops as he gets close enough to see her expression. "Let's go." He opens the car and she's not even buckled before he takes off, cutting across the front of Debra's lot with a bump of toads beneath the tires as he steers away from the woman still shouting behind them. They leave through the back of the RV park.

"I need your phone." Val holds out her hand. Isaac complies. Her fingers are slow and awkward on the keyboard as she Googles Kitty's name along with anything about a fire, or anything related to her name or her father's name. She's hoping for police reports. News articles. Missing child alerts.

There's nothing. Only a few posts about *Mister Magic* on message boards, but nothing legal, nothing official. There's no evidence Val even exists. No evidence anyone looked for her, or accused her or her dad of anything.

And no evidence that anyone ever cared about what happened to Kitty.

Isaac drives until they're out of sight of the RV park, and then he pulls over. Val doesn't realize she's sobbing until he leans between the seats and wraps his arms around her. She cries into his shoulder until her head throbs and her breaths come in desperate spasms.

At last, she's out of tears. She has one hand against his chest, her eyes still pressed into his shirt. He keeps a hand on her shoulder, the other on the back of her head.

Isaac doesn't ask what happened, which somehow makes it easier to open up after thirty years of keeping doors closed on hopes, on fears, on feelings. Thirty years of stubbornly following her father's lead, which had been absolutely unnecessary for both of them. And now he's dead, and she's almost forty, and there's nothing—*nothing*—to show for their lives.

They'd never been keeping any threat out. They'd only been locking themselves in.

Val's voice is raw, all the emotion hollowed out of her. "Debra didn't look for us. She never tried to find me."

Isaac sighs. "I wondered, when I visited her. I tried to give her the benefit of the doubt and assume she'd given up after so long, but . . ." He doesn't need to finish his sentence.

Val lets out a strangled, half-hysterical laugh. Maybe she isn't out of emotions yet, after all. "We were playing a game of hide-and-seek, but no one was seeking. It wasn't only my mom who didn't care where we were. No one did. My dad's stroke, his death. My broken wrist. God, school. A career. A family. Any of it. *All* of it. We could have been living this whole time. Something outside the tiny world we made for ourselves because we thought if we stepped out of it, we'd lose everything. We never needed the ranch. I hate it now, which isn't fair, because I really did love some of it, but it was a prison we chose, a prison we—"

Val can't keep going. Every single aspect of her life is being rewritten by this terrible dramatic irony.

Dad gave up everything to keep them safe from a threat that didn't exist. And because Val was so committed, so fucking stubborn, she stayed the course, too. All it would have taken was a few questions, a careful inquiry, a single stupid Google search, and Val would have known everything.

She lets out another hiccup of a laugh. It's too much.

"What do you want to do?" Isaac asks, once again giving her the choice.

She's always had choices. It took Isaac finding her at last for her to realize that. But what does she want to do? It's such a huge question. She has no formal education. Job skills, sure, but they're pretty specific. Is she going to start from scratch now? Go back to the ranch to regroup, figure out her next step? How can she find her way forward when she still has so little of her past? Because these new revelations don't change that. Even the glimpses she got with her mom are fragmented, confusing. She wants to excavate her own mind. Hopefully, she'll find more of Kitty there.

After all, Val lost so much, but Kitty lost everything. It's not fair. It's not fair that Val lost her sister and all the memories of her, too. Val wants those years back. She wants a life where she grew up with Kitty. Where she was able to protect her. Where Kitty would be the first person she'd call on a day like today, so they could cry and laugh together.

She wants the little girl she's always dreamed of, and she can't have her.

*No.* Val refuses to accept that. Something flares inside, an old fire long reduced to coals, brought back to life with a furious breath. It feels familiar. It feels powerful.

Val wants Kitty back more than she's ever wanted anything in her life. If the only way she can connect with Kitty is through digging up the past, Val will make it happen. No matter what it takes. No matter what it costs.

Val straightens. She's not sad anymore. She's determined.

"Sorry I got your shirt wet," she says.

"I like it better this way. Adds character."

Isaac's the only one who looked for her. He'll help her look for the truth about Kitty. But it will require looking at herself, too. Throwing open the doors to whatever is behind them. She was scared before, but now? Hell itself couldn't stop her.

Val rolls up her sleeves to reveal more of the splotchy scars running from her palms up her forearms. Isaac traces a finger along the damaged skin.

"How did that happen?" he asks.

"Burn scars. But my dad wouldn't say how I got them. Is it possible I'm the one who burned down the studio? And that's how Kitty died?"

Isaac shakes his head quickly. "Kitty didn't die in a fire."

"I thought you couldn't remember what happened."

His nose scrunches, shifting his glasses so only the tops of his eyes are caught in the magnification. "I didn't say I didn't remember. I said it doesn't make sense. But I know it wasn't a fire."

"Then how did I get these scars? They happened before the ranch."

"You didn't have them on the show. I would have noticed."

"So, it happened in the brief window between when I left you, and when my memories begin." Val sighs. She's glad, obviously, that Isaac doesn't think she set a fire that killed her sister. But at least then she would have known what happened. She tugs her sleeves back down, rubbing her itching left palm on her jeans. The mystery of her scars doesn't matter if it has nothing to do with Kitty. Kitty is the priority.

The lack of police reports or news articles nags at her. Something like that should have had some sort of investigation. Unless it was covered up. But there are still people out there who worked on the show. Who will know what happened.

Thanks to the reunion, Val's exactly where she needs to be to access them.

"I want to come to the gala," she says.

Isaac doesn't look enthused by the idea. "You've been through a lot. We should get you to—"

"I don't matter. All that matters is figuring out the truth. Fire or not, what happened to Kitty is my fault."

"No," Isaac says, as emphatic as she's ever heard him. He takes her chin and turns her head so their eyes are locked. So he can be sure she understands. "Listen to me: It wasn't your fault."

"Kitty was only there because I wouldn't do it without her. She was never supposed to be on the show. Look at the house, even—six stories, six families. But I took a spot for my sister. I dragged her into it. My dad knew something was wrong, otherwise he wouldn't have taken me. But he left her. He left all of you there, too. If it wasn't safe, and he knew . . ."

Val shakes her head, fighting the guilt threatening to overwhelm her. Her guilt and shame have served their purpose, reminding her all these years that she has a job to do. She's doing it now, and she needs to focus. So she takes those feelings and puts them behind a door.

"I've always known I did something unforgivable. That's why I blocked out the past, why I went along with what he told me for all these years. I left my sister behind, and she died."

"You were a child."

"So were you, and you still blame yourself." It's Val's turn to hold his eyes.

Isaac has no response to that. He can't meet her gaze anymore. His head turns to stare out of the windshield, into the desert. They're oriented north, the car pointing in a straight line back to the house. She doesn't know how she knows, but she does. It's out there, waiting for them.

"I was the oldest," Isaac whispers. "You were all my responsibility. You still are."

Val can't contradict him, because she understands. Kitty might not be here, but Val owes her. "It feels unfinished, doesn't it? We're all stuck in the show, one way or another. Even I couldn't shut out everything." The songs, the tastes, the way she feels with Isaac. And *Kitty,* in her mind, always.

"Like a door left ajar," Isaac says. "Is this your choice, then? You want to stay?" His hand turns slowly, extending outward, palm up. "We'll close the door at last."

Val puts her hand on top of his, making the deal between the two of them and no one else. "Or we'll throw it all the way open." Val's tired of closing doors.

It's time to unlock everything and invite in whatever is lurking. For Kitty's sake.

From: Greg S. Johnson
Subject: Gala

First, let me remind everyone that all group emails must use BCC, not CC, which I think we understand after this week's reply-all disaster.

Second, let me even more firmly remind everyone that all communication regarding The Show and any developments must come from official channels, not from rumors, and using the email server in that way is a violation of the community charter.

Third, yes. I can confirm that, at last, the circle can be closed once more. I know I share all your relief and joy. Please hold any placement requests and be patient; a lottery for the remaining current and future slots will be held once timing is more certain. Remember that everyone benefits regardless of casting. We do this not for ourselves, but for the edification of our whole country and all the precious, innocent children in it. (Contrary to rumors, I have not already cast my own grandchildren. Again, all official communication will come from official channels, and anyone spreading rumors via the email server or any other means will be brought before the board.)

And finally, Jan would like you to please remember that the gala is black tie and that if you have not sent in your RSVP she cannot guarantee you will get the meal of your choice. But above all, please use caution interacting with the returning cast members. I know we are all excited—and rightfully angry at thirty lost years of blessing the world through quality children's programming—but this is a celebration, not a tribunal.

Warmest regards,
Greg S. Johnson, President of the Board of Bliss,
CEO of MM Entertainment

PS: Jan would also like me to remind you to properly bag trash before setting out your cans on the curb; we've had issues with spillage and no one wants a trashy community. Clean hearts and clean minds, cleanliness at all times!

# TEN

Isaac takes a long route back to Bliss, avoiding the RV park.

"Where's the gala?" Val asks. It's a relief that they have a few hours before it starts. She needs to get her head clear so she can look for answers about Kitty. She'll find everyone who actually worked on the show, and then she'll do whatever she has to in order to get the truth from them.

"The hotel." Isaac pulls to the side of the road outside of Bliss, still in the desert but with that jeweled oasis in sight. He sends a text and his phone immediately chimes in response. "Oh good, Jenny got rooms at the hotel for changing. She says they'll meet us there in a couple hours. She's glad you're coming."

"Shit," Val says. Rooms for changing, but she has nothing to change into. "Can you ask her to bring my funeral dress? It's the only nice thing I have." She doesn't want to wear it again, but it's grimly appropriate to wear something honoring the dead.

"Sure." He drives them to the beautiful old hotel with the wraparound balcony and arched doors. The parking lot is behind the building. It's odd seeing what's hidden by the main street. The desert nudges up against the borders of the manicured green; such a stark line where Bliss ends and reality begins.

The hotel is pristine. Shining tiled floors greet them, leading to a gilt-accented desk behind which stands a smiling blond woman.

Double doors to the side of the lobby show a bustling ballroom where employees are setting up for the gala. There are soaring pillars everywhere. Are they decorative, or structural? Does this entire building depend on them to keep it from crashing down? Val decides she'd rather not know, but she can't stop looking. Names are carved into the base of each of them.

"Do you know what these names mean?" she asks as they walk by one.

"Pillars of the community," Isaac says. He looks pained.

"Oh, it's not *that* bad of a joke." Val elbows him, and then they're at the desk.

Isaac speaks to the clerk there. "Jenny made a reservation."

All it takes is Jenny's first name. They must not get many visitors. The clerk does a bad job of surreptitiously trying to sneak in glances at them, unable to hide her curiosity as she enters something in her computer and pulls out two keys.

"Two oh five and two oh six. Adjoining rooms," she says, sliding keys across the desk. "Can I ask, what—"

"Perfect. Thanks." Isaac grabs them and guides Val toward a grand staircase.

The plush red carpet beneath their feet is vacuumed into neat lines. Val focuses on it as they climb to the second floor of the hotel. She doesn't regret leaving the ranch. She refuses to regret seeing her mother and learning about Kitty. But all the things she knows now, and all the things she *needs* to know, feel so heavy.

Isaac hands her one of the room keys. "Do you want to . . ." He trails off, and she gives him an exhausted smile.

"I'm going to nap."

"Same," he says with a relieved laugh.

Val has a moment of regret when he disappears into his room. She needs quiet time to reset, but does she want to be alone?

The room is fancy in a fussy, performative way. Plush, cream-colored carpet, a bed half covered in floral throw pillows, heavy drapes the same blood red as the carpet on the stairs. A dead-bolted door in the wall connecting her room to Isaac's. Another door to a black-and-white-tiled bathroom. And a wall-mounted TV she refuses to make eye contact with.

Val barely takes it in before throwing the useless decorative pillows on the floor and collapsing onto the bed. If she can rest for a few minutes, she'll be clearer-headed for tonight.

She scratches her itching, burning palm. Her thoughts swirl sluggishly, and she chases them in circles. She'll talk to Marcus, Javi, and Jenny. Press them on what they remember about the last show and the night her dad took her. Ask Javi what he thinks the podcaster's angle is and what she might know. Borrow Isaac's phone and dig into the online theories about the show and how it ended.

Isaac will help her. He has resources, and she trusts that he knows how important this is. Trusts his eyes and his funny smile and his long fingers, trusts—

There's a soft noise. Like a sigh.

Val's eyes open with a start, her heart racing. The room is dark now. The only light comes from the static on the television, which she never turned on. The room is freezing, too, though she can't hear an AC unit running. She can't hear *anything* over the surrounding urgent hum.

Val turns her head to the side. Or her head turns on its own. She doesn't feel in control. The door to the hallway is open. Beyond the threshold, there's only perfect black. It looks deep and soft and warm.

A figure peels away from the darkness. Val's jaw is clenched, her whole body frozen in terror—or anticipation. Is it a mysterious man in a cape and top hat? Does she want it to be him? Would he have answers for her?

But as the figure comes closer, it gets smaller, settling into its borders. It stops at the edge of the bed, staring down at her.

Not *it*. Kitty. Those big blue eyes are the only color in the dark room, like everything else is set to black and white. Kitty leans close, so they're face-to-face. Her eyes are so vivid it hurts to look right at them, but Val can't look away. She wants to ask her where she's been. To say sorry. To swear that Kitty was always in her dreams, even if Val forgot her.

But Val can't do anything. All she can do is stare.

Kitty takes Val's hand and presses her tiny, freezing fingers against her palm. The relief is so instant that Val wants to cry.

"Why are you sleeping, lazybones? There's so much to do." Kitty's voice is the same as the darkness in the doorway, soft and velvet and welcoming. It's the color black. Val once knew what the color black tasted like. She misses it, even without remembering it. There are so many gaping holes in her soul. So many cavernous spaces for the hum and the icy cold to fill. Her throat aches and her eyes burn.

"No crying," Kitty says in a singsong tone. "What do we say about crying?"

Val still can't move, but the song chimes through her head, where it's always been waiting. *Smile! You're not sad. Smile! It's not bad. Smile! You're okay. Smile! That's the way.*

Kitty's own mouth splits into a smile, wider and wider, so wide Val doesn't know how the corners of her lips aren't cracking. Then she walks backward, as though someone hit REWIND, back into the warm, featureless dark.

Val wants to go with her.

When her eyes open, the room isn't dark, and the door isn't open. But the television is on, a multicolor test pattern lighting her hand in cold blue. Her hand—the hand Kitty took, the hand Kitty soothed—is still icy to the touch.

What's the weirdest myth you've ever heard about a children's program? I'm talking Mister Rogers was secretly a military assassin and always wore cardigans to cover his tattoos.

-Tinky-Winky was written to convince children that the "gay lifestyle" was acceptable.

-I'm gay and the sun 100% is a laughing baby, everyone should try it

-Tinky-Winky just accessorized well.

-I can't believe people watched Tellytubbies and thought "gay!" not "DRUGS"

-Steve left Blue's Clues because he died of a drug overdose. Turns out he just didn't want to go bald while hosting a children's show.

-Did he get the drugs from Barney's tail?

-wait people actually thought that the friendly purple dinosaur had drugs in his tail? Why? Like honestly what purpose would that serve? Did they think the guy in the suit was doing them, or they were for the kids, or what?

-I don't think the people starting these rumors care much about logic

-didn't the guy playing Barney get like death threats and stuff?

-Don't do drugs, kids! That's how the dinosaurs went extinct!

-Lindsay Lohan actually had a twin sister, The Parent Trap wasn't special effects. But her sister was murdered and that's why she went off the deep end.

-yeah no other reason imaginable a kid exploited by Hollywood that many years might struggle emotionally, gotta be secret dead twin

-Kitty died on the last episode of Mister Magic and the kids watching saw it happen.

-what like it was broadcasting live or something? Or like the producers were all, well, gotta use the footage, lol

-no seriously my cousin swears she saw it. She wouldn't sleep alone for four years after the end of the show.

-I knew a kid in junior high who claims he saw it, too. He died of an overdose a few years after graduation, I think. Sad. I'll punch the first person to make a Barney joke here.

-This one is just stupid. All it takes is a quick bit of research. There are no police reports, nothing about a missing kid or a kid killed on set. This sort of stuff makes the news. After all, she was a cute white kid, right? They eat that shit up. Now if Marcus had died . . .

-dude too far

-who was Marcus?

-the only Black kid

-We all know it's true.

-Okay but did your quick bit of research turn up anything about the studio behind MM? Or the directors, or producers, or writers, or the actor who played MM? Because that's the real weirdness behind the show. Allegedly it was the longest running show ever, all the kids I knew watched it when we were little, but no one knows any details about it or has any footage of it or anything. Which makes me think something bad did happen and everyone involved buried it. Or HER, in this case.

-I feel like MM is like that stairs in the woods post, just a big joke someone started and everyone else keeps going. No way this was a real show.

-Don't dismiss Millenial culture, you have spookyspaghetti or whatever, we have our own messed up shit, it was just all analog instead of digital

-Not a kids program but I swear half the WB/CW heyday actors went on to start or participate in cults

-yeah that's not even a rumor, it's true

-If Sarah Michelle Gellar starts a cult, I'm there, no questions asked

-pretty sure the Sarah Michelle Gellar cult is the gay lifestyle the Teletubby people were afraid of

# HE'S HERE AGAIN

Val slips out of bed and goes to the door—the one connecting to Isaac's room, not to the hallway. She can't, won't open that door, afraid it will plunge her out of this reality and into Kitty's velvety, lightless realm. It's not fear of the darkness that holds her back; it's fear that she *wants* to follow Kitty there.

The connecting door is open on Isaac's side. Of course he would leave it open for her. The hinges squeak as she enters. He shifts in bed, eyes still closed, and opens the blankets.

An automatic invitation, without questions or qualifications. He's there for her no matter what, even in his sleep. She nestles in, curled against him, and knows this is the way she sleeps best. It's a memory stored in her body, just like the rhyming songs. Just like Kitty. Val's eyes close and she doesn't open them again until Isaac's phone chirps.

"Your hair still tickles." Isaac brushes it away from his face as he looks at his phone. He doesn't have his glasses on, so he squints at the display.

"Five forty-five," Val says.

He drops the phone onto his chest with a sleepy sigh. He's on his back, Val still curled into him, and he's exactly as lanky as he looks. She likes it. She likes everything about him.

"*Still* tickles," she repeats. "Did we room together during the show?"

Isaac reaches over her for his glasses on the nightstand. "We all slept in the same area, yeah. Piled like puppies. You had a lot of nightmares."

*Present tense,* she thinks. Have, not had.

Val knows she should get up, thank him, apologize, do *something*. But she isn't ready to move yet. Moving means going back to reality, and reality has so many demands now. "At least I don't snore?"

"Uh . . ."

"What?" Val sits up. "I don't! Do I?" She's never actually spent the whole night with someone. She's had sex, sure, but she always kept intimacy off-limits.

"Purring. You purr. Like a little kitten."

"Oh my god, I snore."

Isaac laughs, sitting up. "And your feet are almost as icy as your hands."

Val's hand is still cold. Isaac noticed it, too, which should frighten her—evidence that her nightmare was anchored in the real world—but instead it comforts her. She brings her knees up and rests her chin on them, looking at him. "You were waiting for me. When I came in."

He holds her gaze without embarrassment. "I feel like I've always been holding that spot for you."

Should she tell him she feels like she belongs there, too? That everything about him should be surprising, but nothing is? How do you connect with another person after spending a lifetime avoiding it? There's been an Isaac-sized hole at her side when she slept all these years. An Isaac-sized hole in her life. Maybe she dreamed of Kitty's face and not his, but Isaac is still here. Still . . . hers.

His phone chimes. "The others are parking," he says. "They'll be right up."

Val throws her legs over the side of the bed. She'd rather not explain what they were doing in here together. Not because it's secret, but because it feels almost sacred.

Regardless, there's no time to dwell on it. To think what Isaac means to her, or what he could mean. She has to focus on her goal: information. Galas are new and unfamiliar, but she knows how to talk to rich people, how to sway them toward her ideas, just like with Poppy's mom at the ranch.

She catches herself scratching her hand again. Now that the chill has faded, the itching is back. "Do you think Jenny has some sort of allergy cream? My palm is going crazy. I must be allergic to something."

Isaac fixes the bedspread like he doesn't want to answer any questions, either. "I think Jenny has everything in that purse of hers. Allergy cream. Ice packs. A coloring book and markers. A puzzle."

"An emergency flare."

"A picnic blanket."

"A full picnic."

"A full change of clothes."

"A full change of clothes for seven different clothing sizes."

"A spare tire."

"And," Val says, "a tire iron. For changing the tire, or other, less legal purposes."

Isaac laughs. "Yeah, I wouldn't mess with her."

Val retreats to the other room and uses the bathroom before everyone else shows up. When she comes out, the men are already with Isaac, distributing garment bags.

Jenny drags a suitcase through the adjoining doors. Her arms are full of dresses. "You decided to join us." She sounds neither pleased nor annoyed. Mostly tired. She throws the gowns onto the bed. "I stopped at home and grabbed everything I have. Figured you wouldn't want to wear what you wore to your father's funeral."

It's a blunt statement to accompany a thoughtful gesture. Val puts a hand on Jenny's shoulder. "That was really kind. Thank you."

Jenny's eyebrows rise. "Oh. Yeah. You're welcome." She sits on the edge of the bed, picking idly at the pile of gowns. "I think you've told me thank you more in the last day than anyone else has in years. It's like—when there's a stack of dishes, if my husband actually does them, I tell him thank you. But when I do them, no one thanks me, because it's not something nice I did for someone else. It's just what I was supposed to do all along."

Even Gloria has the good grace to acknowledge Val's hard work. Not to pay her fair wages for it, but still. "That sucks," Val says.

Jenny lets out a sharp, surprised laugh. "It does. Come on. Pick a dress."

Val shuffles through them. She and Jenny aren't the same size—Val is taller, with broader shoulders and smaller breasts—but a sleeveless green one has enough forgiveness in the cut. It comes with a little short-sleeved jacket, which Val emphatically opts not to use. She's never worn something this nice. She likes the way it drapes down her, loves the soft swish of the skirt against her muscular calves. Most of the shoes in the suitcase are too small, but some strappy heels aren't agonizing. It's like playing dress-up with a friend, or how she imagined getting ready for prom would be.

Jenny sighs and picks up a matronly maroon dress with boxy short sleeves, an empire waist, and a mid-calf-length skirt all in the same lifeless, matte fabric.

Val removes the dress from Jenny's grasp. "Absolutely not." She chooses a bold red sleeveless number with a low back and a long slit up the leg. "This one."

"I can't wear that!" But Jenny presses it against herself, turning to look in the full-length mirror and running her hands down the material.

"Then why do you have it?"

"I bought it years ago, on a trip when I felt like someone other than me. One of those stupid vacation purchases that feels reasonable until you get back home and realize you're not actually a different person. Real life was just on pause for a minute." She lowers it with a sigh. "It's too immodest. It demands attention. I can't do that."

"Why not?"

"Don't you remember— No, I guess you don't." Jenny makes a face, but it's not Val she's annoyed with. She sets the red dress on the bed, running her fingers down the slinky material. "The three of us—you and me and Kitty—got extra lessons. Extra rules. Separate from the boys. *Cover up, button down, no one likes a flashy clown.*"

"Oh my god," Val says, yet another piece falling into place. "Is that why whenever I'm putting on a bikini, there's a voice in my head cheerily singing, *One piece is better than two! Who's responsible? Only you!* I thought it must have been a radio jingle or something."

"That's our song. One of them, anyway. That was the modesty song. There was the nurturing song. The song about staying sweet. Oh, and the one about how we should be happy where we are, tending to our own garden, not reaching too high because the grass that grows tallest gets cut."

"That's . . . fucked up," Val says.

Jenny frowns. "No. It was to teach us to be happy with what we had. Not to make ourselves miserable with ambition."

"But the boys didn't get that song. They didn't have jingles about not showing skin, or getting cut down for ambition. Did they?"

"It's not about that," Jenny says. Her face is starting to flush. "It's about spheres of influence, you know? And finding ways to be happy. Like the sweetness song. *If you're feeling angry, swallow it right down. No one likes a meanie, no one likes a frown. Keep gentle and sweet, and all that you'll meet, will greet you with a crown.* We liked that one! Remember the crowns we'd get to wear when we bowed our heads?"

Val doesn't want to upset Jenny, but everything about that song feels messed up. She'd never teach her camp girls that lesson. But then again, she used the cleanup song on them. She was affected by these "lessons" they learned, even if she didn't remember where the thoughts came from.

But *then again,* every time she thought of the swimsuit song, she had been gleefully putting on a bikini. It made her feel powerful, contradicting that idea. So maybe the songs had the opposite effect on her: a stubborn defiance. Although she had definitely stayed where she was, never asking for or demanding more. Was it because of those lessons, sinking in so young? The more subtly insidious ones would have been harder to identify and rebel against.

Jenny sits on the edge of the bed, next to the maroon dress. She pinches the material. "I always took the lessons and rules for granted. They were to make us happy so we could grow up and be good people. Good women. Good moms. I followed all the rules. I never showed my shoulders or thighs. I only got one piercing in my ears because that was feminine without being aggressive or suggestive. I went to college to improve myself but I studied child development, because that way it wasn't selfish, it was for other people. Then I dropped out because I got married and my role changed, so my priorities had to change. Wife and mother. The goal, right? Six kids, and I diet and work out all the time so my husband can brag to people that *you'd never guess by looking at her.* And now my oldest is a tween and we're fighting about whether or not she can wear tank tops and, like . . . why not? Why am I telling her that her body is something she owes to other people? That she's responsible for how other people—how boys, how *men*—feel when they look at her?" She rubs her face. "I saw your expression when I sang that song. I know how it sounds, I do. But this is the way to live, you know? In the world, not of the world."

Val sits and nudges her knee. "Please take this as kindly as possible, but what the hell does that mean?"

Jenny cracks up, silent laughter shaking the bed. "I don't know! What *does* it mean?"

"It's nonsense. And you know what else is nonsense? That ghastly maroon dress. You're wearing the red dress tonight, and you're not responsible for how it makes anyone feel. Only how it makes you feel." Val pulls Jenny to her feet, pushes the red dress into her arms, and playfully shoves her into the bathroom.

When Jenny comes out again, she looks equal parts excited and terrified. "Well?"

Val whistles. "Damn, girl. You're not in *or* of, you've jumped straight to *out* of this world."

Jenny's laugh has an adorable snort at the end. "I forgot what a dork you can be. But is it too much?" She looks in the mirror, putting her hand over her stomach, letting her leg peek out of the slit.

"No such thing. You look amazing."

"Only you could make me do this. You're as pushy as ever." Jenny pauses, appraising Val, then a satisfied smile takes over her face. "Just as pushy. Okay, let me do your makeup."

Jenny sits Val down and pulls a kit out of the shoe suitcase. Although Jenny's regular makeup look is subtle, she has a deft hand at dramatic makeovers. By the time she's done, she and Val have expertly lined and smoky eyelids above bold lips.

"Oh my god, we're so hot," Val says as they stand side by side in front of the mirror. What would it have been like, to have Jenny as a friend all these years? To have grown up together instead of being ripped apart?

"We really are." Jenny's smile is longing. She lifts her fingers to the mirror as though looking at something in a storefront window she wants but can't have.

Before Jenny can change her mind or her dress, Val pulls her into the guys' room. All five of them exclaim to one another at the same time, then laugh.

"We all look amazing," Javi says, and it's true. His collar is rakishly undone several buttons under his midnight-blue suit jacket, Marcus's jacket is a dark purple that shows off his broad shoulders, and Isaac's suit is black with a green tie that sets off his hazel eyes.

"Damn, Jenny." Marcus takes her hand and spins her. Jenny laughs self-consciously, but she looks pleased. "It's criminal that you've been wearing knee-length shorts this whole time."

Jenny lightly cuffs his shoulder, but her brilliant smile hasn't dimmed one watt.

Whether it's a trick of the light or his glasses, it looks like Isaac's about to cry, taking them all in.

"Is this what prom was like?" Val asks, aching for all the things she never had, and the people she didn't have them with.

"Oh god, no," Marcus says. "There's not nearly enough Axe body spray killing brain cells for this to be prom."

"And we won't have to sneak in our own booze." Javi takes Jenny by the elbow.

"And I don't have to pretend to enjoy kissing a girl," Marcus adds.

"And it won't be our peers out there, just a bunch of judgy old people." Jenny's smile at last dims.

Javi tugs Jenny toward the door. "Quick, before she can change into a dress my grandma wouldn't be seen dead in. Which is saying something, because my grandma is actually dead."

Val wants to luxuriate in the weirdness of growing up and living the way she did and suddenly being here, in a gorgeous dress, with four people she cares about.

She can't, though. She's about to tell them her plan, when her eyes fall on Jenny, and her dress, and what she said about stopping at *home*. Jenny lives here in Bliss. She's part of everything, still, which might mean she has information. But if she does, she's never shared it. So her loyalties aren't to Kitty's memory, or to Val.

Val glances at the others. There's no way of knowing how connected they still are to the show. Whether they're keeping secrets. Javi tried to warn her about something, but even that could have been a test to see what she remembers. For now, she'll keep her suspicions and her plan to herself.

Isaac links his pinkie finger with hers. It's a bond between them, but also a promise. He's on her side, no matter what. At least she has that.

She hates suspecting any of them, but she has to be smart. Careful. She owes it to Kitty.

"It's not fair that we have to work during the gala," complains one of two white men in their mid-thirties sitting in front of a bank of monitors.

The other shrugs.

"There's not even anyone at the house," the complainer points out.

The other shrugs. "It's our duty, Mike."

Mike flicks idly through the camera feeds, settling on the one in the basement. "I hate missing free food. You don't get it. You have a wife, so your food is always free."

This time in place of a shrug, a questioning look.

"I mean, not free, but, like, you don't have to make it. Or clean up after it. If I want to eat I have to actually do the work myself. I need a wife. You're lucky you snagged one early. Bliss is too small. Right now my only options are a couple of second cousins. First cousins once removed? I can't ever remember. And they're not interested anyway. And all the rest of the single girls are in their mid-twenties. Something wrong with them if they aren't already taken by then, you know?" Mike runs a hand through his thinning hair, his frown showcasing wrinkles around his eyes and deep lines on his forehead.

The other man shrugs.

"I wish there were more girls in the house right now. What do you think of Val? She's kind of hot, in a—"

The audio from the monitor crackles. They both jump in their seats, alert. A small voice, distorted, comes in and out like they're picking up a faint radio signal.

*". . . make a circle, in the dark, close your eyes, and wish with me, keep them closed, keep them closed, keep them closed, keep them closed . . ."*

The voice skips, repeating that line over and over. But the camera itself isn't showing anything. Just a view of the chair in the empty room.

Mike wrinkles his nose in disgust. "Man, I hate it when it picks up the echoes like this." The song fades, still stuck on that one line. After a few minutes, he shakes his head. "I don't know whether I can still hear it, or if I'm just listening so hard for it that I'm imagining things. Can you still hear it?"

The other man shrugs.

Mike leans close to the speakers, trying to catch anything else. They have to log it all.

"Oh hi!"

"Shit!" He jumps back as his chair clatters to the floor. He spins around, heart racing, trying to find the source of the voice. It was so close, so clear. Like a child standing beside him.

A giggle grows farther and farther away. Still nothing on the video feed.

Mike looks at the other man, who, predictably, shrugs. But there's a slight, smug grin on his face. Mike's eyes travel up to the corner and meet the camera. Someone's always watching. Even the watchers get watched.

Wiping his brow, Mike drags his chair back up and sits shakily down. "Listen, I'm sorry I swore," he says, more for the camera than his companion. "It startled me. I don't use language like that. I don't think it needs to be written up."

The other man shushes him, holding up a hand. He's doing his job, listening. The laughter is gone now, and someone is crying somewhere, punctuated by staccato, hiccuping breaths.

"That's static, right?" Mike asks, but he doesn't sound hopeful.

"Shut up," a small voice hisses. "You'll make it hungry again. We just have to wait a little longer. You'll see."

The other man begins tapping notes into his laptop. The date, the time, and then the audio transcription. Records upon records, recordings of recordings. Everything filed, everything saved.

Mike shakes his head, giving it a few more minutes before gratefully clicking away from the basement camera. "I need a new job," he whispers.

# ELEVEN

"Damn," Javi says. The five remaining friends stand together in the entrance to the ballroom. Most of the attendees are in their fifties or older, the women sleeved and kitten-heeled and the men suited and bow-tied. But the homogeneity doesn't end there. It is an absolute sea of white people. Even Val, who has spent her whole life in *Idaho,* notices.

"We really were the token minorities," Marcus says.

Javi turns to the others. "Look at how beautiful we are. We could go be beautiful somewhere else, instead."

Val wants to agree with Javi, but she needs to find people who worked on the show. "Be where you're expected," she starts, picking another rhyme out of her head.

Sure enough, Javi rolls his eyes and continues. "Always be on time."

"Be helpful and caring," Marcus chimes in.

"Or your ass is mine," Javi finishes.

"That's not how it goes!" Jenny snaps. "He never would have taught us that."

Javi beams at her and takes the first step inside. "Speaking of asses, how many of them do you think I'll have to get through to reach the free booze?"

"Oh god, my mom's here." Marcus grabs Javi's arm. He looks around the room for a hiding place, but there's no way for Marcus to blend in. "What is she doing here? I can't deal with her, not right now. Not ever."

"Is she the aggressively blond woman talking to my mother?" Javi asks, eyebrows rising.

Val's heart picks up. Is her mother here, too? She can't imagine Debra owns anything sparkly enough for this crowd. Maybe that's why she's been banished to the RV park outside of town.

But the presence of Javi's and Marcus's moms makes it clear Val was right to keep her plan secret for now. They're still connected to Bliss. She doesn't want to raise suspicions, making people defensive and giving them a chance to coordinate their stories. "Are your parents here, too?" she asks Isaac and Jenny.

Isaac shakes his head. Jenny scowls as something else snags her attention. "I told him to get his suit steamed," she mutters.

A man like mayonnaise in human form stalks toward them, eyes only on Jenny. But not in the way Isaac looks at Val. He's zeroed in on Jenny the same way parents approach Val when their expectations for little riding prodigies aren't being met.

"I don't understand why you had to stay with them at that house," the man says. He must be Jenny's husband, picking up like they're already in the middle of a conversation. He looks about the right age. Val can't help the petty observation that Jenny definitely could have done better. "It's been a nightmare, babysitting for this long."

"Babysitting?" Val asks. Must not be Jenny's husband, after all.

Jenny gestures weakly at him. "Everyone, this is Stuart. My husband. Stuart, this is—"

"Wait, *babysitting*?" Val asks again, confused. "Aren't they your own kids? Isn't babysitting when you look after someone else's kids?"

Stuart's pale face goes splotchy red. He looks at Jenny as though expecting her to explain, but then he stops and actually *looks* at his wife. Val waits for the moment his eyes light up as he appreciates how hot she is. Instead, his face flushes deeper with embarrassment.

"*What* are you wearing?" His tone is low, as though they can't all hear him. Suddenly Jenny's reluctance to dress sexy makes sense. "I can see your boobs," he whispers harshly. "Which means *everyone else can*."

"Lucky us!" Val links her arm through Jenny's, both to support her and to keep her from fleeing. "Nice to meet you. Jenny's going to introduce me to some people now."

"But I—" Stuart starts.

"I'm always curious about grown men who still use the word *boobs,*" Javi says idly, tilting his head at the other man. "Why don't you show me where the drinks are, and you can tell me when to use *boobs* versus *boobies*. I'm not clear on the rules."

"Jenny." Stuart's face is approaching purple. "These are your friends? I don't like their influence on you. I don't like any of this. You've been gone too much; I don't care what the board says, it's not right for a mother to be away from her kids. We're going home. Sarah's been crying nonstop since you left, and—"

Jenny cuts him off. "*No*. You know how important tonight is to me. I've worked a long time for this. You can handle things until I'm done."

Val braces for anger, but after a shocked expression, Stuart deflates and drifts away, without explanation or apology. Maybe that's the best support he can offer his wife: not getting in her way. He seamlessly joins the ranks of a few other bland men in bland suits with white shirts.

"Come on, Jenny. I meant it about introducing me to people," Val says, more confident. It really is a room full of demanding, unhappy parents, and she knows how to work that crowd. Give her a few minutes and she'll have everyone here offering her the information she needs like it was their idea all along.

Marcus grabs Javi's elbow. "Take me with you. I can't do this alone." They ease their way into the ballroom together. Isaac is quickly pulled aside by an older woman who wants to talk to him about her Lasik surgery and how much he'd love it. Val feels bad abandoning him, but desperate times, et cetera.

"Brace yourself." Jenny follows her own advice, her back going ramrod-straight as she leads Val into the fray.

Everyone greets them and then makes excuses to go elsewhere. Bathroom, drinks, food, someone they absolutely need to talk to at that exact moment. Val barely catches names, much less what anyone had to do with the show. She misjudged this. Irate parents at the ranch actually *wanted* to speak to her. How can she get anyone here to tell her secrets if they won't even look at her for longer than a few seconds?

Jenny's no help. She whips them through the room, dropping names without any details. Carols and Dawns, Joes and Daves. Meaningless. Any eye Val catches is always watching her. As soon as they see her looking, their gazes dart away or their glares are replaced with spring-loaded smiles. *Smile! You're not sad,* Val thinks.

"Oh, not them." Jenny tries to steer Val away from a group of people walking toward them, but they're caught.

"Fellow alumni!" A woman with perfectly set hair and coral lipstick takes Val by the shoulders in a weird sort of half hug. She smells like the magazine perfume samples Gloria's daughters used to rub on each other.

"Alumni from the last class," a man adds. He's handsome, balding with a shaved head and big brown eyes. "For now!"

A woman wearing Jenny's terrible maroon dress's twin has the same reflexive, uniformly brilliant smile as the rest of them. Val could swear she has more teeth than she should. "Wasn't it the best? I've always felt so lucky I got to be on it before—well, *you* know." She switches to an exaggerated frown, like she's pantomiming feelings for a toddler. She puts her hand on Val's shoulder. "We don't blame you for the show ending, sweetie."

The others look away, making it clear the sentiment is not shared.

"Why would you blame me?" Val asks, fishing for information.

"Well, on account of how you broke the circle." The woman's expression becomes less cartoonish, her pencil-thin brows taking on a pedantic cast. "You left before your time was finished, and then—"

"And then the show got canceled," the handsome man finishes. There's something sharp in his delivery, echoed in his glance toward the woman. Val's heart picks up. They have a secret.

The toothy woman nods quickly, her smile popping back on. "But you know how things are these days. Everything's getting a reboot! Don't worry about it." She pats Val's shoulder once more, then holds her hand at her side like she doesn't want to touch anything else until she's had a chance to wash it.

"Wasn't it the accident that ended things? Who canceled the show? A network? The showrunner?" Val searches their faces intently.

Instead of answering, they all turn to Jenny like a school of fish on the hunt. "Don't you look special," the toothy woman says. The way she delivers it makes it clear *special* is not a compliment. "Listen, while I have you here, the book club decided to change your pick for this month. We felt like your choice was too . . . exciting." She laughs. "I'll email you." The group disperses as quickly as they gathered, off to hunt elsewhere.

Val tracks them through the room. She's zeroed in on Toothy, determined to get her away from the others.

"So, you know all these people," Val says to Jenny, noting the table where Toothy ends up. She'll wait until the woman heads to the bathroom. Get her alone. Hopefully later in the evening, after she's been drinking.

"I've lived here my whole life. I know all their names, and their kids' names, and what they do for a living, and what cars they drive, and how much money their husbands make, and what their kitchen renovations cost." Jenny glares at a man approaching them. He immediately veers in another direction. "But no. I don't know any of them, and none of them know me."

Jenny puts a hand against her forehead. "Sorry. I'm in a bad mood. Oh no, here comes the mayor. I can't get cornered by him, not again. Not when I'm wearing this." She turns to flee.

The mayor is exactly who Val needs to talk to. The crowd parts around him as he shakes hands and pats backs. He's an older man, extremely tall and almost gaunt, with silver hair in a widow's peak swept back from a high forehead.

Val lets go of Jenny's arm and walks right up to him. "Hi," she says, sticking out her hand. "I'm—"

"I know who you are, little Valentine." He takes her hand and pulls her closer, setting her off balance. She has to crane her neck at an uncomfortable angle to look up at him from this close. Though he *is* very thin, she sees now that it's more a factor of his height than any sort of frailty. His blue eyes are deep-set and piercing, the wrinkles around them formed by smiling, except for the deep crack between his dark brows.

He grips her hand tightly, keeping her almost right up against himself. She can't step back and create a more comfortable distance. Jenny made the correct decision in avoiding him.

His smile is more paternal than anything Dad ever offered her, and it immediately pisses her off. Paternal and patronizing are such close relatives. His words are even and measured, like he's practiced them. "You finally found your way back to the fold."

Val smiles as cheerfully as she can manage. If she feeds his ego, he'll be more likely to let his guard down. "I can't believe what a gem this town is. I'm surprised I never heard of it."

It's the right tactic; the mayor nods, seizing on the topic. "Oh yes, our Bliss! You know the history of how Utah was first settled—a lot of the Southwest, too, all the way down to Mexico—don't you?"

He's ignoring the fact that all those places were already inhabited, but she needs him to keep talking. "Not really, but I'd love to know more about Bliss and its connection to television history."

"We'll get there, we'll get there. See, first you have to go back. You know who Brigham Young was, right?"

"Sure." There are a couple of colleges named after him, something to do with the Mormons, but Val doesn't actually care.

"After they arrived in Utah, he sent his pioneers out from Salt Lake City. Each group was supposed to settle a day's journey from the previous, forming continuous lines of safety for travelers. Like a web around the center, where he sat like a big, fat spider."

Val must look surprised at his unexpected criticism, because the mayor smiles conspiratorially at her before continuing. "What most people don't know is that the men old Brigham didn't like got sent to the worst places. He was in charge and ruled with an iron fist. Any threats to his power, any men who challenged him or were too popular, were sent far away from Salt Lake City. The first families to come to Bliss were assigned this place as a punishment, believe it or not!"

Val makes a noise of disbelief. "But it's so pretty!"

"It is now! It sure wasn't then. Imagine, my great-great-great-great-great grandfather, banished to the unforgiving desert, and told to make a town! But he understood that it wasn't a punishment. He had a vision that truth and power and even *paradise* were out here waiting for those bold enough to ask. Angels were everywhere, if you knew how to recognize them. If you knew how to make a deal. And my family, well. We found a place even better than Brigham could have dreamed of, with all the power he was hoping to keep from everyone else. He tried to silence us, but we ended up more influential than he could ever have been!"

"How do you figure?" she asks.

"Well, our broadcasts, of course! Suffer the children, you know. At first it was small, just our own community and anyone we could bring in to listen and learn. But then technology—miraculous, really—gave us new reach to bless lives. First across the radio waves, and then in the homes of everyone with a television set. And we will be, again."

"You're going to restart the show?" It's the first Val's heard it confirmed. And it means people here have a financial interest in keeping terrible secrets buried.

"In good time. In good time." He pats her hand.

She wants to yank it away, but she can't yet. "But what about the accident that ended it? Don't you think the death of a cast member on set will make a new show controversial?"

Val doesn't know how he'll respond, but she wasn't expecting to see those authoritative eyebrows lift in surprise.

He leans in even closer, his deep-set eyes searching her own. "Who have you been talking to? No one ever died on the set of *Mister Magic*."

MAGIC CIRCLERS BIG BIG NEWS: That reunion podcast just appeared on my app. Everyone subscribe. We gotta get it to the top of the charts so the studios will give the show a reboot!

-Why? Not everything needs a reboot. Can't we just let our childhood memories stay intact?

-No

-go home and cry joylessly into your still-in-the-box Transformers

-just because you don't want it doesn't mean no one does, I got kids, they need this shit

-including the shit where there's a whole song about not using profanity

-fuck yeah especially that shit, someone's got to compensate for my terrible influence in their lives

-lol "clean hearts and clean minds, cleanliness at all times, nothing dirty nothing bad, always happy never sad" fuck yeah love that song

-Oh my god I can't believe it's actually happening. I really thought it was cursed, that it was impossible.

-just a podcast not a new show

-not a new show YET, but this is the age of mining nostalgia! I have hope!

-So are they going to talk about what happened to Kitty?

-Who was Kitty?

-Cast member who died

-ALLEGED castmember who ALLEGEDLY died

-urban legend, I don't remember a Kitty and there's no proof

-cast member everyone says died but actually is a real estate agent in Delaware

-lol Delaware isn't a real place, imaginary businesnesses imaginary people

-the fucking president is from Delaware

-imaginary president

-if you stand in front of your mirror and say Bloody Mary three times she'll show up and tell you the story of what happened to Kitty

-seriously here is a link to Katherine Johnson's real estate page, she was Kitty, the production ended because of an accident but there wasn't any death, my girlfriend and I got our true crime book club to investigate last year and we figured it all out, you can read about it on our blog, link in my bio

-wrong, besides, what about all the other kids who died, why doesn't anyone talk about them

-who let this nutjob back on? Moderator?

-Where can we subscribe? I need a new commute podcast

# TWELVE

The mayor still has Val's hand in his grasp, holding her in place. "I assure you, no one ever died in his care."

"Whose care? The director? Is he here?" Val looks around hopefully, but the mayor laughs.

"You know who I mean. The show was perfect. There was never harm done to any good child. And don't worry, my dear. Now that you're back, all is forgiven." He pats her hand, then strokes it.

She wants to yank it free, her palm hot and itchy and her skin crawling from his prolonged touch. He hasn't given her a straight answer. Maybe Kitty was injured on set so they moved her somewhere else for plausible deniability. They could still claim no one died on set that way. Then again, she spent decades assuming her mom was dead because Dad said she was gone. Was she making the same mistake? Had Debra actually confirmed that Kitty was dead? Val can't remember. But her friends all said Kitty was dead.

"If Kitty didn't die, then what happened? Where is she?"

The mayor frowns. "Well, your father, obviously. It was his fault entirely."

"My *dad* killed Kitty?" That couldn't be true. Not according to the timeline from the others. But they were kids. Maybe they were wrong. Maybe the fire really did happen before she left, maybe Dad took the blame, and—

"No, no. What is all this talk of killing and death? You're working yourself into hysterics. Calm down. You're here now, and you're going to fix it. You're going to make it right." His grip tightens, tugging her against him. "You owe us that much, don't you?"

A woman with hair dyed a lifeless, flat yellow-blond takes the mayor's elbow. "Dear, we have an issue."

"Duty calls! Welcome home, Valentine." The mayor presses a kiss against her forehead before she has time to push him away, and then he's gone.

Javi sidles up to her, Marcus with him. "There's not even alcohol." Marcus glares down at the glass in his hand. "This is sparkling juice. Do they think we're still children just because we were on their kids' show?"

"What did Mayor Handsy say?" Javi asks.

Val wipes her forehead with the back of her arm, wishing she had that stupid little dress jacket after all so she could avoid touching her own skin where the mayor kissed her. "He assured me they only blame my father for what happened to Kitty. But also he said Kitty didn't die on set? *Did* she die? Did my dad do something? Did I?"

Javi shakes his head. "I'm not clear on a lot of things at the end of it all, but I *am* sure that you weren't there when it happened. You were gone."

"You were," Marcus says, nodding.

"But is Kitty dead?" Part of Val dares to hope for a moment. After all, her friends were kids back then. Maybe they remember wrong.

Marcus takes her hand, and with him there's nothing possessive or entitled about the gesture, just the comfort of one friend to another. "I don't like to think about what happened; the pieces don't make sense. But I know she's gone. And I know you weren't there, and neither was your dad. We were alone."

"Who is *we,* though?"

Javi answers. "The circle, and him."

"You mean Mister—"

"Don't say it. Your rule," Javi reminds her.

Val gives up on secrecy. With Javi's warnings and Marcus's reassurances, she trusts that they aren't trying to somehow set her up. "Who was he, though? Can I talk to him? What about the crew on set that day? The director? Are any of them here?"

Marcus shrugs helplessly. "It was a long time ago. I don't remember anyone from the show except the five of us and Kitty."

Javi echoes the shrug, then pulls a flask from his jacket. "Guess I was wrong about not needing to sneak in our own booze. Luckily, I'm always prepared." He takes a swig before passing it to Val. It burns down her throat.

Val wishes Marcus wasn't sure. Wishes she could hope there was a possibility of seeing her sister again. Wishes she *had* opened the hotel room door after her nightmare, just to make sure Kitty wasn't still out there. Waiting.

Javi takes another drink, then hands it to Marcus and glares around the room. "All anyone wants to talk to me about is what an honor it is to be with the firm that asshole predator Harrell worked at before he got appointed to the Supreme Court. You know what was an honor? Locking him in the bathroom at the Christmas party." Javi beams as Marcus lifts the flask in a toast, then passes it back to Val.

No one here will talk about the show. But the mayor denying Kitty died is evidence in and of itself. He's involved, either in the death or in the cover-up. Why else avoid acknowledging it?

"Oh no, here comes my mom." Marcus tenses as one of many bottle blondes weaves through the crowd toward them. "She's going to ask about my ex-wife and talk about how much happier I seemed 'back then,' by which she means how much happier *she* was when I was in the closet."

Javi holds out a hand. "Come on. She can't corner you if we're dancing."

Marcus's face freezes. His voice is soft but firm. "Please don't tease me."

Javi's mischievous smile drops away. It's as though he's shed a layer of skin, revealing the truth underneath. All his nerves and veins, all the tender, delicate parts that keep him alive. "I would never." His voice isn't soft, though. It's fierce.

"Everyone will stare," Marcus says, but he takes Javi's hand.

"They're all staring anyway." Javi leads Marcus to the dance floor. A few older couples are shuffling back and forth to an uninspired playlist of soft 1990s end-credit songs. Javi whispers things that make Marcus laugh and hold his attention. They're beautiful, dancing together.

The older couples move away, as though afraid of being contaminated. With what, Val wonders. Rhythm? Joy?

She's so alone. Dad's dead, and even before he was, she was alone in every way that mattered. Her mother's alive, but couldn't care less that Val is. And once Val's finished here, once she's figured out what happened and—well, she doesn't actually know what her goal is beyond finding the truth. To avenge Kitty, if such a thing is even possible?

Once that's done, what will she have? *Who* will she have?

Val turns to find Isaac behind her. He holds her with those beautifully magnified eyes, and then he's holding her on the dance floor. For a few minutes, her palm doesn't itch and her brain is quiet. She laughs as they twirl around Javi and Marcus. The song switches to something faster, and they break into a dancing circle. Only Marcus is actually good, which somehow makes it better.

The music cuts abruptly. The mayor is on the steps near the entrance, holding a microphone. "Welcome, everyone! What a pleasure it is to have you all here, celebrating our first step back into quality children's programming. Or, as we like to think of it, programming quality children!"

Javi rolls his eyes and Marcus lets out a "boo" so quiet only they can hear it.

Val searches the crowd for Jenny, but she's already rushing in their direction, inexplicably chasing a woman. That woman is in a nightdress rather than a gown.

The mayor is still speaking. "On this, the long-awaited reunion of—"

"You!" the nightdress woman howls, one finger pointed at Val. She doesn't need to push through the crowd; they part for her, giving her a clear path. The woman is as small and fine-boned as a bird, but when she grabs Val by the shoulders, her grip is like talons. "You broke everything!" Spittle flies out of her mouth as she screams. "You broke everything! You—"

Jenny pulls the woman off, but her hold slips. The woman lunges, raking her fingernails down Val's face. Val stumbles backward, trying to protect herself from the onslaught.

Javi, Isaac, and Marcus jump in. It takes the three of them plus Jenny to keep the woman from attacking Val.

Val's eyes are wild as she takes in the scene.

Other than her friends, the entire ballroom is still. No one else has made a move toward them. No one has a phone out to call the cops, or even to film. They're all watching. The mayor, microphone in hand, doesn't say a word. No calls for order, or instructions for handling the woman. His face is deliberately impassive, but Val swears she sees grim approval there. They all approve. Val isn't forgiven, after all. But who is her attacker?

Jenny throws her arms around the straining woman's neck, pulling her close. "Please," she says. "Please, stop it, Mom!"

To: MM204@mm.org
From: MM587@mm.org

Daily report:

Enclosed (1), please find transcripts of today's interviews with Javier and Marcus. A note that Jenny may need to be brought in for a disciplinary council for inappropriate use and contact. The relevant portions have been flagged. While it has been agreed that responses to Jenny are strong enough to allow her to continue with the project, this independent behavior cannot be condoned. Everything must go through the proper chain of authority.

Enclosed (2), please find a summary of all new internet content involving, mentioning, or related to Mister Magic. There has been a noteworthy uptick since posting the intro podcast on all apps; we may want to assign another permanent social media monitoring position, perhaps even two. Podcast subscriptions are already in the thousands with only the teaser. Of note for Tuesday's meeting is the transition of podcast narration for potential permanent outreach, assuming successful restoration of the show, which may lead to a disruption of and/or change to our access. As previously discussed, continuing the podcast independently once the show resumes will allow us to exert more control over the narrative. Social media is a new factor that we can take full advantage of to support Mister Magic's message, as well as monetize effectively to sustain our mission.

Enclosed (3), please find a transcription of unscheduled, spontaneous activity on the screen; audio only. Also included is a graph of the exponential increase in such events since the death of Valentine's father and her rediscovery.

Of note: Mike in Observation used profanity in the workplace. A copy of that transcript will be forwarded to HR with a recommendation of formal censure. His position is a sacred privilege and should be treated as such.

# ALL BY OURSELVES

Jenny's mom is still shouting. The sound pursues Val as she rushes through the hotel lobby and out the front door. But that still feels too exposed. She doesn't want to be found. Not right now, not when she's about to lose it.

The parking lot in back is full of cars but devoid of people. It's bathed in featureless orange light, the tone seeping color and life out of everything. Even her dress looks muddy brown. It feels truer that way, though. Like the beautiful green dress, the hotel, the ballroom were lies all along.

Val walks to the darkest edge of the lot and stands with her toes in the desert, her back to Bliss. Everyone in the gala watched as Jenny's mom attacked her. They approved of it, even if they didn't join in. They hate Val. She suspected as much from how she moved through the room like she was the wrong end of a magnet, repelling everyone there. It was even in the way the mayor held her hand: not an embrace, but restraint.

Whether they hate her for leaving as a child or for something more, it's clear now: No one in Bliss is going to help her find out what happened to Kitty. The mayor knows. The former cast members might, too. Maybe they *all* know. It doesn't do her any good. Anger and entitlement she can work with. But outright hatred? How can she manipulate that to her own advantage?

Tonight wasn't all a waste, though. The mayor said there was no harm to any *good* child. That's a qualifying phrase—an implication that there was harm to kids who weren't good.

But if that's true, why is Val still here and Kitty's not? Because according to Val's mom, Kitty was the good one.

"Val!" Javi runs across the parking lot toward her.

"What was that?" she asks as he reaches her.

He shakes his head, looking around—but upward, at the lights, searching for something. "I have to go back in and help Jenny, but I made an excuse to escape so we could be alone. Be *careful*. Don't talk to anyone. Assume you're being recorded at all times. Something else is going on here."

"What, though?"

"When they reached out to me about the reunion, I got to thinking. Why now? So I did some research. No one ever tried to figure out what happened to Kitty. No one was arrested or prosecuted. There weren't even any newspaper articles about it."

Her brief internet search told her as much, but Javi has more access to legal documents than she ever could. "They didn't care," she whispers.

"I think they're using this reunion and podcast nonsense to build a new narrative. To officially pin Kitty's death on someone and clear themselves before restarting the show."

Val gives him a lifeless smile. "I'm the perfect villain. Her troubled older sister. They can make it a family thing, not a show thing. I even look guilty, running away and staying in hiding ever since. No wonder they're all so glad I'm here."

Javi looks grim; he agrees with her assessment. "We all know you weren't there when . . . when it happened."

"But there's no proof." Val has her first happy realization of the night. "I'll bet anything *they're* the ones who burned down the studio. To destroy all the footage and evidence. It wasn't me."

"There's no evidence, but there are witnesses. Their mistake was in bringing us back, too. We won't let them do this to you."

Val laughs. "Jenny would throw me under the bus. And her mom would be the one driving it, apparently."

"Whatever else she is, Jenny's a loyal friend. She wouldn't do that." Javi squeezes Val's shoulder, then jogs back to the hotel.

He's wrong—none of them really know each other. No matter how good a friend she was when they were kids, Jenny's been part of Bliss this whole time.

Val roots for the desert to sweep in, to cover this whole stupid place in sand and brush, to blast the color and life from the red bricks and green lawns. To erase the lie of Bliss and replace it with the harsh grit of the truth. The desert, unchanged and unchanging, no matter how hard people pretend otherwise.

Val's exhausted. It's cold, and her cheek stings where Jenny's mom clawed her. Maybe Isaac's car is unlocked.

Once again, he comes through for her. She opens the door to the passenger's seat and notices something tossed into the back in a plastic bag. Her rumbling stomach reminds her that she never got a chance to eat at the gala. Maybe it's snacks from the gas station.

It's even better. She laughs as she pulls out that absurd *Mona Lisa* blanket. Isaac got her an inside joke she can literally wrap herself in. She pulls it up over her shoulders and closes her eyes, still hungry but warm now, thanks to Isaac.

A sharp tap on the window startles her. A woman is standing there. Not Jenny's mom, thank god, but Val doesn't trust anyone from Bliss. She can't roll down the window with the car off. Her first impulse is to shake her head and tell the woman to leave.

But . . . the woman doesn't look angry. She looks haunted. And she's not dressed for the gala. She's wearing a cardigan, jeans, sensible sneakers. Val opens the door and steps out cautiously. The woman is white, in her sixties or seventies, tall and lanky but turned in on herself. She has her arms folded tightly across her chest, holding on to something.

"Valentine," the woman whispers.

"Have we met?" But then Val realizes this is the woman who was shouting after Isaac in the RV park. She takes a step back, bumping against the car. Is every person in this town unhinged? Are they all going to take turns attacking her?

"You need this," the woman says. Val relaxes a little at her voice. She sounds sad and a little nervous, but there's no malice. The woman unfolds her arms to reveal a narrow, rectangular black object.

It's an old VHS tape. Unmarked, no box. Val doesn't take it. But she wants to. "What's on it?"

The woman darts a worried glance over her shoulder. "Don't let them know you have it. Not until you've watched."

"Don't let who know? The people in the gala?"

"Your friends. The others from the circle. They don't understand. They can't. Not yet. But you deserve—you all deserve to know."

Heart racing, Val takes the tape. Relieved of her burden, the woman stands a little taller and meets Val's eyes. She's familiar in a way Val can't put her finger on, more than just recognition from the RV park. "Have we met before?" Val asks. "Did you work on the show back when—"

A door bangs open nearby. The woman startles and sprints away through the cars. But instead of going into the town, she heads straight into the desert, quickly swallowed by the night.

Javi's voice drifts toward Val. The others are coming.

Val wraps the tape in the *Mona Lisa* blanket, holding it to her chest like the woman did. Did she cradle it because it was a secret burden, or because it was precious?

Isaac is with Javi. He lopes toward her in a half run. "Are you okay?"

"I'm fine." The lie, easy as ever. But unlike Dad, Isaac doesn't buy it. He watches her closely, concern magnified as he examines the scratches on her face.

Javi catches up. "Marcus is helping Jenny get her stuff from the rooms. She feels awful about everything."

Val shrugs. "Hey, if I had a dollar for every disturbing encounter with someone's mom today, I'd have two dollars."

She's rewarded with a dark laugh from Javi. "Yeah, you managed to avoid mine and Marcus's. Otherwise, you'd be all the way up to four."

"Can we get out of here?" she asks.

"Where do you want to go?" But Isaac's head betrays his desires, as he once again turns to look in the exact direction of the house. Val knows it's out there. She can *feel* it, buzzing in her chest. That unnatural house, standing sentinel in the desert. Waiting.

That unnatural house, with a television and VCR on every floor.

Keeping the tape secret from them feels wrong, but didn't Javi warn her they were always being monitored? No matter how much she trusts Javi and Isaac, the woman's insistence on keeping it secret from them has wriggled inside and infected Val, too. Once she knows what's on the tape, she'll be able to decide what to do. Who to show it to.

"Back to the house, if that's okay with everyone? Nowhere else I'd rather be than with my circle of friends."

Question: Can anyone think of children's programs where the characters were allowed to evolve? Or where the format changed as the show went along? All the ones I can think of are static.

-Avatar: The Last Airbender, and, to a lesser extent because it was more teen programming, Avatar: The Legend of Korra. From the first episode to the last, the kids all grow and change for better and for worse.

-I mean, like, little kids shows. Like how Blue's Clues never changed format. There was no continuous storytelling. Same on Barney.

-Bluey? Some deep shit there.

-I'll check it out.

-Mister Magic?

-Mister Magic was always the same. Kids, circle, magic, playtime.

-Not the last group. I watched my whole childhood. It ended when I was twelve, but I made excuses to keep watching it with my little brother. It definitely changed. They phased out Mister Magic and focused more on just the kids. Maybe that's why it ended? They messed with the format? Tried something new and it didn't work. I liked it, though.

-Interesting. Do you know where I can watch the last season?

-lol no one can watch it. It's nowhere.

-Kids' shows have gotten a lot better. Stuff changes in them now. A lot more cohesive storytelling than just trying to sell new toys or whatever.

-Define better. Also pretty sure all the stuff that changes is still just trying to sell toys. My Little Ponies don't suddenly have new outfits and hair three times a season out of storytelling integrity, my dude.

-If something works, why change it?

-Mister Magic probably agrees with you. See above.

# THIRTEEN

The problem with a house with no doors is that if Val immediately goes upstairs and plays her video, someone is bound to notice.

She doesn't want to go inside at all. She stands on the threshold, holding her tape inside her blanket, staring up at the windows. It's just a place, but it feels like a presence, too. Like how Stormy haunted the barn. Val always knew Stormy was waiting, impatient to terrorize with teeth and hooves.

Impatience. That's what it is. The house has been standing here for decades, but somehow it feels impatient. Val can't explain it, but she accepts it for what it is. Maybe it's that incessant humming buzz, setting her teeth on edge, making it impossible to relax or even focus.

Javi claps his hands together, drawing her attention. "Come on. We're going to make a bonfire."

"With what?" Isaac asks.

"You'll see." Javi's grin promises mischief. Isaac shakes his head but follows him inside. A few minutes later, Javi shouts from somewhere above. "Heads up!" There's a crash around the side of the house. One of the TV stands is smashed on the ground. At least it's not a TV. Though Val only needs one. She wouldn't mind seeing the rest smashed.

"Heads up again!" Another stand sails off a balcony, splintering as it hits near the first. One more is sacrificed, and then an elated Javi and a sheepish Isaac are back down with Val.

Javi surveys his work, nodding in approval. "Wanted to move my TV to a closet anyway," he offers as justification for destroying house furniture. "Damn thing wouldn't turn off. I woke up in the middle of the night and it was glowing. Creepy."

Val is relieved someone else noticed. That meant the glowing TVs were real, not just a nightmare. She stares up at the house, struck by an idea.

She doesn't need *her* television. She'll use the sixth floor. A buffer between her and the rest of the house. If she waits until they're all asleep and turns the volume down low, no one will hear.

Val excuses herself to change. Her instinct is to hide the video on the sixth floor, but she remembers Javi's warning about being watched. Just because she hasn't seen any cameras doesn't mean they aren't there. She can't give anyone enough warning to stop her. So she goes into her room and pretends to drop her blanket next to her bed, using the movement to hide the video beneath her mattress.

She doesn't linger after changing. Being in the house alone is almost as bad as being on the stairs. She rushes back outside, wrapped up in the *Mona Lisa* blanket. Javi's well on his way to having the fire going by the time Jenny and Marcus pull up.

Jenny storms into the house, passing Val without acknowledgment. A loyal friend, Val's ass. Marcus doesn't bother changing, tossing his jacket inside and joining them around the fire. They had bonfires at the ranch, but she avoided them out of fear it would remind her of something she didn't want to know. Now she wants to know everything, but staring at the flames doesn't trigger any memories.

Her impulse is to help—she was always busy on the ranch—but Javi knows what he's doing. He shields the tinder, letting it burn as he waits for the larger pieces to fully catch.

"How do you know how to do this?" Marcus asks. "Boy Scout?"

Javi lets out a dark laugh. "Opposite program, same outcome. I can build a fire, administer basic first aid, and bullshit my way into making older people think I'm trustworthy."

Jenny stomps out in a matching blue pajama set and Ugg boots. She stands right next to Val and holds out a sandwich. It takes Val a few seconds to realize it's for her. She takes it, puzzled.

Jenny glares at the fire, picking up a conversation as though they were in the middle of it. "And Stuart only had one actual job: making sure my mom was watched for the night. Of *course* he couldn't even manage that. He put Emily in charge! An eleven-year-old! In charge of my mother! So not only did she manage to ruin the entire gala, but now Emily is traumatized by the whole thing." She darts a glance at Val. There's something pleading beneath the anger. Jenny isn't upset with Val. She's just plain upset, and this is her way of apologizing. The sandwich is a thoughtful gesture, too. Val's starving after missing dinner.

Val softens. It isn't Jenny's fault that her mother is . . . whatever her mother is. And Jenny might be from Bliss, but she didn't stand back with the others, watching. She was the first person to pull her mother away, the first one to stand between Val and harm.

Val bumps Jenny with her shoulder. "It's okay."

Jenny still sounds angry. "It's not okay, though. He knew tonight was important, and he knew she'd ruin it, and he didn't protect me from that. It's like—it's like he doesn't think about me as a person, you know? None of them do. I'm the mom. I'm even the mom to my own mom. I've never not been a mom." She sighs, leans a little closer to Val. "I know I've been intense about all this reunion stuff. But it's so important to me. When we were together as friends, when we had the show, when we were with him—that's the only time I ever got to be a kid."

"I'm sorry." Val squeezes Jenny, pulling her closer, and the other woman rests her head on Val's shoulder. Val takes a bite. "Oh my god, this sandwich is legitimately delicious?"

"I pickle the onions myself. But wait. Is that—are we burning furniture from the house?" Jenny sounds mildly alarmed.

"In my defense," Javi says, "the TV stands are so ugly. It's like they *wanted* us to burn them."

Jenny surprises them all with a laugh. "Sure. Whatever. Go get some chairs, too."

"For burning?" Marcus asks, confused.

"No, for sitting. We can't stand here all night. And bring some snacks."

"I have booze," Javi says. "If that's okay with you, Isaac?"

Isaac nods. "I'm good. I'll help get chairs." He follows the other men inside. They do better than chairs, though, grunting as they maneuver the first-floor couch out. They heft it on the ground in front of the fire.

Jenny sits, tucking her feet beneath her. "Maybe we can burn this if we get drunk enough."

Within half an hour, the fire is roaring, music is blasting from Isaac's car stereo, and Val is happily tucked onto a couch between Jenny and Isaac. Across from them are Javi and Marcus, whose couch is only slightly broken after being dropped from the second-floor balcony.

"And because of his phobia of shitting where anyone can hear," Javi says, gesticulating with his glass while not spilling a drop, "it was the farthest bathroom from the party. No one found Chief Justice Harrell for two whole hours."

"Amazing," Marcus says fondly. Then he shakes his head. "I can't get over the fact that a justice who has done his damnedest to take away privacy rights refuses to use a bathroom where it's possible someone might hear him."

"Right?" Javi laughs. "When my grandfather found out, of course he knew it was me. But the important thing was, he couldn't prove it, so his belt had to stay around his waist."

Val and Marcus share a troubled look across the fire. "Would he still beat you? Even now?" she asks.

"He'd probably try. Honestly, I'm with Jenny. The show was the only good part of my childhood. Maybe if we'd stayed on it longer, I could have learned the lesson the man in the cape kept trying to teach me. Would have made my life a lot easier."

"What lesson?" Val asks.

"You know." Javi tips his head up like someone has put their fingers under his chin. "Be obedient. Do what you're supposed to. Don't be a little shit."

"There was also a lesson about not swearing," Jenny chides, but there's no force behind it. She's finally relaxed, maybe because of the fire or the absurdity of destroying the couches for one evening of fun. But most likely because of the alcohol. Val once heard Gloria say that all alcohol did was give people permission to be themselves. She had expected Jenny to snap at them and be colder than ever, but drunk Jenny is so much *softer.*

"Yeah, fucked up that lesson, too." Javi lifts his glass to Jenny and she rolls her eyes. "Anyway, the show was a lot gentler than camp."

"Camp?" Marcus asks.

Javi gestures toward the fire. "Have you ever heard of those wilderness camps they send bad teens to?"

"Like conversion therapy camps?" Marcus's expression is bleak.

"That was definitely an element. My grandpa hated my girlfriends almost as much as he hated my boyfriends. But these camps are more general. It's a whole industry. They kidnap you in the middle of the night, carry you out of the house kicking and screaming and begging as your mother watches, wine in hand, just so you know she approves of it. And then they take you across state lines, into the wilderness, where no one can reach you or advocate for you or even give you a hug, and they make it very clear that they will let you get hurt—or hurt you, if they have to, to keep you *safe*—until you finally do what you're told. And you still fight them, so they take your shoes. And then they take your shirt. And then they take your pants. You're fifteen, skinny, shaking with the cold in the wilderness with no sleeping bag and no tent and no clothes and no food or even fire *privileges,* and you break. You give up. You finally admit that the people who are supposed to love you will do anything to keep you in line. Will let anyone do anything to you if it means you stop fucking up their lives. And you don't forget *that* lesson, don't forget how it felt to stand in your dirty boxers, begging for clothes, while your family slept comfortably hundreds of miles away. Not when you go home, not when you go to college, not when you go to law school. Not when you marry the woman they chose for you, do the job they chose for you, pose and smile for the photo ops they chose for you. You never forget the lesson that they would rather destroy you than let you inconvenience them."

Marcus shakes his head. "Jesus."

"I'm so sorry," Isaac says. "I wish—" He doesn't finish it.

Javi just nods. "It was a lot gentler, learning lessons on the show. I wish I had learned them well enough."

Marcus stares into the fire. "My mom knew what I was. I think even before I did. She didn't know how to have a kid who was Black *and* gay. Even one of those was too much for her. So she flattened me. I became the dullest, saddest version of myself. On the show, I got to be so many people, and I hate that I ended up as this." He gestures to himself in disgust. "It was unfair to everyone. My ex-wife, my kid. How could I be there for them when I couldn't even stand myself? I finally gave up pretending, but now I don't know how to create the version of Marcus I want to be. I miss the ease of slipping into roles on the show, the joy of being an artist. That creative power that felt like actual, real power. I'm afraid it's too late to get any of it back, though. And I'm terrified my son will think I'm selfish."

"Isn't it funny?" Isaac's gaze is fixed on the crackling flames. "We have kids and our most desperate hope is that they won't be like us, but . . . they're already ours. I sometimes wonder what poison I passed to Charlotte in her DNA. What damage I did just by being her father."

"That's not fair." Val takes his hand. "You're breaking away from your parents' patterns. It's hard, and you're doing it anyway, for her."

Isaac nods, but she can't see his eyes. Only the reflection of the fire in his glasses. "I'm going to give her what she needs. No matter what."

"No matter what," Jenny echoes on Val's other side.

"We'll protect our kids the way our parents didn't protect us," Javi says.

Val scratches her palm, slowly, rhythmically. It makes the itching turn to an agonizing burn, but she can't stop. There's something about the fire, how it makes the night all around them featureless. An infinite, empty black. The best kind. She feels sealed in here, with these strangers. Her best and only friends.

"My dad thought he was protecting me," she says. "But I found out today that no one was ever looking for us. We weren't hiding from anything. Maybe he was—maybe he was sick, you know? Maybe after what happened to Kitty, he was scared he'd lose me, too." That might explain why he couldn't stand to look at her. It reminded him of the daughter he hadn't saved.

It didn't excuse it, though. He could have talked to her about Kitty. Could have explained what they lost. "He made my life so small. I could never leave, never be anything else. *Try* anything else. I couldn't ask questions. Couldn't even *dream,* you know? I was going to leave a few years ago, but then he was sick and how could I? I had to keep everything shut away, every door closed, eyes only on what was right in front of me, otherwise I'd tip over the edge into absolute—"

She stops, because she's already falling. She found the edge of despair, and she's falling, and she doesn't know what will happen when at last she hits the bottom.

Isaac takes her left hand. She closes her eyes with a small sigh of relief. She can't scratch it now. Jenny scoots closer on her other side, snuggling in.

Javi holds out his drink. "May we recover from how bad our

parents fucked us up, and never find out how badly we're fucking up our own children." He takes a long swig.

Jenny laughs, but it's not the bright bray of earlier. It's low, gasping, and bleak. "Oh, I know exactly how I'm fucking my girls up, because I'm making them into me. I look at them and I love them so much I want to eat them whole, and also they're such little shits I want to strangle them. And they don't care about either feeling, because they don't care about my feelings, because I'm not a person to them."

Marcus has one arm across his chest, his hand on his own shoulder, cheek resting there. "No one tells you how hard it is to be a parent, but they also never tell you how terrifying it is. My ex has our son half the time and I spend every minute he's gone vaguely panicked about whether he's sad or scared or hurt, and I don't know about it and can't help him. And then when he's with me—" He pauses to take a long drink before continuing. "When he's with me, I sometimes count down the hours until he's gone again, because at least then I know *what* I'm afraid of. When he's with me, I'm still afraid, and I don't know why. Or how to be what he needs. What he deserves."

Isaac nods. "Are you ever terrified you're not protecting them? That there's something obvious, something easy you should be doing, but you haven't done it and they're going to suffer because of it?"

Jenny gestures to the night around them. "The fact that we're out here in the middle of the desert trying to unearth our own childhoods rather than taking care of theirs is probably all the answer you need. Bad mom. I'm a bad mom."

Javi stands, emphatic. "You're not a bad mom, you just don't have any help. And I don't mean fucking useless Stuart. I mean real help, like what we had. That magic, that safety, that friendship. If I can't go back to it, at least I could give it to my kids, you know? Give them what we had when we were all happy."

Val doesn't feel left out because she's not a parent. She feels left out because she can't agree with this sentiment. Not only because she doesn't remember what it was like to be on the show. But also because she doesn't think Isaac's right about why she forgot. Kids don't block out memories of an entire childhood because they're too *happy*.

As though reading her thoughts—or maybe her face—Marcus waggles a finger at her. "No, Val. You were happy then. You might not remember, but we do. We were all happy, together."

Val gives a shrug of a smile, the same gesture as her shoulders. There and then gone. "Maybe I was. Maybe I'm projecting my current pain onto my past self. I'm not happy now, so I couldn't have been then."

Jenny points at her. "Yes! Like taping over what was there with something new. Maybe you got sad sometimes, but what kid doesn't? The important thing is you remind them they aren't really sad, then distract them and keep them from feeling that way."

That doesn't seem right, but Jenny doesn't notice Val's dubious look. She's too busy nodding to herself. Then she springs to her feet, mimicking Javi's posture. "Let's swear."

Javi holds out his arms dramatically, shouting, "Fucktrumpet! Shitgibbon! Cockwomble!" to the night.

Jenny stomps her foot. "Be serious for once! Let's all join hands around this fire and swear we're going to do better. Be better. Make a better life for our own kids. If we get nothing else out of this whole weird mess, we'll at least have that."

The fire seems more alive in Isaac's glasses than in reality, flickering hypnotically. He stands. "We'll make magic for our children, whatever it costs us." He reaches for Marcus, whose hand is already waiting.

Javi and Marcus are clasped hand in hand on the other side of the fire. Javi grabs Jenny's hand, tugging them all slightly too close to the flames. It feels dangerous to Val, especially considering everyone except Isaac has been drinking. "We'll protect them," Javi says.

"We won't let them be sad," Marcus says, "or lonely, or scared."

Isaac holds out his hand, silently asking. Val is the only link in the chain who hasn't connected yet. She slowly rises, staring at the fire in his glasses until it grows and blocks out anything else. She knows sometimes kids have to be sad. But she's been sad and lonely and scared for so long. She doesn't want it anymore. Not for herself. Not for any of them.

"For Kitty, too," Isaac says softly. "Because no one did this for her. We'll fix the world for all of them."

Val takes his hand. Jenny squeezes her other. Val doesn't have kids, will probably never have kids, but *this* is what she wants. This circle, these friends, this belonging. Val to Isaac to Marcus to Javi to Jenny to Val. A circle, almost complete. They stare into the fire, standing too close, the heat almost unbearable on their faces. But they bear it. They bear it as witness that they're going to do better. For the kids who are still here, and the one who isn't.

Jenny starts humming a tune Val knows down to her core. Her stomach clenches and suddenly the fire isn't hot enough, can never be hot enough to warm her. The surrounding darkness no longer feels safe. It's infinite and hungry and buzzing, and she's small. She's so small.

"Oh no!" Jenny slaps her forehead, breaking the circle. "Isaac, your interview! You missed it this afternoon! You need to go down right now!"

"But she won't be awake, will she?" Val asks.

Jenny waves dismissively. "She's waiting for Isaac. Gotta take our turns. *Take your turn, bide your time, sit so still, wait in line, be so patient, be so good, do just what you know you should!*"

Isaac stands. Val holds out her blanket. "Take it. It's colder inside."

Their fingers brush as she passes him *Mona Lisa*. She wants him to stay here, with her. She wants to curl into him so she can forget who she is and who she'll never be. But Isaac's head turns inexorably toward the house, and he goes inside.

What is this hold it has on all of them? And who is the interviewer, available all hours of the day to talk about a kids' show? Have they all talked about Kitty without her?

She desperately searches their faces. "Do you remember what

exactly happened to Kitty? Because my mom—she said she wasn't watching, and my dad never said a word about her, and the mayor said Kitty isn't dead, and I—I need to know. I need to know what happened to her."

The others fall silent. No one meets her gaze.

"Could she still be alive?" Val presses. "Is that even possible?"

Javi shakes his head, but then stops, tilting his chin up.

Marcus has a hand on his own shoulder again. But his eyes are closed. "I don't remember," he whispers, over and over, like a chant to reassure himself.

Jenny turns toward Val. Her eyes are filled with tears, but they're also fierce and burning. "Kitty never left the show," she says. "Maybe she was the lucky one, after all."

Val can't deal with this. She stands, but the only place for her to retreat is the house. Still, it's better than out here, romanticizing a past that stole everything from her. Inside, an icy draft spills upward from the basement. Val deliberately doesn't look at the stairs, some childlike sense that if she doesn't acknowledge them, whatever is down there won't notice her, either.

A light pulses on the kitchen counter and then disappears. Isaac left his phone. Val idly picks it up, needing to talk to the one person she can never talk to again. "Dad," she whispers. It's both longing and accusation.

As though summoned, the phone silently flashes again with a call. Val frowns. She knows that number. It's the *only* number she knows. She answers.

"Gloria?"

"Val? Val, is that you?"

"Hi, Gloria. Is everything okay? It's so late, and—"

"Where are you?" Gloria sounds frantic.

"Utah. With some friends." Val can't explain better than that. Not even to herself.

"Can you get back? Or I can meet you. Anywhere."

Val feels awful. She should have been sending updates. "Not right now. It's complicated, and I don't have—"

"It's okay, it'll be okay," Gloria interrupts. "I set aside the money. All of it, thirty years of wages for both of you. And I have IDs, documents. We can get you settled again."

Val's speechless. She'd always been under the impression that they were only working for room and board. She has money and legal documents? Both of which mean she has options for a real life. She's both furious—why didn't Gloria tell her earlier?—and astonished. For a few seconds her imagination swells with possibilities.

A cold draft tugs her back to reality. She can't leave yet. Not until she knows. Not until she's found Kitty again and laid her memory to rest.

"Thank you, but I'm fine. I'm sorry I haven't called. That wasn't very thoughtful of me."

"Val, please. Tell me where you are. It's not safe."

Val shakes her head, leaning against the counter. "My dad was wrong. No one was ever looking for us. My mom didn't care that he took me. We never needed to hide. There are no police reports, no arrest warrants, nothing."

"He was never hiding you from the police," Gloria says, and Val hears muffled sounds like she's getting dressed, then a jingling of keys.

"He told you that? Then who was he hiding from?"

"Anyone who was looking for you, anyone who took the trouble to find you: They're not your friend. You have to get out of there. *Now.*"

“Isaac.” The name is a sigh of affection. And then the lights flicker on, illuminating him.

“Hi.” Isaac drops the blanket at the bottom of the stairs, then lopes toward the screen, still all arms and legs as he sits down. His gaze is open and clear. “Are you— Who am I talking to?”

There’s a giggle, and then the interviewer says in a teasing note, “You’re going to talk to the whole *world,* Isaac.”

He runs a hand through his long hair, more out of habit than to push it back from his forehead. “So . . . why are we doing this?”

“For the podcast, of course! They said it was important. Do you want to hear your intro?”

His smile encourages without patronizing or questioning. “Sure.”

*Even if you didn’t have an older brother, every time you sat in front of your television and joined that circle of friends, you did.*

*Let’s summon him together:*

Isaac.

*Saying his name makes you feel safe. Protected. Like someone’s going to show you the ropes and help you when you can’t do it yourself. He wasn’t the funniest, or the most playful, or the best at pretending or creating, or even the leader, but he always picked up Kitty if she fell, or comforted Marcus when he pretended too much and got lost in it, or helped cheer up Javi when he felt bad about what he'd done.*

*Isaac was never dismissive, never teased the other kids, never pushed them around. He was the oldest, and he took it seriously. Those magnified hazel eyes watched everyone, always, keeping tabs to make sure all the friends were okay. Keeping them safe.*

*And if he ever did look away*—Why did Kitty fall in the first place? Why did Marcus go so far that he got lost? Why did Javi misbehave? Why did the circle break? Because Isaac wasn't watching, of course—*Mister Magic put his hand on top of Isaac's head and turned it the right direction, so he would see what he needed to with those funny glasses.*

*Isaac still has glasses, though there are more lines around his eyes, and a beard on his face, and his short hair has grown long because he's too sad and guilty to do anything simple and kind for himself, like get a haircut. He can still watch out for everyone, though. Still make up for his failure. He just needs a chance to prove it.*

Isaac doesn't react to his introduction. There's no surprise or offense or disapproval.

"Well?" the interviewer prods.

"I'm sorry I looked away," Isaac says. "I'm not looking away now."

"Good."

"But I think Val's going to leave."

There's a burst of static, spikes of painful, piercing sound. Isaac doesn't even flinch.

*"What?"*

He takes off his glasses and uses his shirt hem to clean the lenses. "She's not the same, anyway. When her dad pulled her away from us, she lost so much of herself. I don't think she belongs anymore. We can do it without—"

That same white-noise static flares louder. It's a wall of buzzing so overwhelming all other senses shut down. Isaac drops his glasses, puts his hands over his ears.

It lasts only seconds, but the air pulses with its absence when it cuts off. "We're not finished," the interviewer says, her tone light and pleasant.

Isaac picks up his glasses. But he doesn't put them on. He keeps his eyes down, a way of distancing himself. "Val didn't want to be found. We should have respected that."

"She was happy to be found!"

He shakes his head.

"Put on your glasses."

Isaac does as he's told, but keeps his gaze on his hands, resting palms-up on his knees. "She doesn't remember anything, so it won't matter anyway. Maybe we could—"

"You made a deal. *This is the deal.*" The voice warps, dropping lower, then reverts to its cheery, childlike tone. "We have to see it through to the end, together! You can't drop halfway to the bottom and then just stop. You have to sink all the way to the inkiest depths, sit in the silt and the mud, feel it suctioning onto you. Let the pressure above and around you push in, push, push, push, until your lungs and your head and your heart can't take it anymore, and then—and *then*—you'll let go enough."

Isaac keeps his own tone carefully neutral. "Let go enough for what?"

"You can't get better until you've hit rock bottom. You know that. Val will learn, too. We'll push her to the bottom and then she'll remember, and she'll be our *friend* again."

The word *friend* is sharp when the interviewer says it, so razor-edged it could be wielded as a weapon. Isaac glances toward the stairs. Toward the blanket waiting for him there, her warmth still lingering inside.

His name is whispered in the softest hiss, like the first hint of a kettle beginning to boil.

Isaac's head turns straight forward, guided back to what he

needs to focus on. Back to the screen. His eyes are clear, though. He's not swallowed up by what he sees there, not lost in a dream or a promise. He already made his deal, after all.

"She needs to remember," the interviewer says. "She can't be whole until she does. None of you can."

"What if forgetting is a gift? People act like it's a tragedy, how much we forget. I forgot, while I was in there. I forgot all about what the world was like, how much it hurt. And as soon as it was over, as soon as I was forced back into the light, I remembered everything, and it was too much. I lost Val, and I lost—" He gestures weakly at the screen. "It was my fault. I wish I *could* forget it. I tried to, for a lot of years."

The interviewer's voice perks up. "But you're doing better now! And you'll be good. You'll be so good. You'll be what they need you to be. What *we* need you to be. What Charlotte needs you to be."

"Charlotte," Isaac whispers, a prayer or an incantation or a promise. His fingers close over his open palms. His head doesn't turn, his eyes don't drift away. He's facing exactly where he needs to be facing.

Another happy, satisfied sigh. "We missed you, Isaac. We're so glad you're ours again."

# FOURTEEN

"Val?" Marcus calls from outside.

Val startles, nearly dropping Isaac's phone.

"Val?" Gloria echoes.

"I'll be safe, I promise," Val says. "I'll call you again soon. But don't call this number anymore, okay?" She hangs up as fast as she can and stares at the phone as though it will tell her what to do next. But Isaac—who leaves everything open between them, always—doesn't have a passcode.

She goes to the call logs. Gloria has called so many times since yesterday. Her stomach keeps sinking, no bottom to be found. In the messaging app where Val texted Gloria yesterday, there are dozens of frantic responses, alternately pleading for Val to answer and threatening whoever owns the phone.

They've all been seen and left unanswered.

Val deletes the call history from tonight so Isaac won't know that she picked up, then sets the phone back on the counter.

What should she do?

A deeper chill cuts through her. She turns, holding her breath. It's dark in the house, so all she can see is a figure standing at the entrance to the basement stairs. He's wearing a cape.

It's Isaac, wrapped in her blanket. She knows it's him, knows it's her blanket, *tells* herself it's her blanket. Promises herself it's only Isaac, her Isaac.

*Anyone who was looking for you is not your friend,* Gloria said. But the people here are her oldest friends. Her only friends. And the only people who ever looked for her.

Gloria could be as paranoid as her dad. Strange ideas about the government, about surveillance, about cabals of powerful people in league with malevolent forces. She was an odd duck already, and maybe Dad's delusion spread to her.

But.

None of her friends will tell her what happened to Kitty. They all say they were there, and yet not a single one of them can give her any details.

And Isaac is still standing there in the dark, silent, nearly invisible. He shifts, the edge of the blanket opening to invite her in. To give her a place tucked into his side. The only place she ever felt truly safe, truly loved.

She can't give that up. Not again. She'll let him explain everything. Val takes a step toward the thick darkness, toward the humming stairs and Isaac waiting for her.

"Val!" Marcus shouts again, laughing. "We need you."

She turns toward the open front door, annoyed. "What do you need me for?" she answers, then glances back over her shoulder at Isaac.

No one's there.

The top of the stairs is empty. He was there. He was *right there.* Wasn't he? Maybe it was a shadow, or a play of light on the wall from the fire outside. Or maybe he was there, but he went upstairs and wants her to follow.

Or back downstairs and wants her to follow.

"Val?" Marcus puts a hand on her shoulder. She whirls around.

"You need me?" Val tries to keep her tone light, fighting panic. What would have happened if she had crossed this dark space in answer to the invitation? What would she have found waiting for her in the stairwell?

Is it still there, just past where she can see?

"Of course we need you," Marcus says, eyes bright, tone warm. He raises his voice. "We're arguing about what drinking game to play, and you have to take my side. Javi and Jenny are bullying me."

"We are not!" Jenny shouts from outside. "And don't try to use Val! She's not in charge anymore!"

"When was I ever in charge?" Val asks.

Marcus laughs like it's the stupidest question he's ever heard. It's exactly what she's been trying to ignore: All of them act like they know her, when she doesn't know them. She might want to, might even feel like she does, but they brush off her attempts to get actual information.

If she asks Isaac about Gloria's calls and texts, he'll have a non-answer that feels comforting but doesn't actually tell her the truth. Maybe she *is* being set up, like Javi warned. But maybe the culprits are much closer. After all, even Javi said they were the only witnesses. What if they all decide to tell the same story? A different one than they've been telling her?

She waves for Marcus to go without her. "I'm pretty exhausted. Think I'll turn in."

"Boo!" Javi says from outside the door, Jenny right behind him.

"We can find more things to burn!" Marcus offers. They're crowding in, blocking Val from the exit. A veritable wall of friendship between her and the way out.

She backs up, smiling. "We've got to keep some of the furniture, don't we? I'll see you in the morning." The temptation to look down the stairs, to check if Isaac is waiting there, is strong. But not stronger than her dread.

Instead she launches herself up the stairs, taking them two at a time as though speed will protect her. Safe—or safe enough, for now—on her floor, she longs for a door to separate her from the rest of the house. To seal herself away from the cold, from the hum, from the basement. She ends up in the bathroom, sitting in the tub, thinking and trying not to think at the same time.

She'd give almost anything to erase that phone call. To purge the doubt and fear Gloria poisoned her with. Didn't Dad do the same thing? Trap Val in his own paranoia? Maybe that's why Isaac didn't tell her about the texts and the calls. Maybe he knew that it was Val's prison, reaching out to reclaim her.

But it always felt like Isaac was giving her choices. So why wouldn't he give her the choice to respond to Gloria?

For a long while sounds drift up, laughter and the occasional raised voice. Then a few rushes of plumbing beneath her. At last, nothing. There's no way to be sure they're all in bed, but at least they aren't wandering. And there's no reason for any of them to go up to the sixth floor.

Val leaves the bathroom. The only glow is from the television's black screen. How can something so lightless still provide illumination? Val grabs the tape, then, as an afterthought, drags her bedspread free and throws it over the television. It makes her feel better. She creeps to the stairs and pauses for a few breathless seconds before stepping out onto the landing.

One thing to be said for the house: The maddening ambient hum dampens any stair noise. She pads upward, feeling vulnerable and unsteady, like the basement is closer than it should be. The sixth floor is dark except for the black glow of its television screen. Val adjusts the volume as low as it can go before it's silent. Then she pushes the tape into the VCR.

It fuzzes to life immediately, mid-scene, and Val finds herself staring at . . .

Herself.

Val, a beautiful child with thick, dark hair and dramatically furrowed eyebrows, stares directly at the camera.

Little Isaac—gangly, with glasses that magnify his hazel eyes—stands closest to her, laughing at something Jenny just said. Dots of light swirl in the distance, coalescing into a tiny girl. She twirls into focus, wearing a pale-pink leotard with white tights, tutu floating around her waist like a cloud.

"Kitty," Val says. Her eyes leave the camera and a smile softens her intensity. "Have you been practicing?"

Kitty twirls once more, moving through a series of complicated ballet poses as Marcus sings, "*Practice makes perfect, and perfect's the crown! Anything else is letting us down!*"

But on her big finish, Kitty stumbles. Her eyes well with tears and she flinches, looking furtively around as though expecting something to come out of the darkness. The stage is still a perfect, featureless black, only the children visible.

Kitty stammers. "I tried, I did, but—"

"You did a wonderful job. Marcus," Val commands, her voice tight and efficient. "Magic show."

Marcus bows with a flourish. He holds his hands up, waving them like a conductor. A stage melts into existence, with curtains so red and creamy they look frosted onto the walls. The boards of the stage floor are polished and gleaming, a spotlight trained on the center. Jenny appears in a tuxedo with a red bow tie, striding confidently across the stage.

She points to the space above her lip. Marcus laughs and scurries over, using his finger to draw a curling brown mustache on her face. The hairs shift as Jenny beams.

"Ah yes." Jenny strokes her mustache dramatically. "Much better." The others giggle and she clears her throat, glowering seriously at them until they quiet down. "Today, to amaze and delight you, I shall make my lovely assistant—" She points to Kitty, still in her ballet dress. "—disappear!"

"But I don't want to disappear." Kitty crosses her arms over her chest.

"Kitty," Jenny hisses. "Don't ruin the show!"

Kitty looks to Val, who nods in encouragement. The littlest girl relents. Jenny waves a hand, then taps it lightly on Kitty's head. "Abracadabra!" Jenny frowns in frustration, then tries again. "Alacazam!" Nothing happens.

Jenny stomps her foot and glares at Val. "I need the cape. How am I supposed to do magic without a cape?"

Marcus steps forward, hands raised, but Jenny shakes her head. "Not one of your capes. I need a *real* cape."

Val answers. "No."

Jenny's voice rises, face flushing red. "It's not fair that you're in charge. I should be in charge sometimes, too! He likes me best, anyway."

Isaac puts a hand on her arm. Unlike the other children, Isaac doesn't do any flourishes. There's no element of performance in his movements. His voice is so soft it's barely audible, meant only for Jenny. "Calm down. You don't want to make him come."

"Maybe I do!" Jenny shouts. "Maybe I want him to come all the time! We never voted on it!"

Isaac looks at Val. "Please? They all need more playtime. And Jenny won't be happy until she finishes her magic show."

Val sighs. "Only for a little bit." She reaches into the darkness at her side—not off camera, but still impossible to see—and suddenly she's holding a shimmering length of black cloth. She solemnly walks to Jenny and drapes it carefully across her shoulders.

The transformation is astonishing. Jenny looks taller. She angles her head differently, shifts her eyebrows, juts her chin. This time when she extends her hand, a traditional magic wand with white tips appears there. Her voice drops, still a child's but somehow stronger, deeper. A voice that can command.

*"Till the ground and plant the seed, I will give you what you need, close your eyes and count to three, what you want is what you'll see!"*

Jenny closes her eyes, and everyone else does, too. When none of them are looking, when they're all busy counting to three to call up the magic, Val turns and stares directly into the camera.

Her eyes widen once, a flash, a soundless plea.

Then Jenny taps Kitty on the head with the magic wand and, without a poof of smoke or shower of sparks, Kitty is *gone.*

Jenny's flushed with success, beaming beneath her twirling mustache. "And now, for my second act, I'll make her reappear!" She waves the wand with a flourish, taps the air, and . . . nothing happens. She does it again, frowning.

Nothing.

"Jenny," Val says, worry edging her voice. "Where is she? Where did you send her?"

"I don't know, I—"

"Abracalacazam!" a voice shouts. From behind the curtains, two children giggle. Javi swaggers out, also wearing a tux and a mustache. He bows with a flourish as he parts the curtains to reveal Kitty, sparkling in a puffy-sleeved dress.

Jenny scowls. "You messed up my trick."

"Did I?" He produces a bouquet of fresh flowers every color of the rainbow, which he presents to Jenny. But the flowers aren't flowers—they're butterflies that fly up and circle her head like a crown. She can't help but smile, and then laugh as her mustache tickles her nose.

"That's enough cape time." Val steps forward, hand extended to take it back.

"But my show isn't done yet!" Jenny lifts her arms, eyes twinkling with mischief normally saved for Javi. "Can't have it back until you find me!" She lowers her arms and disappears. The curtains fall to the floor, revealing a new set behind them. It's an ancient temple, filled with treasure and statues and dozens of hiding places.

Val sighs, a long-suffering look on her face as everyone begins the hunt for Jenny.

Javi tries various tricks to lure her out, at one point even meowing like a lost kitten. Isaac searches with a worried expression on his face—he doesn't like it when they aren't all together. Marcus changes their outfits to explorer costumes, complete with binoculars and walkie-talkies. Kitty uses her walkie-talkie to tell nonsense knock-knock jokes while they look.

Val's in the middle, calling out for Jenny and smiling at Kitty. But when everyone else peers into a newly discovered cavern—hidden behind a painting of Magician Jenny and her Marvelous Mustache—Val's expression changes. One second she's there, playing, and the next she's so sad and so, so, tired . . . and she's gone.

The kids notice, but pretend they don't. They're still looking for Jenny, smiling and laughing and playing along the way, but there's a frantic energy to it. They find Jenny at last. She bursts out of a treasure chest with crowns and jewels for all of them, but no one can manage more than the barest pretense at excitement.

Because Val's not back.

"Val?" Isaac calls. "Please, Val. We need to stop."

Javi walks around the temple with Marcus, hands around his mouth as he shouts. "Valentina, Valentina, come out come out wherever you are. The game is over."

Jenny stands in the center of the room, hands full of treasure, still wrapped in her cape. Her plans are ruined because Val is missing. They're still in the ancient temple, but the edges have gotten blurry. The corners are darker than they were. Marcus fixes it where he can, but it's like holding back the tide. They're losing the temple, and something else is seeping in to take its place.

"We need Val," Javi whispers, as though trying to keep it secret. Marcus is busy holding the room intact, Kitty is on the verge of tears, and Isaac has wandered off camera, too. Jenny's next to a pedestal holding a giant vase painted with the six friends. She tips it over. It crashes to the floor with a terrible din.

Kitty gasps. "Jenny! No!"

Jenny's smile grows. "Hey, Val!" she shouts. "I'm making a mess! And a mess is an invitation!" She kicks over a plant. Dirt spills across the shiny tiled floor of Marcus's temple. Where it falls, the floor disappears, turning pure black. The cape twitches on Jenny's shoulders, tugged from the corner by an unseen hand.

All the kids peer into the darkness at the edge of the world. The borders of their play shrink as black ripples closer and closer, like rising floodwaters. Jenny's cape floats. It's being lifted, slowly, slowly, slowly away from her. She reaches up to her throat to unclasp it and set it free.

Val's voice rings through the darkness, closer and louder than the others. "Stop."

Everything does. The room stops shrinking. The cape falls flat and lifeless. Jenny drops her hand, a flicker of frustration on her face quickly replaced with smug triumph. "Found you."

"No, Isaac found me."

Sure enough, they emerge together from somewhere off camera, holding hands. Isaac whispers something in Val's ear, and she nods. Then her serious expression blossoms into a huge, playful smile.

"You found me! Great job! You didn't give up, even when it got hard and a little scary. Sometimes things *are* hard and scary. That's when we need each other the most. I'm so proud of you all! Now the game is over, and it's time to stop."

Jenny's lips turn into a pout, her mustache drooping. "But I wanted him to—"

Val sings to Jenny. "*Only when we need him, only when we ask! Only when we six just aren't up to the task!*" She holds out her hand. Jenny unfastens the cape and solemnly relinquishes it.

Val beams at her. "We're up to this task, aren't we? Together, we can do anything! Let's clean up!"

Jenny relents, smiling. Isaac directs the tasks and soon enough the entire space is wiped clean, both of Jenny's destruction and of the temple. Kitty finishes singing their cleanup song, and the friends are once more standing in a featureless black void.

"Maybe we could have him come and say good night?" Jenny asks, hopeful. Her mustache melts, as does Javi's. The kids are in regular clothes again, tees and shorts in neon ice cream colors.

Val wraps Jenny in a hug. "You know he never says good night, and we don't need any lessons. We're doing great. *You* did so great today, Jenny!"

Jenny nods into her shoulder. Val passes Jenny to Marcus, who hugs her while Val carefully folds the cape smaller, and smaller, and smaller. It's a magic trick of her own, how small the cloak can fold. When it's the size of her palm, she closes her fingers over it and whispers. When she opens her fingers again, the cloak is gone.

All six children sigh and slump like someone has cut their strings. In the last second before the screen goes black, Val once again looks directly at the camera. This time there's no silent plea in her eyes, only a weary, glazed look of resignation.

The lights disappear. The children disappear.

The darkness flickers once more and immediately the children are back, laughing, as Jenny and Marcus teach them a clapping game with a rhyme about doing what you're told.

# DON'T BE SEEN

"What the fuck," Val whispers. She presses a button on the VCR. Everything moves in fast-forward, a blur of childhood games and joy and magic. She pauses it at random, freezing the screen on a children's vision of a tropical beach. The water is so vividly blue it practically glows, the sand is crayon yellow, the palm trees straight lines with green spikes at the top. Jenny has Kitty buried up to her neck in the sand and is sculpting a new mermaid body over her while Val, Marcus, and Isaac hit a beach ball and Javi sneaks behind them with buckets of cold water.

It doesn't make any sense.

As far as she can tell, there are no cuts. Only one camera, but somehow it gets angles and views that should be impossible. No visible mics or equipment, no edits or breaks while the scenery and costumes change. There's also no music, other than what the kids sing. All of which might make sense if this was unedited footage, but there are special effects. Astonishingly good special effects.

Val looks down at her watch and swears again. It's been seventy minutes. How was a single episode seventy minutes? There was no intro, no credits, no commercial breaks. No self-contained story. It just seemed to *go*. Like watching kids playing, if you could see their actual imaginations.

And she can't get past the visual effects. Val hasn't watched many things, but she's sneaked enough glimpses of shows to know that, for the early '90s, that level of sophistication was . . . impossible. It's probably impossible by today's standards, at least without an astronomical budget. The way Marcus painted the background and it appeared around them wasn't only seamless, it was *beautiful*. Lavish and wondrous and magical.

Val leans back, wanting to put distance between herself and the television. The glass between them isn't enough. Not after how real the show looked.

How real it *felt*.

If being on it was half as overwhelming as watching it, no wonder the others haven't gotten past their time on *Mister Magic*. But where *was* Mister Magic? He didn't appear once. Why did they go out of their way to make sure they didn't bring him on-screen on a show named after him?

Val is haunted by this glimpse of the past. Not by Kitty, but by her own face, thirty years younger, staring directly into the camera. She was the only one who broke the fourth wall. She was pleading. Begging, even. But begging for what?

*We watched,* her mother said. *We could see it was working. We could see you were happy.* But Val has seen now, too, and she knows her own face well enough to know: She wasn't happy in there.

Why did the woman in the parking lot give this to her? And how did she even have it? According to everyone Val's met, and the internet as a whole, this recording shouldn't exist.

Her first impulse is to talk to Isaac, which breaks her heart all over again. Javi, then. She'll trust that he was warning her in good faith. She has to. She carefully sneaks down to Javi's floor and tiptoes across his family room. His darkly glowing television is now resting on the floor. Why didn't he move it into his closet, like he said he would?

The answer is soon obvious. His bed is empty. Which means he's either still outside, or in bed with someone else. Defeated, Val turns to go back upstairs. But the light in the room has changed.

She flinches, expecting to be discovered. It's only the television, though. In place of that barely visible black screen is a rainbow test pattern.

Feeling pursued, she rushes back upstairs. She wants to linger on Isaac's floor, to slip into his bed. She wishes she'd never talked to Gloria, never seen Isaac's phone. Wishes she had gone back out and played games around the bonfire like the stupid, carefree teens they had never been allowed to be.

Gravity feels stronger the higher up she goes, like the basement is exerting extra effort on tugging her downward. The sixth floor feels impossibly far away. She stops at the fifth. She doesn't want the video with her, anyway. She feels infected. Already, she can't forget how the things little Marcus created felt more alive than the room around her. Than the whole world around her. Everything is dingy and tired and broken down compared with what they all lived and dreamed, together.

She's glad she doesn't remember anything, that it's all contained on a single tape instead of inside her. But she's also devastatingly happy that she got to watch Kitty. Val crawls into her bed and closes her eyes. She hopes she'll dream of her sister. But she can't escape the sensation of being observed. Maybe it's a lingering effect of seeing the show, watching her own childhood like a stranger might. Oh god, like strangers *had*. Who knew how many people watched her and Kitty as children? It's an oily sensation across her brain, a film she can't wipe away. She was packaged and presented to the whole world before she was old enough to understand what that meant. They all were.

As if her thoughts aren't aggravating enough, her hand itches, the burning torture worsening the longer she tries to lie still and ignore it.

She sits up on the edge of the bed, abandoning sleep. The test pattern on her television provides enough light to see as she scrapes her fingernails over her palm.

Under the skin, beneath the swollen, red scarring, *there's something there*. Val flinches in disgust. A single black thread grows like a hair in the center of the irritation. Did her incessant scratching break the skin? Maybe something from her clothes worked its way underneath and is now festering its way back to the surface.

She pinches the thread between her fingers and gives an exploratory tug, afraid of losing her grip on it. But the string keeps coming. A half inch, an inch, three inches. The smell of rot and infection lurks beneath her skin.

Val keeps going. She should move into the bathroom for more light, for soap. But she can't stop, not while any of it is still inside her. The string doesn't end. It's connected to something bigger.

Val sobs, grabbing onto it and pulling. Pulling. Pulling. More and more soft black material tears free of her skin, pooling wet and stinking on her lap. At last, with one terrible effort that rips out something vitally connected to her body, she has it all.

She wants to throw it out the window, never look at it again. Never think about it again. But she can't stop, any more than she could stop once she had started tugging. Val grasps the length of black horror she gouged from her hand, and holds it up.

It's a cape.

A cape she knows as well as the back of her hand. Or the palm of it, in this case. She flings it away with a cry. But the cloak doesn't flop wetly to the ground like a discarded, filthy washrag. It floats elegantly downward. When it lands on the floor, it drapes, a slow, sensual reveal of something crouched beneath.

Val doesn't move. She doesn't blink. She doesn't breathe. It's a trick of the light. It has to be. There was nothing on the floor. She would have noticed, she would have seen it.

Val pulls her feet slowly upward, away from the carpet, from the cape, from whatever is under it. If she can get the blanket over herself, she can shut the door on this horror, she can pretend—

The cape scuttles forward.

Val screams so hard it wakes her up. She's covered in sweat, still under the blankets. *Her hand.* She flips it to look at the damage to her palm, but . . . it's smooth. No sign of any irritation, and no gaping hole where a cape was pulled free. It doesn't even itch anymore.

She can't forget that sound, though, or the smell of rot. There's a hint of it, still. And her room is freezing, her teeth chattering, sweat chilling her straight through.

She'll go back to sleep. Pretend it was only a dream, close her eyes, close this door, close—

"No," Val says. She's not closing doors anymore. Not even if what's behind them is horrific.

She leans over the side of the bed, letting the floor slowly reveal itself. It's only the ugly carpet. But there are so many places to hide. Under the bed, in the closet, behind the television. Just like in their game on the show. A cape can hide anywhere in the darkness, because it's made of the same material.

"I am losing my mind." But even as she whispers it, Val doesn't quite believe it. Maybe watching the show put new ideas in her head, or maybe it reminded her of truths she had locked away. There are answers here. Answers to what happened to Kitty. Answers to what happened to *her.* No bad dreams are going to keep her from that, just like no betrayal or lies will.

Val retrieves her video from upstairs and leaves the house. She sits on the smoke-stained couch outside and waits for the sun to restore reality. In the light, she'll feel in control once more.

And, the part that she doesn't admit to herself, in the light she'll be safe from that cape.

There's a giggle and an exaggerated shushing before the lights click on. Javi and Marcus are revealed, arms around each other for balance in the dark.

"Hello?" Javi stage-whispers. They look at the screen and seem satisfied that it's off.

Marcus walks closer, slightly unsteady. "Do you see a remote? Or anything with buttons. Or a touch screen. Do you think it's a touch screen?" He peers intently, but then backs up. He doesn't try to touch it.

"I don't see anything. Only that camera." Javi points up at the lens trained right on them, then wanders the borders of the blank white room, trailing his fingers along the walls. "Is it just me, or is this stone? Shouldn't it be drywall?" Javi tries for the chair, doesn't quite make it, ends up half falling to the floor. Marcus joins him. They sit knee-to-knee, closer than they need to. Neither moves.

Marcus nods toward the screen. "I was hoping we'd be able to watch it. The show."

"Did she tell you she has recordings?"

Marcus nods, his expression somber and worried. "Yeah, she did. But I don't want to watch it with her, you know?"

Javi knows. His jaw clenches, his brows drawing low as he stares at the screen where there is only darkness. Infinite, warm, inviting darkness, stretching forever.

"She's weird, right?" Marcus asks.

"Super weird. But anyone obsessed with our show would have to be." Javi nudges Marcus with his shoulder and they laugh, but use it as an excuse to sit even closer. Neither mentions that they've both agreed to a deal with her. Both agreed to remember the song, to sing it.

Marcus starts humming, as though now that he's here again, he can't help it. Or maybe just to drown out the other humming.

Javi interrupts him in a rush. "What do you actually remember? About the last time? The last circle?"

Marcus's gaze goes blank. His eyes track back and forth, watching a memory. And then he flinches, putting a hand on his own shoulder before closing it into a fist. "Nothing," he lies.

"Yeah." Javi's eyes are flat and lifeless, his tone dead. His chin drops to his chest, leaving no space there for long, spindly fingers to tip his head up and remind him to behave. "Yeah, me neither." He crosses his legs. Marcus does the same. They sit on the floor, staring up at the screen like kids waiting for their favorite show to come on.

Nothing happens. It's not time yet.

"I missed you the most," Javi says quietly. A single tear traces down the far side of Marcus's face, where Javi couldn't see it even if he looked away from the screen. Maybe Marcus can't tell if Javi is talking to him, or talking to the empty warm nothingness pulsing in front of them.

Marcus leans against Javi's arm. They're still for so long that the motion sensors shut off. Darkness settles around them like an embrace. There's the softest sigh of static from beyond the screen, and then only silence.

# FIFTEEN

"What is this?" a voice demands.

Val's eyes peel open. Her mouth is dry, her head pounding, and it's unreasonably bright.

She's outside, asleep on the couch next to the bonfire's ashes. She sits up in a rush, flinging her left hand away from her like it's contaminated. But daylight reveals a perfectly smooth palm. Only her regular scars, and it doesn't itch anymore. The cape got away last night.

Val shakes her head, trying to fully wake up.

"What is *this*?" Jenny demands again. She's fully dressed, her hair immaculate, looking none the worse for wear after last night. But it's not Jenny's knee-length khaki shorts or pale-pink button-up top that catches Val's attention.

Jenny's got Val's tape.

"That's mine." Val holds her hand out for it.

Jenny raises it above her head. She looks ridiculous, in her fussy middle-aged-woman clothes, holding the tape up out of reach like a child throwing a fit. "Tell me what it is! Tell me where you got it!" Her eyes blaze as brightly and painfully as the sun.

Val sits up wearily, scraping her hair back from where dried sweat has plastered strands to her forehead. She needs a shower. She needs a meal. And she needs that tape, because it's all she has left of Kitty. Even if she can never bring herself to watch it again, she'll know she has it.

Jenny backs up quickly when Val stands, like she's afraid Val might chase her down and tackle her.

Val holds up her hands in a truce. "I want it back," she says, "but you should watch it first." She has a moment of irrational fear that the tape will be different for them than it was for her. A feeling that she should watch it with them to make sure it's the same.

Then again, they probably *will* see something different no matter what. After all, that tape is their childhood. An experience shared, but not an identical one. They talked about how wonderful the show was, but Val's seen it now. She wasn't happy.

The show was the worst kind of bad. The kind that makes you pretend so hard that everything is okay, you forget yourself in the pretending. Bad that insists you look right at it and call it good until you believe it.

Val knows all about that kind of bad. She hopes the others recognize it, too.

Jenny's clutching the tape to her chest. "No. No, it's a trick. You're going to ruin everything again, like you did before."

That old familiar sludge of shame churns back to life. Val wishes she could tug it free and throw it, stinking and repulsive, to the floor. Maybe there *is* something wrong with her, though. Maybe she's always been too broken to enjoy a magical childhood experience. Maybe she had to destroy it for everyone else, the same way she dragged Kitty along in the first place. Maybe the problem was never the show, but Val herself.

Maybe she's looking for something sinister because it would be a relief to be able to blame it for this terrible, formless guilt that has haunted her forever. To blame it for the wasteland of her life.

Val's too tired to argue. "Watch it or give it back to me. I don't care. All I know is my sister died, and someone out there knows what happened. I'm not going to stop until I have the truth."

"This isn't about Kitty! I'm sorry we lost her, I really am, but this is about *us,* about what *we* need." Jenny points to the house. "Go do your interview."

"What?" Of all the responses Val anticipated, this is not one of them.

"Go downstairs and do your interview!" Jenny's voice is high and strained.

"Why would I do an interview?"

"Because I need you to remember! I need you to be the Val you were, the Val in our circle. My friend Val." Jenny trembles with some combination of rage and desperation.

"I don't want to be her," Val says. Not after seeing the tape. Maybe Isaac was right that forgetting was for the best; she's free from the chains of nostalgia. She can't romanticize a childhood she doesn't remember, she can only engage with the truth of what she saw.

Besides, Jenny's "friend" dragged Kitty into all of this. Without Val's stubborn insistence, Kitty never would have been on the show. She'd still be alive.

Val's exhausted and heartsick and scared. It's the last one that surprises her. Her instinct is to ignore it, put it behind a door. But look where that's gotten her. Val holds on to the feeling instead, honoring her fear. This house, the show: They scare her. Bad things happened here. But houses don't have memories, and so there's nothing left for her inside.

If Javi's right, then whoever is in charge wants to pin what happened to Kitty on her. They can't pin her if they can't find her, though. She'll run. Take the money Gloria saved for her and hide.

But she won't stay hidden forever. Not like Dad did. She'll get somewhere safe, and then she'll go on the attack. They're going to regret finding her.

"I'm leaving." Val stalks into the house to get her things.

Jenny follows, practically stepping on her. "You have to do your interview! She's waiting for you!"

Val stops in the middle of the kitchen, suddenly wary. What if she tries to go up the stairs but Jenny throws her down them? Val's cheek still hurts from where Jenny's mom attacked her.

Val eases around the counter, keeping it between herself and the other woman.

Jenny frowns, then realization dawns on her features. Her anger turns to desperation. "I can't force you to do it. But I *need* you to do this for me. For us. Please, Val. Please go do your interview. Please! You can keep this tape, I don't care, just—just please, help me." Jenny throws the tape onto the counter, clasping her hands together like she's praying to Val.

"What's going on?" Isaac's at the entrance to the stairs, that liminal space that's both up and down at the same time. He doesn't know he's vulnerable there; how can he not feel it?

"This fucking house," Val mutters.

"Please, Isaac, she wants to leave." Jenny turns to him, beseeching. "She needs to do her interview. Help me!"

Isaac looks at Val. The moment their eyes met again for the first time changed her whole world. Renewed her past, and opened up a future. She wanted him in that future.

She still does, but. *Anyone who was looking for you isn't your friend.*

Isaac nods. Not to Jenny, but to Val. "I'll drive you," he says. "Or you can take the car. Whatever you want." He reaches into his pocket and tosses her the keys.

Jenny's high-pitched panic is now a low bleat of despair. "No. Val, please."

"What's wrong?" Javi asks from the stairs above Isaac.

Val grabs the tape from the counter. "Javi, come here." She's unwilling to go on the stairs. Just in case. Javi eases past Isaac, who hasn't taken a step toward Val. Always inviting her into his space, never demanding hers.

"Weird vibe in here, guys," Javi says. Marcus appears on the stairs behind him, pausing there as though unsure whether he should continue.

Val shoves the tape into Javi's hands. "It's the show. Some of it, anyway. I want it back. I'll find you when I've got information on—"

A frigid draft brushes her hair away from her face. It came from the basement. There are answers down there. She has no doubt about it.

But she also has no doubt that it's a trap.

"Anyone who wants to can come with me." Once again, it's Val leaving the rest of her friends behind. She's abandoning them, and they're going to get hurt, and it will be her fault.

"Please," she whispers. "Please, come with me. Nothing here is good for you."

No one moves.

Val walks out on her friends. Isaac's car is waiting in silent judgment. She climbs in and slams her palm against the steering wheel. It doesn't split open. Nothing comes out of it. It's just skin. Her scars are still a mystery. Maybe everything always will be.

Val puts the key in the ignition, watching the front door. Hoping. She extends her hand, wanting to ask, but knowing the cost of asking. Her hand and the doorway both remain empty. That house, that terrible, wretched desert parasite, looks down at her, smug and sated and humming. She flips it off, then turns the key.

And nothing happens.

**The Blogcast Review**

The latest episode of *Gnarly '90s*—which, if you're a longtime reader of my reviews, you'll know I don't usually love on account of their tendency to be overly critical—is my favorite they've ever done. More because of subject material than actual content or presentation, because for once they delivered news I actually want.

*Mister Magic* is coming back.

In podcast form, at least. A reunion episode to start out with, which, eh. But I'll take whatever I can get. If you don't remember, *Mister Magic* was a long-running children's program. I watched it religiously. As in it was basically my religion. I swear every lesson I learned in life I learned not in kindergarten (shout-out to Ms. Craft, who hated me: I hate you, too), but from Mister Magic.

The show was always on when I needed it to be. My mom worked late and I was by myself a lot, and it was always there to keep me company. We lived in a sketchy area and I couldn't run around and play outside, but I always had friends on the television. I know that sounds sad but it wasn't. It helped me so much.

I have some weird memories of it, too. I swear the show was somehow in between channels. When you turned the knobs, you always found it halfway between clicks. Maybe that was a quirk of our old junky television. And one time—I probably dreamed this, but it's such a vivid memory—I was awake in the middle of the night, scared from a nightmare. I didn't want to wake my mom up, so I sat down in front of the television, hoping *Mister Magic* was on. What kind of kids' show is on at 2 AM? But when I found that sweet spot between channels, there it was.

Only it wasn't a regular episode. It was also the middle of the night in the show. The kids, my friends, were all piled up sleeping. And again, I know it sounds weird, but it was comforting, watching them breathing in and out, holding hands. I curled up on the floor with my own hand pressed against the television, the hum lulling me to sleep. My mom found me there in the morning and yelled at me about wasting electricity. That's how I know at least part of the memory is real.

So, waking or sleeping, *Mister Magic* was always there for me, until it was gone. No cancellation has affected me as deeply since. I can't wait to hear from the cast, to finally get some closure. To relive that time in my life when I could always find friends just by turning on the television. And—if rumors are to be believed, and I desperately want to believe them, because I have kids of my own now who need some magic friends, who need those special lessons—the podcast will break news of a reboot.

Our friends, here for us once again, when we need them the most.

Link **here** to the *Mister Magic* podcast; first full episode isn't live yet but you bet I'll keep hovering between channels, waiting for it to appear.

# SIXTEEN

Val checks the engine. She's done enough work on ranch equipment and their fleet of battered old trucks to have some knowledge, but as far as she can tell the issue is the battery. It's dead.

Her brain sparks the way the battery doesn't, roaring to life with conspiracy theories. But the answer is simpler than that. She closes the hood and then rests her forehead on it, bent over with despair. Last night, blaring the radio during the bonfire. No one killed the car on purpose; they were just idiots.

She checks the trunk, but there are no jumper cables. Val tiptoes up to Jenny's van like it might yell at her on behalf of its owner. The back windows offer no glimpse of cables. Doesn't mean there aren't any, but the van is locked, so she can't search without permission. And she needs the keys, anyway, if she's going to get a jump.

Val trudges back to the house. She opens the door but doesn't step inside. The others are gathered around the kitchen counter, an argument cut off mid-word as they turn to her.

"Battery's dead," Val says. "I need a jump."

"Oh, I can—" Marcus starts, but Jenny cuts him off.

"No."

"Jenny," Javi chides.

Jenny shakes her head, mouth a hard, flat line. "I don't have cables."

Isaac doesn't meet Val's eyes. He looks exhausted, everything magnified by his glasses. "We can drive her to the nearest—"

"No," Jenny snaps again. "It's *my* van. If Val wants to abandon us again, fine, but I'm not helping her."

Marcus puts a hand on her arm. "Jenny."

Jenny shakes him off. "Stop saying my name that way! Don't look at me like *I'm* the one who's being a bitch. All we're asking her is to walk down those stairs and talk about the show. It's not a big request! After everything we went through because of her, because of what she—" Jenny stops, throws her hands in the air. "You all act like she's special, like we need to be careful with her, when really *she* should be going out of her way to help *us*. To fix things. But no. She's Valentine. She does what she wants, and makes the rest of us do it, too. Well, not this time. Not anymore."

Javi pulls out his phone. "I'll call someone to bring a battery here."

Jenny smiles meanly. "Good luck with that. Even if you find someone willing to come all the way out here, it'll take hours. Get comfortable, Val." She stomps into her room and slams the door.

"I'll talk to her," Isaac says.

If Val still has to be here, she wants to talk with him. Ask him why he didn't tell her Gloria was trying to get ahold of her. Why he *really* worked so hard to find her.

But before she can tell him to wait, he slips inside Jenny's bedroom and closes the door again. Their conversation is inaudible over the ambient hum, which Val swears has gotten louder.

Marcus rubs a hand wearily down his face. "Why do I feel like I went to sleep in one reality and woke up in another? What happened last night?"

Javi leans on the counter, watching her thoughtfully. "I think you should go down."

"What?" Val shakes her head. "No. Absolutely not."

"They're going to frame this however they want. With this

podcast, they're the ones controlling the narrative, shaping it for listeners, leading them along to a preexisting conclusion so it feels like it was the listener's idea all along. But if you do an interview, maybe you can get new information? Or maybe you can figure out from her questions whether I'm right and they're trying to frame you, or whether I'm paranoid after years of living with my vindictive, evil family."

Val doesn't want to go down the stairs, not for anything. But her gaze is drawn to them. To the lure of what's there, the promise of answers. This is why she needs to leave. If she stays, she'll end up down there. She knows it.

"Hold up," Marcus says. "You think the podcast is, what, trying to blame Val for what happened to Kitty?"

Javi pinches the bridge of his nose. He looks older than when she first met him, even though it's only been two days. "They need to clear up any controversy if they want to restart the show, which it sounds like they do. But no one was ever charged or even investigated for Kitty's death."

"What the hell? How is that possible?" Anger narrows Marcus's beautiful eyes, reshaping the kindness of his face into something almost holy in its rage. "I'll go down with you, Val. I can come into the interview, or wait at the bottom of the stairs where she can't see me. Back you up if things get weird."

Val's touched by his offer. Though he's not scared of the basement the same way she is, it still means a lot that he'd go with her. "You don't blame me, too? For how it ended?"

"No," Marcus says, his expression still angry. Then it gets soft—so soft it hurts her, almost makes her want to recoil from the love and understanding there. She's been alone in her guilt for so long. But Marcus is with her in that terrible private space. "Kitty was my friend. I miss her. She deserves justice."

Marcus and Javi are on her side. She was wrong to suspect them. The way that ballroom reacted to both of them was enough to make it clear Bliss didn't want them. That whatever happened with the show, they're not part of it.

It makes Val feel stronger, knowing she isn't alone. She never has been.

Val tried to run again, to deal with this by herself, and it didn't work. So, she'll stay, and she'll get the truth. Because Marcus is right—Kitty deserves justice, but they all deserve closure. She can't take that away from them.

She takes a deep breath, holding it until it burns. Irrational fears are often rooted in something real. It's time to find out why she's so afraid of where those stairs lead. "Thank you, but there's something even more important you can do for me right now. Watch this video. Both of you. Tell me whether I saw what I think I saw."

Marcus nods. Javi flashes her a tight, encouraging smile, and they both walk her to the stairs, standing at the top. On guard up here.

Javi holds the tape as evidence that, for once, he'll do as he's told. "We'll stay on this floor, so we can hear you if you need us. It's a single room with a screen down there. No doors, no way to lock you in or sneak up on you or anything. No one can hurt you."

Val wishes she shared that confidence. She finally looks down. The vertigo washes over her, a terrible dilation stretching and narrowing the stairs, contracting into the darkness like a throat swallowing.

She takes a step, and another step. Gravity hungrily seizes her, each stair sinking her deeper.

And then suddenly she's at the bottom. It's just a flight of stairs. Javi and Marcus are still waiting for her on the landing. She hasn't been swallowed; she could turn around and race right back to the top. She gives them a weak thumbs-up, which they return. The arched doorway down here has no door, but there aren't any lights. It's pitch black beyond the threshold.

"The lights are motion-activated," Javi calls.

Val steps inside. There's a hissing noise, like a length of cloth being drawn across a floor, and then the lights flash on with blinding brightness.

The room is featureless save a single wooden chair in the center.

White walls, shiny white floor, blazing lights set into the ceiling. One of the lights isn't working, but she realizes that's because it's not a light. It's a camera designed to look like one.

Another doorway is in the wall to her right, a perfect rectangle. It's an opening into nothing, pure darkness beyond it. There shouldn't be a doorway there; Javi said there was only one door. And the house doesn't extend in that direction. So unless the basement is larger than the foundation of the house, or she's somehow gotten turned around . . .

Val doesn't step toward the doorway. She won't. She *can't.* All the bravery and determination that got her down here have been swallowed by the emptiness beyond that gaping door.

She's numb with fear. No, more than fear. The air is so cold she can see her breath; her finger joints ache with it. Her scars are brilliant white, memories her body holds even if her mind does not.

When she looks back up, a woman is standing in the doorway. There's something flattened and featureless about her, like she has a face designed by committee. Val could pass her on the street tomorrow and not recognize her, or she could find her in every woman she sees for the rest of her life. Either. Both.

"How long have you been down here?" Val asks, shocked.

"Oh, forever," the woman says. There's a slight lag, her voice coming through before her expressions and movements can catch up. Val tries to shake off her disorientation. It's not a door. It can't be a door, because none of the brilliant light from this room is traveling through it. There would be a square of light, at least, on the floor. Where the woman is, there's only darkness.

It's a screen. Val grasps hold of the realization, uses it to reorient herself to reality. It's a screen on the wall, not a door. The basement is exactly the size it should be. The interview is just an interview.

"You got old." There's a note of betrayal in the woman's high, clear voice. She scowls, a child's expression on an adult's face, and Val would laugh if she could. But there's still something about this woman ringing warning bells.

"Yeah, it happens." Val shrugs. "So, the interview. For the podcast. I guess you know who I am. I'd like to know who you are."

"Intro first!" The woman's voice shifts, becomes more animated as she narrates.

*Val sang the songs, and she held the hands, and she played the games, and she followed the rules. She did everything right, always. She listened and obeyed, she knew all the things to say and all the ways to say them. She never got in trouble. She never had to be cautioned, or dimmed, or comforted, or directed, or watched. She was the very best of the friends, the lock that hooked together all the links in the chain of the circle, the one you never worried about, the one you never wondered about, the perfect child among such good children. The leader.*

"That seems—" Val starts, but the woman keeps talking, the recitation uninterrupted.

*It was Val's hands that held everyone there, that squeezed, that kept them in place. Unlike the circles that came before, it was Val's absolute determination, her irrepressible will, that kept the magic going. It was Val who reached into the darkness and pulled out what they needed. Do you remember now? Who it was that pulled out the cape, threw the cape, every time? Who it was that decided to keep Mister Magic* out of his own circle*?*

Val frowns. It was true, wasn't it? In the episodes she had seen, Mister Magic hadn't even appeared. But how was that her doing? It was a show. Surely there were writers, directors.

*Val! It was our little Valentine. The most important part of the circle. If you could see her now, you'd see she has the same thick, shiny brown hair in that long braid you loved to tug on to tease her. You would see she has the same beautiful eyes, lashes and brows boldly framing them. You would see she has the same freckles, even more of them now. You would see she's grown from a pretty little girl you wanted to be just like into a beautiful woman you don't know. She won't let you know her. She ran away so no one could. Even now, her arms are crossed. Her eyes are narrowed. She's made certain there's no room for us. Marcus was the dreamer. Javi was the instigator. Isaac was the protector. Jenny was the friend. And Val?*

"Who was Val?" Val whispers.

The woman smiles, and in a flashing glitch of the screen, she looks like Val's nightmare of Kitty, with a smile too wide, too many teeth. And then her smile snaps closed and her tone goes colder than the basement.

*Val was the liar who broke the circle and ended the magic.*

There it is. The blame. At least now Val doesn't have to pretend to be friendly. She stands behind the chair, more comfortable keeping it between them even though the woman is behind a screen. "I want to know what happened to Kitty."

There's a burst of static so sudden and loud it feels like a physical object stabbing into her. Val flinches, but by the time her hands are up to protect her ears, it's over.

"You left," the interviewer says.

"Yeah, which is why I need to know what happened."

"I already told you. You *left*. That's what happened. You were supposed to hold her hand, but you were gone. And Mister Magic—"

"We don't say that," Val says automatically.

"Why not? They're just words." The interviewer's tone is teasing, her mouth curled around small, white teeth. Too small. They look like baby teeth. "All words are imaginary. Sounds that we attached to meaning, images and emotions conjured out of the air. So really, all words are magic. Something from nothing. Forcing others to feel things, to think things, to understand things simply by uttering the right combination of noises. You were always good at words, weren't you? Good at making the others do what you wanted."

Val refuses to be baited. "You tell me."

The interviewer's tone turns petulant. She slouches, seeming to grow shorter. Smaller. Like she's farther from the screen. "I'm tired of talking. They gave us so much to learn, so much to do to help them so they can help us. They conjure words out of nothing, as easy as breathing, but we have to carve them free, dredge them up from where they're cold and sleepy at the bottom. Most of the words aren't even ours. Magpie words, stolen and brought back to the nest." She leans forward and her eyes are revealed to be brilliantly, painfully blue. "Say it. Say his name."

Val forces a casual shrug. "Why does it matter, if all words are imaginary?"

The interviewer laughs, and now Val's sure: She has baby teeth, tiny perfect pearls in her mouth. Her hair looks softer, too. Curlier. And her eyes. Val's seen those eyes before, realizes now what she couldn't put her finger on.

The interviewer looks like Kitty.

"No." Val shakes her head, because this is too fucked up, too cruel. They've manipulated Val, forced her to look at this twisted image of her lost little sister. If they're trying to break her, it's working. Val backs toward the stairs. She doesn't dare take her eyes off the screen, afraid of how the image might change. Afraid that if she looks over her shoulder, the stairs will be gone.

She has to trust that they'll be there. She reaches behind herself, holding out a hand. Needing the stairs. Willing reality to reassert itself, to give her a way out.

Val steps into the stairwell, and the lights click off. The screen should still be on. She should still see that monstrous version of her sister, but there's nothing visible now. Only that voice, high and sweet and terrible, calling after Val.

"Words *are* imaginary," she says. "Didn't you learn from Mister Magic? Nothing is more powerful than imagination!"

In the beginning, they stand in a circle and they sing the song. Val always pulls the cape from the darkness, and it always drifts down exactly right to reveal Mister Magic in the center.

He observes all their games, half in the darkness on the edges until they need him to step in. They're so young, so open and exuberant. Their play is filled with laughter and singing and fun. The episodes pass in a blur, easy to get lost in.

But, watching one after the other after the other, it becomes clear: As the games and lessons progress, the friends in the circle get smaller. Less distinct. More like each other and less like themselves.

Every time Javi is corrected, his smile becomes less impish, his eyes duller. Every time Marcus is pulled back from losing himself in creating, his scenery gets blander, his characters carbon copies of the ones that came before. Jenny stops having actual fun, instead doing and saying exactly what she should so she can get another hug from Mister Magic. Kitty's boundless energy turns to sleepy, smiling obedience, more like a doll than a child. Isaac stops playing, standing at Mister Magic's side, watching. Doing as he does, a shadow to a shadow.

And Val?

Val gets *annoyed*. She watches her friends, and she notices the changes. Eventually, when Mister Magic approaches her, she refuses to acknowledge him. She scowls at the camera with stubborn determination instead. She stops playing his games. When he leans down to whisper the rules in her ear, she skips away, pulling Kitty with her, drawing the others to a new activity.

And then, between one episode and the next, everything changes. The children gather in their circle, but as they start to sing, Val stops them.

"Not for this game," she says, her tone confident. "We don't need him for this one."

Marcus looks confused. "But he's the magic."

Val's eyes twinkle with the mischief that Javi's lost. "No. We are." She screws her face up in concentration, reaches into the darkness, and pulls out the cloak. But instead of tossing it up so it drifts down to reveal Mister Magic, she drapes it across the floor like a picnic blanket. She nudges Marcus. "Let's go to the water park today and teach Kitty about water safety!"

Marcus is hesitant, but he lifts his hands and begins to paint. When it works, his eyes light up and his painting gets bigger, more elaborate. No one is going to pull him back. An incredible water park appears before them with towering, twisting slides, lounge chairs, and a crashing wave pool. The children run in, elated.

Jenny pauses to look back at Val. She alone is uncertain.

"It's okay," Val reassures her.

"But Mis—"

"New rule!" Val chirps. "We don't say his name. He needs a rest, so we don't want to wake him." She winks at the others, then turns and stares directly at the camera again, smile gone, face set in defiance. And then she's back to being a child, skipping forward with the others to play.

After that, the episodes are different. When things get too out of control, or if anyone ever cries or fights, a shape lurches forward from the darkness, but Mister Magic is never as dashing as he had been, never as omnipresent. Val takes charge, guiding their play, directing the magic. Marcus's art and characters are once again larger than life, Javi's mischief is back in full force, Isaac plays and takes care of the others rather than just observing and worrying, Kitty is wild with energy and happiness, and even Jenny has fun rather than constantly looking for approval. Though she misses Mister Magic and brings him up occasionally.

It's the same show, but it's not. Episodes blend one into the next, game after game, exploration and adventures and lessons on friendship and kindness. The children are happy, vibrant, thriving. But Val is exhausted. It shows in the way her hand trembles when she reaches into the darkness and demands what she wants from it, in the way the darkness is echoed in the hollows beneath her eyes.

And it shows when she starts to disappear, first for a few minutes at a time, then for more. Whenever Val is gone too long, Mister Magic appears, his hat so tall it stretches into the darkness above them, his fingers so long they reach across the screen, his cape so dark it swallows all the light around it.

But Isaac always finds her, and Val always comes back, and they keep playing.

They just keep playing.

# DON'T BE MEAN

Val bursts out of the stairwell onto the first floor. The twisted mockery of her dead sister's face is blazed onto her mind like the afterimage of staring into the sun.

Javi and Marcus are sitting on the floor in front of the television, Jenny and Isaac behind them. They're all watching the tape, transfixed.

Val stumbles over, feeling boneless and light-headed after the heaviness of the basement. "She looked like Kitty, she looked like—"

Javi turns to her, eyes bloodshot. "We started at the beginning."

Val glances at the screen. It's the same beach scene she stopped on. But she started watching in the middle of the tape. It took her over an hour to get that far. How are they already there?

She rushes to the front door and flings it open. It's late afternoon.

"I couldn't have been downstairs for that long." Val tugs on her braid. She feels like she's been tricked, like something vital has been stolen from her when she wasn't paying attention.

"The show changed," Jenny says. Gone is the anger. She looks drained. Diminished, even. "As it went on. He was in it less and less."

"*He* as in—" Val prods.

Marcus nods. "Yeah. Because of you. You changed the show."

Jenny bites her nails, eyes fixed on the screen. "It's not . . . it's not how I remember."

Isaac takes off his glasses, rendering his world blurry and unknowable. "I thought we were happier when he was part of it," he whispers. "I really did."

"We *were* happy." Javi leans close to the television and pushes FAST-FORWARD, their games playing out in triple speed. "We were, I know we were."

"Why is it like this?" Marcus asks.

"We all chose what to remember." Isaac doesn't put his glasses back on. He doesn't want to see anymore. "Or what to forget."

"Stop! Pause it!" Jenny shouts. Javi pushes PAUSE. She raises a trembling finger, her cuticles raw where she's bitten them down too far. "Look."

The kids are standing in a circle in the blank black space. Val doesn't understand why this is any different from what came before, until she sees what Jenny noticed.

Val isn't there anymore.

"This is the last time," Marcus whispers.

Jenny lets out a low moan, clutching her stomach. "No, no no no, don't—I don't want to see it. Don't push PLAY. Please, let's just—let's just go. Let's leave. Let's rewind to the beginning, when it was working, when it was fun. Don't. Don't."

Val drops to her knees on the carpet next to Javi. She puts her fingers against the television screen, not surprised to find it icy to the touch. There, in little dots of light, for the last time: her sister. Val should be next to her, holding her hand. That was where her place was in the circle. Kitty on one side, Isaac on the other.

Isaac and Jenny are holding Kitty's hands, Javi and Marcus on the other side of the circle with their backs to the camera. Jenny's face is in full view. She looks excited. Proud, even. Isaac looks sick. And Kitty looks worried, her button nose wrinkled, her face turned to the side, brilliant blue eyes searching the darkness around them for something.

For someone.

Val remembers the feel of Kitty's tiny hand in hers. Her fingers curl around the sensation, dragging other memories free from where she's locked them away. All the strength of will that she used to stubbornly keep doors closed her whole life, to keep everything out and keep herself in, that sheer dedication to sealing away what she couldn't have and wasn't allowed to want—that's what she'd used on the show.

It was never just a show.

Val led the circle, because she was the only one strong enough to call form out of the darkness. She was the one who reached out and pulled the cape so he could come and be bound to what they needed him to be.

Mister Magic was real, but *she made him that way.*

Val wishes she could push through the screen and take Kitty in her arms. Take her from that circle. Bring her out.

But it all happened thirty years ago. It's already over. She just hasn't seen the ending yet.

"I have to know." Val pushes PLAY.

Little Jenny holds her head high, eyes narrowed, shoulders back. She has a new role, and she's determined to do a good job. She lets go of Kitty's hand to reach behind herself.

Val shakes her head, mouthing the word *no*. She never let go of Kitty's hand to reach out into the darkness. Always Isaac's hand. It's wrong, it's all wrong.

Little Jenny's forehead wrinkles in concentration. She searches behind herself, reaching, reaching, until at last her fingers find purchase. She tugs the cape free from the darkness. It makes the exact same tearing sound it had in Val's dream when she pulled it out of her hand.

Little Jenny takes Kitty's hand again, the cloak between them instead of between Val and Isaac, as it should be. Then they begin singing, eyes closed.

"No," Marcus whispers, shaking his head, grabbing Javi's hand like he wants to drag both of them up and away from what they're about to witness. None of them can stop watching, though.

The song isn't right. Their singing is off tempo, off tune. They can't get the words to match up. Marcus on screen is mirroring Marcus out here, shaking his head with a worried expression. Little Javi sings louder to compensate, and tears stream down Isaac's face beneath his glasses. Kitty's squeezing his hand, asking him a question that can't be heard over the song. Jenny sings louder, higher, trying her hardest to do it right. To claim this role.

The song ends, trailing discordant and tentative into the darkness. Jenny takes the cape, tosses it up in the air, and—

Val remembers how this part went. She knows exactly how it should go, now that she's at last seeing how it went wrong.

*Val* led the song.

Everyone sang the same words at the same time, buoying her up, echoing her intention. Everyone had their eyes closed. Val pulled the cape from the darkness, as easily as tugging a tissue from a box. She wanted it and she needed it and it was there.

She tossed the cape into the air, as quick as she could before taking Isaac's hand once more. And then they all squeezed, bound, a single chain of hope and wonder and togetherness, holding the darkness out, holding the magic in. Binding it where it needed to be. Always, always with their eyes closed. That chill would pour in, that icy scent flooding them all to herald the change, and then he would be there.

But that's not how it goes on the screen. Not with Val gone, and the song wrong, and Jenny struggling with the darkness.

The cape doesn't drift down, finding *his* form where nothing had been before. Instead it lurches from one side to the other, careening wildly before dropping into the ground and blending seamlessly with the black.

"Dad?" little Jenny whispers, staring down at the emptiness where Mister Magic failed to appear. "Daddy?"

"Turn it off," Jenny begs, but she doesn't close her eyes. None of them do.

In the circle, little Jenny lets go of Kitty's hand and reaches toward the center. The blackness surges like a wave, sweeping straight into and over the smallest member of the circle, the most vulnerable, the easiest to take. Kitty disappears beneath it, only her hands still visible, one clasping Isaac's hand and the other empty. Reaching. Pleading. Jenny screams, backing away. Isaac lets go of Javi, grabbing Kitty with both hands. He falls to his knees, dragged along as Kitty is yanked backward.

"Help me!" Isaac shouts.

But Jenny just stands there, screaming. Javi tugs on Marcus, trying to get him to run with him. Finally, Javi gives up, sprinting away from the center of the circle. Marcus, eyes shut tight, begins walking backward, wailing with an incoherent keen of fear and anguish.

Isaac can't hold on any longer. Kitty's hand slips from his and she's *gone*. There's no more Kitty, no hint of movement or shape in the darkness where she disappeared. Isaac stays on his knees, head bowed, shoulders shaking with sobs. Jenny's still screaming, hands out now, begging for someone to take them. Javi and Marcus keep fleeing in opposite directions, farther and farther and farther. There are no walls to pen them in, nothing to stop them.

Only the darkness and their flight into it.

Only the darkness that swallowed Kitty as though she never existed at all.

Only the darkness that looked and moved exactly like what Val pulled out of her hand in a nightmare.

The screaming doesn't stop, either, the screaming and the crying, as loud as if each child were right next to Val, as if it's happening right now. As if it never stopped happening, has been happening this whole time, all these years.

Val is hollowed out by the horror of it, a void inside herself expanding bigger and bigger to contain all that screaming. All that terror and desperation and brokenness. All that loss.

She pushes PAUSE, knowing it won't help. Knowing she'll carry those images, those sounds, with her forever.

But there's still screaming.

No. Not screaming.

Singing.

Drifting up from the basement beneath them.

The lights don't turn on, but the camera does, recording the voice in the darkness. Is it one voice, or several? It's hard to tell, but the song comes through crystal-clear:

*Take my hand*
*Stand on your mark*
*Make a circle*
*In the dark*
*Close your eyes*
*And wish with me*
*Keep them closed*
*And now we see*
*Magic Man!*
*Magic Man!*
*Magic Man!*
*He's here for me!*

There's a giggle, and then a shushing sound. "We have to be on our mark! It's time!" A whimper sounds farther away than the voice. "Shh, don't worry! We'll always be friends, and soon we'll be together again. And we'll be with new friends, too! They'll turn on their televisions, and we'll find them. We'll find them all."

# SEVENTEEN

They collectively ignore the voice coming from the basement.

Val thinks it's reasonable. It *seems* reasonable in this moment, given that they have more pressing things to discuss.

Marcus shakes out his hands as he paces, avoiding going too close to the stairs. "I remembered what happened to Kitty. I remembered it, but I thought it had to be wrong. That it couldn't be real. It *can't* be real. Tell me it's not real." He looks from face to face, pleading.

Javi's still sitting on the floor in front of the television. "I remembered the same thing," he says softly. "You did other shows, Marcus. Does that tape seem like it would have been possible to film at the time?"

Marcus doesn't answer, and it's answer enough.

"Maybe it's a deepfake," Javi says. "Maybe it's . . ."

Val shakes her head and Javi trails off. She remembers enough now to know. It's real. It's realer than any of them let themselves remember. But at least this explains why none of them could articulate what happened to Kitty. They probably spent all these years thinking they were insane, doubting their own memories. She feels as sad for them as she does for herself. But for Kitty, she just feels *angry*.

"Where did you get this recording?" Isaac sounds calmer than anyone else.

Val looks at his face without the glasses. It makes him seem less himself. But he does, at last, look like the woman in the parking lot. "Your mother," she says. Val had been wrong when she thought Isaac didn't have a parent represented in Bliss.

Javi barks a laugh. "Three dollars! One for every unhinged mother you met yesterday. Now I wish you had met mine and Marcus's, completed the whole set."

Isaac doesn't seem surprised by this information. "Oh. Yeah. She's trying to make amends. She's been trying for a while."

"Fuck me." Marcus leans forward, hands behind his neck as he tries to take deep breaths. "Fuck me, fuck me. Fuck all of us."

"We need to—" Val starts.

Jenny shakes her head, eyes open wide with urgency.

Val can't deal with her right now. Not after what they've seen. "Jenny, we're leaving. We're taking your van, and if we have to steal it, we will."

Jenny hisses, holding her finger up over her mouth. She twists her shoulder in an effort to shield what she's doing as she points, incomprehensibly, at the microwave. *Not—out—loud,* she mouths with exaggeration so they understand.

But it's too late.

There's a popping noise and then relative silence that takes them a few moments to understand. Every sound under and around the hum—the fridge, the lights, the actual AC—is gone.

Marcus stares at his phone. "The Wi-Fi is dead. No signal without it."

"Crap," Jenny says. "Let's go, now." She rushes out the front door and the others follow. Val pauses on the threshold, something tickling her senses, like she's walked through a spider's web. She glances back.

The power is off, but the television still glows with a promise of more memories.

"Absolutely not," she says, then steps out. Jenny is sprinting for the van, keys in hand, but—

"Too late." Javi nods toward the only road in or out. Several cars are parked a hundred yards away, blocking their escape route.

"Behind the house?" Marcus asks. But there's nothing out there. No roads, no towns, nothing but empty, unforgiving terrain for countless miles around them. Even if Jenny's van could handle it, who knows how long it would take to reach somewhere inhabited?

A Jeep and an off-roading vehicle slowly edge forward past the blockade of cars, a clear message that there will be no escape into the desert.

Jenny's gripping her keys so hard her knuckles are white. "I'm sorry. I'm so, so sorry. I didn't know."

They all knew, really. Or at least Val did. From the moment they pulled up to this house. But she stubbornly ignored it, and now it's too late. Val puts her arm around Jenny. Jenny lets out a hiccup of a sob, then lets Val pass her to Marcus, who wraps her up in a hug.

As though pulling on perfectly broken-in boots, Val steps back into her role. She's in charge. These are her friends, and she's going to protect them. She stomps toward the line of cars alone. Javi and Isaac move to follow, but she holds up a hand.

"I'll see what they want."

She's not surprised when the mayor emerges from an SUV near the back of the barricade. She's also not surprised when other men stand by their cars, rifles in hand. After what she's seen in that house, it's hard to feel surprised anymore. She's curious about what they think they're going to get out of this, though.

The mayor strides forward to meet her, flanked by two of the rifle-toting men. "Valentine," he says with that same paternalistic, possessive smile.

"Mayor," Val says, then nods to his companions. "Fuckface. Fuckface junior."

The mayor's smile sours. "There's no call for language like that."

Val plants her feet and folds her arms. The more she digs in, the less she responds how he expects her to, the angrier he'll get. She didn't deploy this option often on the ranch, but she knows how to do it. Angry people are unpredictable, but they're also stupid. They make mistakes.

Something tickles in the back of her memory, a warning that this stubborn defiance was what got her on the show in the first place. This was what her mother couldn't handle, what Mister Magic was supposed to fix.

She smiles.

The mayor waits.

She waits.

He's waiting for her to ask what he wants, but she doesn't care what he wants. She's not going to let him dictate how this goes. Finally, he lets out a frustrated huff. "You can't leave."

Val raises a single eyebrow. "I noticed."

"We won't allow it."

She stares impassively at him. He squirms a little under it. His face reddens and he takes a step forward, jabbing his finger on every other word for emphasis.

"We want it back. We want what you broke. It's your responsibility to fix it."

She gives him a long, lazy shrug. "Dunno what I did, dunno how to fix it, don't really care."

"You're going to care!" His tongue darts out, wetting his pale lips. "This is your fault! You ruined generations of tradition, *generations* of teaching. First you changed it, and then you broke it. None of the new children have worked because of what you took when you left!"

Val's left hand twitches, but she doesn't look down at it, doesn't betray any emotion. "What do you mean, new children?"

He lets out a phlegmy huff of derision. "We tried to fix it without you. To restart. Such a waste. And don't play dumb. We know you've seen the show, that Isaac's mother betrayed our trust. I always said we shouldn't take applicants. That we should keep the cast in the community." He sighs, shaking his head. "Bad mothers make bad children."

Val squints upward. The sun's getting low. Time to bargain. The tape is vital, damning evidence. But she's as old-school Idaho as Gloria, because she knows justice for Kitty won't come through the legal system. So she doesn't really care what happens to the tape now. *She's* going to make them pay. But they don't need to know that.

Val unfolds her arms, holding them wide. "Seems to me like we have evidence now that unsupervised, dangerous conditions on set resulted in the death of my sister. That's a pretty big liability for anyone involved. I think you *want* us to leave. Us in Jenny's van and you in your cars. Once we're back at the highway, we'll give you the tape and go our separate ways. I'll disappear again like a good girl. You can even blame me for what happened to Kitty. I don't care."

The moment he laughs, low and dry and self-satisfied, Val realizes she's fucked.

He shakes his head, still smiling. "We always need a stubborn one. Usually, the stubborn ones are my favorite. I love watching them learn their lessons."

Val fights the shiver of disgust that runs down the back of her neck.

The mayor sighs and sticks his hands in his pockets. "Guess you weren't on the show long enough to wear down those sharp edges. Make you soft and good like little girls ought to be. We should have pulled you the moment you started making changes, but logistically that was tricky, and we were curious. Hindsight and whatnot. Listen, girl. We don't want the tape. We want the *show.* We want Mister Magic back where he belongs, back in homes everywhere. Someone has to fix the direction of this holy country." He nods, more to himself than to her, chest puffing up. "Tell your friends their kids are on the way. They'll be here soon. One way or another, someone is forming the circle tonight. Up to you whether or not it actually works this time."

*No good children were ever harmed,* Val thinks. Children, plural. They tried to make the show work again with new kids, and it never did.

"Kitty wasn't the only one lost," she whispers.

The mayor shrugs. "Not all children can be saved. Sad fact of life. Better to die innocent, though, than to grow up dirty and broken. Don't you think?"

Val takes an involuntary step back, needing to physically distance herself from what he said. From what he believes. "*No.*"

"Well, irregardless, you can make up for what you did. Atone. Or let your friends' kids try their luck with the mess you left. Your choice." He turns and goes back to his SUV. The two men with rifles don't move, watching her from behind mirrored sunglasses.

Val walks mechanically back to the others. They're waiting where she left them.

"You all heard that?" she asks. Their stricken faces indicate as much already, but they all nod. "Do we agree that the show was never really a show?" Val wishes they wouldn't agree. That one of them could offer an explanation or argument that would snap them back into a reality that follows accepted logic.

The others nod again, hollowly.

Val tugs on her braid. There will be no running away. Not this time.

The house welcomes them back with a frigid caress of air and a satisfied hum. It's dim inside, the power still off but the television glowing. Val knows without checking that all the other televisions will be on, too. She eyes the stairs. "We need to figure out what happened when I left. How I left, what I did that broke the circle. But the tape didn't show it."

"The interviewer promised to show us footage," Marcus says. He has his useless phone out, looking at photos of his son.

"She might have recordings." Javi's prowling like a caged animal. Val's worried he'll do something stupid. Isaac must be thinking the same thing, because he gestures for Jenny to put her van keys away. She slides them into her pocket.

"Okay, let's go." Val walks to the stairs and goes straight down, ignoring the dread. Even though the lights don't power on, the screen holding the image of their interviewer is working. She floats, the only light in a solid wall of darkness. For a few breaths Val feels the room around them expanding, pushing outward, defying space. Then the others arrive, their phone lights giving dimension to the room once more. Forcing it to stay within its boundaries.

"What the fuck?" Javi stops dead when he sees the interviewer. "She didn't look like that before."

The interviewer is like a child's drawing of an adult, none of the features quite right. The nose too small, the forehead enormous, the mouth too wide and filled with too many tiny teeth. She's a stretched, distorted vision of Kitty, with the same brown pigtails and LED-brilliant blue eyes.

"Hi!" she chirps.

"Stop it." Jenny's voice trembles. "Stop looking like that."

Val stands directly in front of the screen. "Have they tried to restart the show before now? With other children?"

The interviewer nods eagerly. "Oh, yes! A few times."

"What happened?"

She lets out a long, bored sigh, then glances over her shoulder into empty blackness. Reassured that she's alone, she leans closer to Val and whispers in the loud, conspiratorial manner of a child, "*It gets hungry.*"

Jenny gags, then runs for the stairs. They all wait quietly while she vomits. When she comes back in, her voice is even more ragged. "I never knew about that. I didn't know they sent in other children. I thought—I really thought the show was good. I thought it was good for us, good for kids, they taught me my whole life that it was the ideal, I thought—"

"It's okay, Jenny," Val says. "It's not your fault." She turns back to the screen.

"You're all here now," the interviewer says brightly. "Are you ready?"

"Not quite. Is there footage from when I left?"

"Oh yes! I can show you!" Her eyes narrow slyly. "But we have to make a deal first. After I show you, you sing the song with me. Everyone else already made the deal. Swear you will, too."

"Val," Isaac cautions, his voice reaching for her like a hand in the darkness.

"I will," Val says without hesitating.

"Yay!" The interviewer claps, beaming. "Close your eyes!"

"How can we watch it if we close our eyes?" Val asks.

"It's already in your head, silly. I'll help you find it. Shut your eyes."

Val does as instructed. At first it's only the soft, amorphous afterglow of the screen, with two bright dots where the interviewer's eyes burned. Then the blobs begin to move with purpose, re-forming themselves. A rush of dizzy disorientation threatens to overwhelm Val. She grits her teeth and plants her feet.

"You're not helping," the interviewer says in an annoyed singsong tone.

"I don't know what to do."

"Open up!" she snaps.

All Val's doors, sealed tightly. She imagines following the bobbing light in front of her, letting it take her to something she's kept in the darkness for so long she can't find it on her own anymore. It's hypnotic, watching it shift and double and re-form as it leads her deeper and deeper. And then, so suddenly it's all Val can do not to open her eyes in shock, she sees.

Val has kept the cape away from Mister Magic all this time, and it's hard. It's so hard. But she does it. She folds it up, smaller and smaller, then closes her fingers around it. When she opens her hand once more, the cape is gone.

"Taa-daa!" she says, because she always says that, so the others think it's a game. Think it's easy.

Isaac watches. He knows the truth. But it's nice that he knows. He shares the burden and helps keep things fun for their friends. Finds her when it's too much and she has to crawl away and rest.

It's exhausting, holding back the hunger of this place.

They never used to sleep, but she makes them now. It helps the others hold on to themselves. With the cape nestled inside her, everything disappears into softest black. The cold presses in, cold with teeth, cold with fingers, cold with lies promising the most beautiful dreams. The friends tumble into a pile, like a litter of abandoned puppies. Val tucks Kitty against her, and then she tucks into Isaac, who curls around her to help her stay warm. Marcus, Javi, and Jenny finish the pile, everyone breathing short, sharp breaths practically in unison. Val imagines their breaths like a bubble of warmth around them, and because she has the cape inside her and imagines it so well, it's true.

They'll sleep, and then they'll play again, and Val will make sure that the darkness doesn't crush them. She's in charge, not it.

*She's in charge.* Nothing out there can tell her what to be or do or feel.

She's almost asleep, content and warm enough for now, when the hands appear. At first she's afraid she messed up and called *him* somehow, and now she'll have to send him away. But these hands are human. They're already turning red and raw with the cold, blisters forming on the fingers.

Disentangling carefully from Isaac and Kitty, Val crawls toward the hands. She doesn't want the others to wake up, but she needs to examine what new weirdness the darkness is attempting. It's always trying to trick control away from her, to bring *him* back. To convince her that she wants him to come back.

This doesn't seem like much of a threat at all. It's almost funny, how sad the hands look, how powerless. They're going to freeze soon and be useless.

But then one grabs her wrist.

Val looks down in horror. If she screams, she'll wake the others. She might even wake him. She seals her lips and tugs at the hand. But then she sees the ring. A wide gold band with a simple etched line pattern. She loved tracing that line. She knows this ring. She knows . . .

"Dad?" she whispers, a flood of memories washing in. She's forgotten so much—they all have, in this place where there is no day or night, no before or after, only each other. But she knows him. "Dad?" she asks again with even more urgency, searching the darkness, but it's only his hands. They're reaching through a weak spot that she hasn't found yet.

The hands tighten, and tug. He's going to pull her out. He's going to save her.

But he won't be able to last much longer. Dark patches are already growing on his skin where the cold is killing it. Val's own wrist is freezing around his grip, but she can feel it now. The way out. She can get out.

Her pile of puppies. Her friends. Her sister. She can't—she won't—leave them. Not to the hunger, not to *him*. None of them can do it without her. They have no idea how much she protects them from. But now she knows where to go. How to get out. She can get them all out.

Val pulls back against Dad's grip. She frees her wrist but he knows where she is now, and his hands grab her ankles, dragging her backward. Val claws at the darkness, tries to find hold. Half her body is out now. It's heavy, and it hurts. She closes her eyes, reaching for Isaac, begging him to see her and help. Reaching for Kitty, so she can take her sister with her.

"Val!" Isaac whispers. Val opens her eyes. But he's too far away. And if he leaves the circle, if he breaks their shield of breath, the cold will gobble them up. Tears freezing in her eyes, she motions for him to stay, then uses everything left in her to imagine her friends are warm.

Her own hands are no longer shielded by the circle's love. Cold eats at her, so deep it burns.

Val's head pops free and she screams at the light, at the sound, at the pain. Her arms disappear at the elbows, still in that other place. Her skin is burning, freezing, her hands in fists. *The cape.* She has to leave them the cape she trained, the one she shaped. But she can't feel her fingers to set it free. And then it's too late.

Her father holds her in a white room that's so small, so confined by reality that she can't process it. She's alone. *She's alone.* She failed them all. Val closes every door and sits in the dark in her head, because it's the only place that isn't terrifying. It's the only place that doesn't break her little heart.

# EIGHTEEN

Val opens her eyes. Tears stream down her face as she stares down at her scarred hands.

"I know their story now," she says. "All this time, I thought I'd done something unforgivable. That these scars were evidence of my guilt. But I got them trying to stay. I never wanted to leave any of you behind. I just wasn't strong enough to stop him from taking me away."

Jenny lets out a sob. "I'm sorry. I blamed you because I couldn't see what this place was. What it took from us."

"It's okay." Val opens her arms and Jenny hugs her. Marcus and Javi and Isaac join, re-forming their union, their combined breath a shield against the cold. "It's okay," she whispers, because, at last, it is.

None of this was Val's fault. Dad saved her, but he couldn't save them all. That was what he saw when he looked at her: not her own guilt and shame and badness, but his own regret.

She wishes he had talked to her. She wishes she had let herself keep her memories, let herself feel things. She had been so stubborn. But that was why she was here now. Why she was in that place to begin with. Her goddamn stubborn refusal to do anything she doesn't want to.

Val remembers what it felt like to be that determined and intractable. She's still that girl, despite the world's best efforts. Val pats Jenny and slowly disentangles herself from the group embrace. "Only I made this deal," she says. "The rest of you should go outside and wait for your kids. Try to talk some sense into the mayor, or at least buy me time."

Javi shakes his head. There's no trace of teasing on his face. He looks scared. "I didn't know what I was doing, but I made a deal, too. I'd sing the song if she let me watch the show."

"Same," Marcus whispers.

"But she didn't keep her end of the deal." Val gives them an encouraging smile. "You're off the hook. I'll figure it out from here. You go upstairs and—"

The interviewer giggles behind them. "How do you think Isaac's mother taped all that? Who do you think sent it to her television? I said they could see the show again, and they saw the show. A deal's a deal."

"They didn't know what they were agreeing to!" Val snaps.

"I knew when I agreed." Jenny's arms are wrapped around herself. She's almost doubled over, eyes on the floor. "I wanted it for my— No, I pretended I wanted it for my girls. But I wanted it for me. I knew it wasn't a show. And I still wanted to go back. *He's my dad.*" She says it like she's vomiting the information after holding it for so long. "The angel— The magic— The whatever—" She gestures noncommittally, but it looks like a cape floating in the air. "It needs children's energies, feeds off them, *fixes* them. Makes them better, happier."

"Bullshit," Javi says.

Jenny shakes her head, still looking down. "I'm telling you what they told me, what they taught me. What I've been given as truth since I could understand. They found it, out here in the desert, generations ago. A hum. It was a hum, and they followed it."

"So, not the AC," Val says dryly.

Jenny continues. "They followed the hum, and then they found the veil."

"The veil?" Marcus asks.

Jenny shrugs. "A hole, a tear in the world. Where the veil was thinner, where they could transcend to another plane. And it needed us to shape the hum. To become angels and use it. The first man who went in *became* the hum. Gave it meaning. He was our first pillar. Our first angel. And he called for the children. Suffer the children, so the children wouldn't suffer. They sent in their kids, and he used that power to shape them, to correct them, to teach them the rules. How to be happy, how to be good, how to *be*. The kids came out better than they went in, docile and obedient and perfect, exactly how their parents wanted them. They wanted to share this gift with the whole world, and that's what the hum wanted, too. When radio swept across the world it found those signals, and then television came along and it adapted once more, with our help."

"So your dad's . . . hundreds of years old?" Val asks.

"What? No. That's insane."

Javi raises an eyebrow. "As opposed to anything else about this?"

Jenny lets out a snort of a laugh, but then gets serious again. "After a while it breaks down the grown-ups who go in. Because they aren't pure." Jenny visibly fights against what she's been taught. "No. I don't know why it breaks them down. They need a specially chosen Mister Magic to hold the hum, to guide it so it teaches children, shapes them and whittles them into perfection instead of eating them up. Like the world would eat kids up if we didn't teach them the right ways." Jenny pauses for a moment, lost. "That's what they say. We're saving children. A child goes in first to get the space ready with their need, and then a new Mister Magic can follow them and take his place in the new circle. But only the kids ever make it back out. It's the holiest calling, a noble sacrifice, a—" She bites her lip. "It's not. I know that. I *know* that. They told me they picked my dad because he was so good. He was part of a circle when he was young. He learned all the lessons, always did what he was told, so he believed them when they said it was the best thing he could do for his kids. For me. For the world. A perfect example for us."

"Your dad," Marcus says in disbelief.

"He wasn't anymore, though. Not really." Jenny's arms go back around herself. "I wanted him to be my dad still. But even I knew it was better when Val stopped letting him be in charge."

Isaac's eyes are narrowed, but his gaze is unfocused. Like he's picked a point in the dark room and locked onto it. "What happens if there's no one to take on that role?"

"My guess is exactly what we saw." Javi gestures upward, where the television squats like a toad on the floor above them. "No holiest sacrifice, so when Val left, there was no one who could control the . . ." Javi trails off, unsure what he's describing.

"It gets so hungry," the interviewer says, yawning sleepily. They all stare at her in horror.

"Who are you?" Marcus asks, his voice gentle, like he's talking to a small child.

She shrugs irritably. "The men promised we could go to sleep if we helped them get you back inside. Hurry up. We're so tired."

"Fuck." Javi brushes his arms like he's trying to wipe away something clinging and foul. "That's really it. That's the other place. The show. Right there on the screen. We've been talking to it this whole time."

Val throws back her shoulders. If she can wrangle Stormy and stable parents alike, what's an alternate dimension of hungry darkness to her? "I could control it then. I'll control it now, fix it. No one else has to come."

Isaac steps between Val and the screen. "You're all here because I found you. Because *I* brought you. I'm so sorry, Val. I knew, too. I knew exactly what deal I was making. I remembered more than any of you. Not all of it, but enough to know it was never just a show. I still found you for them. They promised—" He lowers his head, his hair falling forward to hide his face. "This was how I got Charlotte back. This was how I kept my little girl safe. I traded all of you for that. Let me go in alone."

Isaac wilts into the smallest, saddest version of himself. The version the show wanted him to be. A boy who looked exactly where they told him to look, who did exactly what they told him to do, who made sure the other kids did, too.

He thought he was finding Val for these people, but Val had needed him to find her, too. Without him, she'd be on the ranch, living her tiny life with all the doors closed. Kitty would stay lost, both to the world and to Val.

Isaac wasn't so different from his childhood self. He was still looking out for all of them. Still feeling responsible. Still desperately trying to take care of the vulnerable in whatever way he could. They were *all* making the same mistakes they had as kids—confusing obedience for love, confusing arbitrary rules for actual goodness. Playing parts so they wouldn't be punished.

All the same mistakes, only now there were so many more consequences.

So, yes. Isaac lied to her. He helped get them all out here. But . . . she had asked to come. And he offered to drive her away from here. Multiple times. He would have done it, too. He never demanded she take the space he held for her; she slipped into it, because it was where she wanted to be.

*He's* where she wants to be.

Val hooks her pinkie finger through his. A child's promise, the only kind they could ever make to each other. The most powerful kind, though, made with their whole hearts. "I forgive you," Val says.

Isaac blinks, shocked. Val takes in his beloved face, then looks one by one at her friends. Her oldest friends, her only friends. The only other ones who could ever understand what shaped them, why they were the way they were.

"We were *all* lied to. We were all trapped, carved into the dullest versions of ourselves for other people's benefit. My dad tried to save me, but he ended up doing the exact same thing, just in a different prison. If the only way to get out of this, to save your kids, is to face what killed—"

Val stops. She whirls around. The interviewer is watching, blue eyes wide, expression impassive. The mayor said Kitty wasn't killed. Insisted no child *ever died* on the show.

"Is Kitty still in there?" Val asks.

The interviewer tugs on one brown curl. "Never left."

Her sister—her dream—is alive in there. "I'm going in," Val says. "Now." She still has that spark her mother couldn't stand. She's going to save her sister, and then let that spark build an inferno that will burn this place down.

"Fuck," Javi whispers. "*Fuck.*"

"I'm going with you," Marcus says. "We're the circle. We do this together."

"Together," Isaac and Jenny echo.

Val takes Isaac's hand. Jenny takes his other, then Marcus takes hers. He reaches for Javi's.

Javi has his hands in the air, then on his forehead, then back in the air. "You all realize this is insane, right? This is how we *die*."

They shrug in a line, hands rising and falling together. Javi laughs, a sound like a chick falling from a nest, then joins the line. "Fine. At least I'll go out doing what I love: being an absolute fuckwit making the worst possible choice."

"No," Val says, her voice solemn. "Being an absolute fuckwit making the worst possible choice *in the best possible company*."

Jenny bursts into giggles. Isaac shakes his head, but he's smiling again. He stares down at Val in wonder, no force capable of turning him to look another way. Val doesn't want to close herself off from any feeling, not ever again. She puts her free hand—her left hand, her hand that ripped magic and power away from an impossible place, that claimed it for her own and would claim this now, too—on his cheek. She goes onto her toes and presses her lips to his. It's a whisper of a kiss. A promise between children who found refuge in each other's hearts turned into adults who hope to do the same.

He kisses her back, and it's as sad and sweet and aching as the color indigo. Indigo like the day's light slipping into darkness. An ending of one thing. Perhaps a beginning of another.

"Indigo," he murmurs. They understand each other perfectly.

Javi grabs Marcus. "I've wanted to do this my whole life." Marcus lets out a surprised noise before enthusiastically returning the kiss, which is neither as short nor as simple as Val and Isaac's.

Jenny lets out an aggrieved sigh. "If no one is going to kiss me, can we please get a move on?"

Val obliges, spinning Jenny into her arms and kissing her the way she deserves to be kissed. Sometimes a kiss is a promise, and sometimes it's just fun. When Val lets her go, Jenny looks dizzy.

"Is that how it was always supposed to feel? Great. Now I'm even angrier at all the things I missed because of this stupid desert *cult*. I'm ready to break things."

Val links fingers with Isaac again, pulling him close. "Okay," she says. "We're doing this the way we should have ended it thirty years ago. Together."

"Together," the others repeat, everyone taking hands once more.

Marcus frowns. "Wait. We don't know how to get back in."

The interviewer huffs in annoyance behind them. "I've been trying to show you the whole time. I told you to practice. Take my hand, stand on your mark . . ." She holds out her hand. The others are still in a chain, linked, with Val in front.

They sing. And, with Val leading the song, they mean it. They mean it with everything they are, closing their eyes, imagining. Remembering. At last realizing how much of reality is simply belief. The skin on old pudding, Val thinks. That thin, that easy to break through.

Eyes still closed, Val reaches toward the screen. It's not there. It was never there. She was right the first time she saw it: This is a door.

A tiny, freezing hand takes her own, and then *pulls*.

*Dear Charlotte,*

*I'm hiding this in your favorite book, the copy of* Bunnicula *we used to read together. You probably don't remember, but I do. Maybe you'll find it if you ever go through my things. Maybe you won't. It feels absurd to leave it here and hope, but the world is an absurd place.*

*As a child,* everything *is absurd, made up of complex rules and systems that you don't understand, that you follow because you're told to by the grown-ups around you. You're given arbitrary rules that are arbitrarily enforced.*

*Maybe, like me, you're given a god who watches everything, who also has extra sets of rules, just to make sure things go according to plan in this life and the next.*

*Maybe you're given a parent who has no rules, who can't be bothered to care, who leaves you on your own to try to figure out how to navigate this lawless and nonsensical reality.*

*Maybe your god is a lot like that, too.*

*Maybe you cling to the rules as a way to keep yourself safe. And it works, until it doesn't.*

*Maybe you defy the rules as a way to push your own will outward onto the world. And it never works.*

*Either way, the rules defining this biting, lonely reality mold you, shape you, then break you. Tell you that you deserve to be broken, you're better off broken, you should be grateful to be broken. God or society or some twisted combination of the two is watching.*

*Someone is* always *watching.*

*I'm sorry for everything. I wish I had more to offer you than I do. I hope you can forgive me someday. All I've wanted is for you to be better than I ever could have been. And that's a terrible burden to place on a child, isn't it?*

*So: happiness. I wish you happiness, and joy, whatever shapes those take for you, wherever you can find them. And I wish you secret places in your head and your heart where you can feel safe. Unwatched, but always loved.*

*Love, always,*
*Dad*

# STAY SO CLEAN

Val's on firm ground, for the first time in forever. She remembers it now, the sensation of standing here. The cold pressing in all around, but not quite touching her.

It's a good feeling. A safe feeling.

How much she loved the possibility of this space rushes back in. It isn't black like nighttime or darkness, it's black like *blankness*. Like infinite options. A pure palette for the imagination, where they can project whatever they want onto the world.

*No*. That isn't true. They were never the only ones projecting. They were being projected onto. It's still happening. Val focuses through the darkness and finds the interviewer. She slinks backward, getting smaller, splitting, shadows rejoining the darkness until a single child is left. Kitty's face, now. Kitty entirely. So small, exactly like the last time any of them saw her.

"Kitty?" Val asks, tentative. If this is a trick, she doesn't have it in her to resist.

"I'm tired." Kitty sits and the darkness rises to meet her, blanketing her until only her face is visible. Her bottom lip sticks out in a pout. "It's not fair. You all left me."

"I didn't leave." Val takes a step toward her, but Kitty remains just out of reach. "I was taken. I never would have left you."

Isaac sinks to his knees. It's a perfect re-creation of his last pose on the tape. He's been dropped right back into his despair. "I'm so sorry. I tried to hold on."

Jenny moans, wrapping her arms around herself. "He's not here. I wanted him to be here."

"Shit. Shit!" Marcus spins in a circle. "The door's gone. The door's fucking gone!"

"Don't swear!" Javi's panicked. "It's against the rules, and if we don't follow the rules . . ."

"Then he comes." Val looks around, but there's nothing here besides them. That they can see, anyway.

Javi puts a hand on Marcus's shoulder, but Marcus jerks away as though burned. "Don't touch me! Not there. Not like that, while we're here." He puts his hands over his own shoulders, blocking them as he spins, searching the surrounding emptiness. "He's going to come, and he's going to make me go back to who I had to pretend to be." Marcus's face looks painfully young.

"I won't let anything happen to you." Javi stares out as though daring anything to come at him. But his posture betrays him—chin tucked tight against his chest, guarding it from a long finger tilting his head up and correcting him.

Jenny's pupils have dilated to match their surroundings. Her attention settles on Kitty and her eyebrows rise in surprise. Then she smiles as easily as she ever has. "Hi, Kitty. I missed you. What do you want to do?"

The darkness inks its way up Kitty's neck, swallowing her brown curls. "You're supposed to fix things. They said you'd come and fix it." She glares at Val.

Val still can't remember many details. She closed the doors too firmly for any of those memories to survive. But the *feelings*. Now that she's through that impossible door, all her feelings are back as though they never left. They couldn't leave, could they? She locked them away, and now here they are, perfectly preserved, waiting all this time. Just like Kitty.

Fear, hopelessness, exhaustion. And *also* joy, and wonder, and that easy, wild happiness that she hasn't experienced since. She focuses on Kitty's eyes, holds on to the blue of them as an anchor.

"How do we fix things?" Val asks. "We need to bring him back?"

"Say it," Kitty goads her, a child teasing another on the playground. "Say who. That was never a real rule, only *your* rule. Your rule so you could pretend like he wasn't real. You're the one who made him imaginary in here."

Val's throat constricts around the sounds. Her jaw clenches. This is the door she sealed firmest of all, the first door she closed. But if she's going to fix things, she'll have to face him. She'll have to make him real again by letting herself believe that it's possible.

She looks to her friends for confirmation that she's doing the right thing, but they're all lost to their own memories. They feel as far away and impossible to reach as Kitty.

"Mister Magic," Val says with a sigh.

The ground swings up and swallows them whole.

It's simultaneously living it and watching themselves live it. The way childhood memories get Frankensteined into something that never actually happened, but *feels* real. Val struggles to hold on to herself in the flood of memories threatening to pull her under. Because here he is, at last.

Mister Magic.

Summoned by their circle, there when they need him—whether they want him or not. Speaking in a language without words, without a tongue, his commands slithering through his touch into their very souls. The hum is here, too, but it's *him*. Constant. Everywhere, always.

He's not a character in their play; he's the backdrop. The canvas on which Marcus paints his wondrous stories, the games Javi makes, the toys Kitty asks for. His is the love, great and terrible, that everything within their children's kingdom runs on. He's everything, he's nothing.

But he's not benign.

Because even as they remake the world with their imaginations, he remakes them. Paints onto and over them. Whispers new ideas, plants seeds, shapes and directs and whittles them. Once he is summoned, certain actions and emotions tug him from the darkness like a creature snuffling to the surface in search of food. Mischief.

Defiance. Crying. Most of all, *need*. He's there when they need him. He's drawn to help them, designed for it. But he always decides what help they need, and how they should get it.

Watching, Val can see the type of father he must have been, because it's painfully similar to her own. Only engaging when he had to, and then always on his own terms. Demanding that his children take the shape he's already decided they should.

But he isn't only Jenny's dad, or even mostly Jenny's dad anymore. Mister Magic is older than that, bigger, constantly seeping out of the boundaries given to it.

That part is drawn to chaos, *ravenous* for it, devouring and leaving the children hollowed out and weak afterward. That's why Marcus paints structures, why Jenny leads them in carefully planned pretend, why Isaac watches over everyone, why Javi creates distractions, why Val calls him and then dismisses him with such care. Why they all look out for Kitty, who isn't old enough to understand the rules yet and sometimes invites chaos simply by being so young.

But this is all *during*. In the middle of their time here, one infinite blur of play and learning and friendship. Before Val takes control, before she stops letting Mister Magic out at all. It's not what she needs to see, and Val can't let herself get stuck here, watching, much as she wants to. She doesn't need a middle or even the ending.

She drags herself further, drags them all with her, like pressing REWIND on the VCR. She needs to see the beginning, where it started. And there—she finds it. The first circle. *Their* first circle, at least.

But it isn't what Val was expecting. She's ready for terrified, crying children. For confusion and pain as they adjust. But at the start, when they make the first circle and he appears in the middle, he's *exactly* what they want.

Mister Magic hugs Jenny in the dark so she never has to be alone with herself. Mister Magic takes Kitty's tears and tantrums and whispers them away. Mister Magic helps Isaac, replacing all his grief and trauma with responsibility, because children shouldn't be sad. Mister Magic feeds off Javi's energy, letting him know exactly how far he can push it before that finger will find his chin and correct him. Mister Magic lets Marcus create wonder and beauty, but is always there with a hand on his shoulder to teach him how to dim himself, so he doesn't make others uncomfortable.

And Val.

A little girl who doesn't understand why the world is the way it is, why everyone tries to tell her she can't want or feel the things she does. Why her mother never sees what she needs, only hates her for asking. Why, when she reaches out a hand and demands, she's met with pain and rejection. Here, when she reaches out and demands? Magic. And at such a small cost.

Val nearly loses herself in watching again, the past scratching an itch so deep inside her she didn't know it was there. But none of this is what Val needs to see now, because they're already in the circle. She needs to see their arrival.

Val pushes once more. Drags them to the beginning of the beginning, and watches.

Little Val, the stubborn one, the one who makes impossible demands, is sent through first. A child alone in the endless humming dark. She puts her hands over her ears, spinning, trying to find something to hold on to. Someone to help her.

The new Mister Magic follows, but as soon as she sees him, he's already being unmade. The darkness stitches him into something new. Little Val's seen the show. They made her watch before sending her in, so she knows what he's supposed to look like.

But something's wrong.

He's looming taller and taller, stretching and expanding into the space all around them. The hum is so loud she can't think, and his hands are reaching out toward her, the fingers extending into knives of darkness. Little Val wants to scream, or run, or sit down and cover her eyes.

But Kitty's coming next. She has to make it better for Kitty. It's up to her to keep Kitty safe.

Little Val closes her eyes. "*No,*" she says. They told her she had to decide what it was like in here, that she had to control it. It was up to her, since she went in first. So she refuses to be scared, refuses to hear the hum, to let it vibrate her right out of herself. She won't listen to it. No one can make her listen if she doesn't want to.

She puts out a hand and grabs the darkness, shakes it out like she's flinging wrinkles from a blanket. A cape. She'll make the darkness pooling around Mister Magic into a cape. A cape to contain him, a cape to define him, a cape to hide what's scary about him so Kitty won't see.

When she opens her eyes, Mister Magic is there, waiting. She gives him a top hat to complete the image. He bows to her with a flourish and holds out his hand.

They make a deal, in their own wordless way. She'll be in charge of demanding obedience from the hum behind the darkness, the power beneath Mister Magic's skin, the endless hunger around them. And, in exchange for his help, she'll throw open all the doors in her mind and let Mister Magic walk through at will. She'll let him use her.

Together, they'll shape their world. Little Val turns and waits for the others to arrive. Her excitement bleeds outward, replacing the dread and the cold with anticipation. And when the others come, the show is ready for them. It's easy. It's the easiest thing she's ever done, being here with her friends, being here with Kitty. Being where she's wanted. Where she belongs.

Val watches it all happen, and it's wonderful, now that the scary part is over. She could watch forever as they take hands, as they sing, as they play. They're so young and happy and safe. They're so safe. She's holding hands with Kitty again. Back together, at last. She has everything she needs. It's easy, watching. It feels so good.

Someone lets out a pleading whisper. But that doesn't make sense. Val made their world good. No one is sad, no one is—

This isn't them. It's who they *were*. Val's nearly subsumed by the wonder and impossibility of their childhoods. She knows exactly what that pleading whisper was for. Her friends want to stay here, too. Forget who they are, go back to who they were. Watch forever.

Val distances herself, lets herself *see* instead of just watching. Little Val is lit with fire and determination. She's a creature fueled by pure will, but that will isn't informed by experience, so it's easily manipulated. Little Val thinks she's creating the world for her sister and friends, but really, she's being used.

That's the big lie this entire place is built on. The lie that *experience,* that actual life, ruins children. But Val's grown up enough to see that the burden placed on them in here wasn't for their own good. It was to serve the sick purposes and ideals of the grown-ups safely outside.

The same ones still outside, armed and waiting. She'd almost forgotten. This place is a trap, a honeyed lie. Val doesn't blame any of the kids for believing it. They had to survive, after all. But Val refuses to lose herself again. She's seen how they got here now. How did the others leave, after she was pulled free, after they lost Kitty?

Val clings to her desperation, thinking of the guns. Thinking of the kids on their way here now. She rips them all free once more, drags them forward, blurring through their adventures, flinging them past where little Val stops bringing out Mister Magic, past where little Val takes over the magic herself to protect her friends. Forward and forward until they're slammed to a stop by the ending.

Isaac kneeling, Marcus walking backward, Javi and Jenny running, Kitty devoured. Val already gone. The others—besides Kitty—just sort of fade. Not swallowed by the magic, but rejected by it.

It doesn't give Val any solutions. Because they may have left this place, but this place didn't leave *them.* Not really. It lingered, a hum too low to hear, a fantasy of perfect childhood. A wound on their minds that no amount of time would heal, because they couldn't even see that it was injury, not idyll.

And she has no hope that this place will reject them again. She's exhausted fighting it just to get this small amount of control. "We have to—" Val starts, but something slithers over her feet. A part of the darkness coming alive, wrapping around her, and—

Everything snaps backward again, into the middle of a game.

"Sparkles!" Kitty cries out, holding open her arms.

"Sparkles isn't a color!" Jenny complains, but it doesn't stop sparkles from raining down around them, a glitterfall bursting on their tongues. It tastes like the delicious tension of opening a present, getting that first peek, and knowing it's exactly what you've always wanted.

"Chartreuse!" Javi yells, then grumbles in disappointment. "I thought it would be grosser." They laugh and play in the rain that tastes like living as wild things on a forest floor, looking for burrows, curling up in the moss.

That inspires a game. Marcus paints the trees around them, so tall their tops are lost to shadow. Everyone is in elaborate costumes. Kitty's a speckled fawn, Jenny a velvety rabbit, Javi a luxuriously tailed fox, Marcus a jay with flashing blue plumage, Isaac an owl perched on a branch, and Val a badger, patrolling their territory.

Only on the very edges can she even sense that hungry, humming, endless cold. It's so far away though, it doesn't matter. They're safe, and they're together, and they'll play in their forest until they find another game. And another, and another, and another.

The six of them, the circle of friends, happy and free. Val looks up at Isaac. He's watching her, glasses magnifying his eyes, so young. So perfect.

*No.*

Val kicks back against the thought, the way it slithers in as truth when she *knows* it isn't.

This version of him *isn't* perfect. None of them are. New isn't the same as perfect. Growing up isn't inherently loss, it's just change. Maybe she can't taste sparkles anymore, but she has a lifetime of moments that *feel* like that. The first buds of spring after another long winter. Hanging suspended above a lake, about to release the rope swing. Good sex. Watching a student the first time they triumph at a new task. A perfectly ripe, sun-warmed blackberry bursting on her tongue.

Linking fingers with someone who feels like home.

She doesn't want this incomplete memory of Isaac. She likes Isaac as he is now. All of him. He's sadder, older, has struggled through terrible things. Is still struggling. But that doesn't make him *less* than this unformed child in front of her.

Val wants the real Isaac. She needs to find him, the way he's always found her. She can't tell if her friends are with her anymore or not. If they're hidden by the darkness or if they've been lost to their own childhood selves, become them again.

The scene around her plays on, desperately trying to lure her back in. But she won't let this place swallow her with dreams of the past. It lied to her then, and it's lying to her now.

She reaches into the darkness, extending all the hope, all the want, all the *need* she's closed the doors on for the last thirty years. That's the difference between being a child and being herself. The humming can't lie to her anymore, can't distract or divert her. Val knows who she is, and no one and nothing can tell her otherwise.

"Give me my fucking friends back," she growls as she punches through the darkness.

# NINETEEN

The scene shatters, the ambient hum spiking into a wall of furious static buzz. The ground tilts. Val stumbles and the others appear around her, falling to their hands and knees. Kitty's there again. Maybe she was there the whole time. Her eyes are closed, only a circle of her face left.

Val takes a step toward her sister and the darkness plays its game, moving Kitty one more step away. "I can play, too," Val says. The darkness is a rug, the slippery one Gloria insisted on putting in the entry that Val had to move back into place every damn day. Val grabs ahold, pulling hand by hand to drag Kitty toward her. Sure enough, just like the rug, Kitty slides right to her.

Val embraces her, not caring about the freezing cold Kitty's cocooned in. At least she can see Kitty's face. She's always loved this face, even when she didn't remember why. Kitty is the piece of her heart she left behind but never got over. She's also the source of the dread and shame that kept Val trapped and afraid.

What happened here wasn't Val's fault. None of them were to blame. But that doesn't mean it isn't on her to fix it now. She doesn't trust anyone else to do it.

"Kitty," Val says. "Kitty-bug. Tell me how to get you out of here. Tell me how to fix it."

"*I* don't know," Kitty mumbles sleepily, opening her eyes into small glares. "No one tells me anything, and if they do, I don't remember. It's this place. The humming, and the darkness. They need to be controlled again. They can't be without *you*." She glares harder, with all the fervor she can pack into the expression.

Whatever this place is—a pocket universe, a sentient nightmare, fuck if Val knows—it hasn't stopped existing because they left. The hum was always here, Jenny said. They just figured out how to shape it.

Val sent Mister Magic away and then she never summoned him again. And when her dad pulled her free, she took the cape with her. The cape she made out of a piece of this place, to control it. It hasn't been controllable since.

"I think we're supposed to remake the circle," Val says.

"Yes," Jenny says quickly, at the same time Javi and Marcus say, "No."

Val turns to Isaac as tiebreaker. He's watching over his shoulder, absolutely defeated. Val follows his gaze.

Far away, like they're looking across a street and into someone else's bedroom window to pick out what's playing on their television, there's a small square of light. Framed in that light are several figures. One tall and gaunt and handsy.

"They're watching," Isaac says simply. "And they want us to know."

Val tries not to panic. "Damn it."

"Don't swear!" Javi says.

"Sorry. I need some time to figure this out." There's movement in her peripheral vision, a subtle seething of black on black. They're not ready. Val can't control it, which means she can't protect anyone from it. It could unstitch them, remake them like it did Jenny's dad. Or swallow them whole like it did with Kitty.

What if she fails her friends again? What if everything that made her special as a child has been leached out of her by her unremarkable life?

"I believe in you," Marcus says, his voice filled with conviction.

"You protected us all back then, when we didn't even know you were doing it. Let us help you now."

"We have to buy her time," Jenny says, wringing her hands. "Otherwise, they might send our kids in just to see what happens. And to punish us."

A smile slowly spreads across Javi's face. "We should do what we do best." He whispers in Marcus's ear. Marcus smiles, then whispers in Jenny's.

She rolls her eyes, dubious. Javi nudges her and she at last gives a begrudging shrug. "Do you think you can still do it?"

Marcus flexes his fingers. "It's all still here."

Jenny nods brusquely, all business now. "Isaac, you help Val."

Javi winks, then the three of them take a few steps back. "Let's summon a demon!" he declares.

Before Val and Isaac can ask what's going on, Marcus throws his hands up in a subtle gesture. No one who didn't know what he was capable of would even notice it. The air in front of Val and Isaac shimmers. And then, like they're viewing from behind a waterfall, they see versions of themselves walk forward and join the others in a circle.

"No," that imaginary Val says. "We need to figure it out first. Make sure we're doing everything right. We only have one chance."

"This is so trippy!" Javi draws the attention to himself so no one will notice that Marcus's imaginary Val and Isaac don't move quite right. "And stupid. I think it's mold."

"What?" Jenny asks, confused. Then Javi and Jenny get into an argument about whether or not they're having a group hallucination triggered by black mold in the house.

They're buying her time. Val's relieved *and* impressed. Her friends haven't forgotten who they were, but they're even better at it now. Javi is fucking with people who don't have his best interests at heart, Marcus is creating the reality those in power need to see in order to keep himself and his friends safe for the moment, and Jenny is supporting all of them—even though Val knows Jenny wants Mister Magic back.

Jenny really is a good friend when it comes down to it. The best friend.

"I still have the cape. Somewhere." Val looks down at her hands. "That was how we summoned him, how I controlled the magic. If I can get it out, then we can call Jenny's dad back. Bind him again. That should fix it, right? Stabilize things. And then I can take Kitty and—"

Kitty scowls. "It won't work, dummyrabbit."

"*Kitty,*" Val scolds.

Kitty's scowl turns to a penitent pout. "I just mean, he's gone. You took away his power and then broke the circle. He got all ate up."

"But you're still here."

"We last longer than grown-ups." Kitty tilts her head to the side. Crowding the edges of Val's vision are other little kids, or at least the *idea* of them. The ones that broke off of Kitty when the illusion of the interviewer went away. Val can't look right at them or they disappear.

"The kids they sent in, after." Val's heart breaks. They never even had the good times in here. Only terror.

"Other ones, too. Older ones. Say hi, Lemuel." Kitty's voice changes as a tiny, faraway whisper says, "*Hello.*" Kitty wrinkles her nose, then sneezes. Her voice is back to normal. "Sometimes kids couldn't get fixed enough to be good, so they let Mister Magic keep them forever."

Val wants to strangle someone. To punch them. To punch the whole world. But she takes a deep breath and tries to stay calm for Kitty's sake. "That's okay. We'll get them out, with you."

Kitty's eyes well with tears. "We can't leave. It gobbles up our futures. That's why we're still here, but Jenny's dad is gone. He chose this, so he didn't have much future to eat. But it snacks and snacks on us, and it hurts, and I hate it." Her brows descend in fury. "And it's *boring,*" she adds, the worst condemnation she can think of.

Val looks desperately at Isaac.

He links his pinkie with hers. "We'll get them out. I promise, no one will leave Kitty behind this time."

She nods, throat aching. Those monsters outside decided some children were an acceptable cost in their paternalistic fetishization of innocence, their singular definition of "good."

Fuck *good*. These children were *real*. They needed love and protection and nurturing, and everyone in their lives failed them.

The fake performance behind them is still going strong. Marcus holds the pretend versions of Val and Isaac in place while Javi and Jenny argue about the tune of the song. Javi keeps humming it in a minor key, while Jenny chastises him for goofing around and not taking this seriously enough. Either she actually wants to strangle him, or she's fully back in playing pretend mode. It's a virtuoso performance by all three, and Val's proud of her friends.

And terrified she won't be able to use this time they're buying her.

"Just get the cape out," Isaac says, reassuring. "Then we'll go from there."

"But what good will the cape even do us? We can't summon Mister Magic if he's not here anymore."

Kitty huffs. "You don't remember how to play. It's like tag. Pick a new man to be it."

"It?" Val asks, but realization closes in on her, making it hard to breathe, hard to think. The people of Bliss need a new Mister Magic. A new *noble sacrifice* to contain the power of this place. To shape it so the hum once more becomes a focused broadcast for all of their lessons. All of their teachings.

"Who?" she whispers.

"You already know," Kitty groans, annoyed. "It's obvious."

Isaac lets go of Val's hand. He takes off his glasses. Maybe to blur the edges so he doesn't have to see what's about to happen. But he still tilts his head down toward Val. Asking for permission.

She takes a step away from him. "No. No way. There's another option. There's got to be something."

"It was always supposed to be me." Isaac's voice is without fear, without anger. Only acceptance. "He was teaching me, even back then. How to watch out for everyone. How to see what they needed."

Val closes her eyes, but the blackness of this place is there, too. It's everywhere. She's standing on it, in it, breathing it in. She can even taste it now, and she wants to weep at how much she missed the taste of the color black.

The taste of home.

"Please," Isaac says. "It showed me what it would be like. Let me show you." He puts his glasses over Val's eyes. Magnified in the lenses, she sees a whole future crafted for them. A gift.

It's as simple as knowing exactly what she wants and asking for it.

Val reaches into herself and retrieves the cape. It isn't a real cape. It's never been a cape, just a piece of the magic of this place. This wondrous, miraculous place.

She kisses Isaac once more, and then she gathers the others. They can see what needs to happen, and so they help. They make their circle, they sing their song. Even though they aren't children anymore, even though they're faded and broken and diminished, it's enough. When they fasten the cape around Isaac's shoulders, they give the magic to him and give him to the magic. He smiles in relief and gratitude, and then he's gone.

And *he* is back.

Mister Magic tips his hat. It's still him, but with a difference. Now he has magnified eyes that reflect light, shining out of the darkness. Val clings to that, clings to the knowledge that Isaac—their Isaac, *her* Isaac—will be the one watching the kids. Guiding them. Teaching them.

Isaac brings the cape up with a flourish, then disappears. The circle of old, tired friends find a door waiting. This isn't a place for them anymore. They walk out, back into the basement, back into the house.

Val doesn't want to leave, not now that Isaac is here. Javi and Marcus and Jenny choose the same. It's a gentle, hopeful discussion, held among friends who remember how happy they were, in there, together. Charlotte belongs with her father, but they won't send her in alone. Their kids will only stay as long as they need to, as long as is good for them. And when they come out, everything will be better.

After all, Isaac's in there now. They fixed it. Their kids will be safe.

Jenny takes the lead, her two youngest entering hand in hand with Marcus's son. Then Javi's twins. Last is Isaac's little Charlotte. Val sends her in with a pinkie promise, knowing how Isaac's love will envelop her. It will nourish those children, guide and protect them, let them grow in a perfect environment. All the poison in Isaac's genes, all the trauma of Javi's family, all the damage of pretending in Marcus's, all the worry in Jenny's: Isaac will take care of it. That place, that magic, will protect the children.

And teach others, of course. Because the rules apply everywhere, to any child, in the circle or not. Every child deserves to spend time with Mister Magic, to learn important lessons. To see how to be good.

And so the old circle stays, stacked snugly one on top of the other. But they watch alone, sitting on the floor in front of their televisions, hungry to see the children thriving. Never sad. Never scared. Never wanting. A perfect childhood for perfect children who will grow into perfect adults, exactly the way their parents hope.

Val is at home, enveloped in the hum of happiness and peace. She puts her hand against the screen, smiling, waiting for that flash of Mister Magic's eyes, the one that lets her know Isaac is still there as he takes care of all the kids.

But—but it's *not* all of them. Someone's missing. She's forgotten about someone, again. Shame and dread bubble up from deep inside. Val promised. She promised, and she forgot.

Kitty.

Val leans closer to her screen. "*Where is Kitty?*"

There's a flash of lenses in the dark, like headlights on a midnight highway, looking right at her. Val yanks her hand back.

"No," she whispers. "No, this is a lie."

# TWENTY

Val takes off the glasses. She wipes them on her shirt, careful to get rid of the blackness coating them, the magic of this place showing them beautiful, toxic lies.

When she's certain that every bit of it is cleaned off, she puts the glasses back on Isaac. He blinks rapidly, as though waking up.

"Charlotte," he whispers.

"It's not better in here, Isaac. I know it feels like it could be, but it's not. It never was. We were *performing* childhood, not experiencing it. And the show was teaching other kids to perform it, too. In that future, the one this place wants, we're all still prisoners. You'd be molding Charlotte, instead of being her dad and nurturing whoever she actually is. And we'd all be trapped watching the kids, lying to ourselves that we'd done the right thing because it was easy."

Like Debra in her trailer, in front of the television. Claiming she was a good mom because she *watched*. She chose a system that promised to change her children to make her own life easier. She wanted dolls, not daughters.

Isaac twitches, shaking his head. "I was ten," he gasps. "I was ten years old and they let me think it was my fault Kitty was lost and you were taken away. They taught me I had to spend my entire life atoning for it. But they were always making me into the next Mister Magic. They were sacrificing me from the start. Just like Jenny's dad."

Val holds him. He leans his face into her shoulder, crying.

"You didn't fail anything. Your parents—our parents, this system, this cult—failed *us*. You'd never put this sort of blame on Charlotte, would you?"

"No. *God* no, she's a child."

"So were we. We didn't deserve the burden or the blame. None of us." Val at last releases the remnants of her shame.

"This place taught me to closet myself before I even knew what I was," Marcus says. Val looks up in surprise and alarm. Marcus, Javi, and Jenny have joined them. Marcus waves dismissively, pointing backward. The performance he painted is still going strong. "This part was Javi's idea."

The fake versions of all five of them are sitting in a circle, doing a rock-paper-scissors tournament to decide who will be the new Mister Magic. But fake Javi keeps cheating, so they have to start over.

"That's gotta be driving them insane to watch." Javi's smile is satisfied. But then he gets serious. "This place taught me I would only have value if I did what I was supposed to."

Jenny throws her arms wide to encompass the space around them. "I loved *everything* here! I've spent my whole life trying to get back a fraction of what I had then. I'm nothing—" She gasps, tears streaming down her face in agony. "I'm nothing without it. I've never been anything without it. Without all of you. I've tried so hard to replace it. But nothing in my life ever loves me as much as I love it. Not since we left."

Marcus and Javi wrap her up in a hug. "That's what they taught you," Marcus says. "That being alone is bad. That you aren't whole by yourself. You have to be what others need you to be."

Javi strokes Jenny's hair. "You've always been enough by yourself. No one has ever been as loyal and smart and funny and fierce and deeply, deeply annoying as you."

Jenny lets out a gasp of a laugh, trying her hardest to hit Javi, but he's holding her too close for it to have any impact. Her face falls and she squeezes her eyes shut. "I don't want this place anymore. I want to be a person. Whole. Happy with just myself. But how do we do that?"

"Therapy," Javi suggests.

Marcus suddenly has round glasses on, his goatee silver. He has a pad of paper and an elaborate feather quill in his hands, and when he speaks, it comes out in an exaggerated German accent. "In today's session, I'd like to revisit the period of your childhood that was controlled by a minor deity in a pocket universe."

"You're all so stupid," Jenny says through hysterical giggles. "That's not what I mean. I mean how do we do *this*? How do we get out? How do we keep our kids out?"

Val's seen the only way out. If they make a new Mister Magic, there will be no room for them in here anymore. It's a very small pocket universe, after all. Only space for one minor deity, and only hungry for children's futures. Val steps closer to Kitty, imagines the darkness around her sister like an orange peel. She begins gently taking it off.

"Maybe I can make us a way out?" Marcus lifts his hands. The darkness shimmers with doors of every kind imaginable. Big brass doors, secret garden doors, wardrobe doors, even a garage door. But they're all images. Pretend. The doors come faster, his panic showing, the edges bleeding and blending together. He's afraid now, and it affects everything. All his illusions melt away, including the pretend circle. Anyone watching can see them again. "No, no, I can do it," he says, sweat breaking out on his brow.

Javi puts a hand on Marcus's arm. "It's okay. None of us can do it, either. We never did get out on our own."

"That's not true," Jenny says. "At least not all the way true. Val used to find places to hide. Maybe you can find another one?"

Val curses herself for losing the details in her carefully locked-up mind. "I think I used to make burrows. Little spaces where I could rest. But I can't remember how I did it."

She looks at Isaac. At her friends. And then she realizes: The vision in Isaac's glasses already told her what to do. *It's as simple as, at last, knowing exactly what she wants and asking for it.*

Val reaches inside herself, searching. Not for Mister Magic, or a cape, but for *herself.* Asking for a future. Asking for a way out.

It isn't enough. She looks at Kitty, who wrinkles her nose and sticks out her tongue. Kitty's hands are free now, and Val reaches out and takes one. She holds on to her sister, and thinks of everything she locked away. Everything she refused to think about, or remember, or feel. Every want and need she denied because she was *supposed* to. Everything that was too big—too much bad *or* too much good—for her to let in.

Val stands in the center of everything she is, and she opens all the doors at once.

Behind this door, a mother who doesn't know how to deal with her. Always radiating irritation when Val's sad, or when she needs help, or when she's defiant. Next to her, a father who feels everything so strongly, he constantly has to retreat and disconnect. Look away and hope for the best because looking right at what is happening hurts too much.

Behind this door, Val standing at the top of the stairs in this unnatural house, terrified. Then feeling Kitty's hand in hers and knowing she can do it if she isn't alone. She can do it for Kitty, to keep Kitty safe at her side.

Behind this door, the happiness with her friends. Because she *was* happy, so happy. Most of the time.

Behind this door, Isaac, finding her in one of her hiding spaces. Curling up with her and letting her rest, safe knowing he was there. Isaac. Her Isaac.

Her little holes, her burrows, didn't have endings. She could have wriggled all the way through. She could have escaped. But it would have meant leaving behind Kitty, leaving her friends, and she wouldn't, couldn't do that.

Someone else does it for her.

Behind this door, the year of silence. Sitting, stunned, in a bright and grating world with so many demands. She has to eat. She has to pee. She has to sleep alone. All these things that feel useless and impossible, overseen by a father who watches her like she might disappear at any moment. He's both heroic for saving her and cowardly for putting her in another prison.

But she pities him, because he's so afraid. He's right to be afraid. She can still hear that low hum, still feel it, at the edge of her senses: something waiting for her to *ask*.

But she's also afraid, and she's guilty, and she's stubborn. She'll never ask for anything else again. She closes the door back to Mister Magic, back to everything that had come before. And she's true to her word. She never asks for anything, until that day with the open door when her dad at last left her behind, alone.

Maybe that was the opening this place needed to reach out and ensnare her. Maybe that was the beginning of the end. It doesn't matter now. All her doors are open, and Val only has one more to look through.

Behind this last one, blazing so bright it hurts, is *hope*. She loves all the people here, her oldest, truest friends, and she deserves a future with them. A future with Isaac. A life of knowing and being known, of raising his daughter, maybe even having a little girl of her own. It isn't too late, not yet. Not for that. But no matter how long she looks into that doorway, the little girl she imagines is only ever Kitty.

That final door blisters her skin, burns itself into her with everything she wants. She holds on to that desperate swelling ache. She has so much future ahead of her. An infinite expanse of it.

Val knows what she wants. What she's always wanted. And now she lets herself want it so fiercely and so powerfully that no petty rules in a shitty pocket universe can possibly stand in her way.

She opens her eyes, opens her hand, and opens a hole in the fabric between realities.

# DARKNESS PLENTY

Val takes Marcus by the hand. "I love you, and I'm so proud of you," she says, and flings him through first without explanation. There isn't much time. The darkness around them is getting more active, twitching and shuddering. The shadow children have scattered, hiding. Only Kitty remains, held in place by Val.

Javi kisses her cheek. "You came back for us after all, Valentina. I always knew you would."

"Really?" she asks.

"No," he says, laughing. "But I love being wrong. I'm really good at it." He follows Marcus through the tear.

Jenny's trembling, looking around as though considering staying. Val knows what—*who*—she's searching for.

"He's gone," Val says. "You've always been good enough. You can do this alone." Val holds on to the magic like only she can, and imbues her words with so much strength that they become a command. Jenny nods. She *can* do it alone. Val takes her hand and pushes her out.

"You're leaving me again," Kitty says. It breaks Val's heart, how Kitty doesn't sound upset, or even surprised. Just resigned and tired. More tired than any little girl should ever have to be.

"Never again," Val vows.

"Come on, Kitty." Isaac holds out his arms to her. "We're taking you with us."

But Kitty isn't really Kitty. Not anymore. And she hasn't been for so long. She sighs, the darkness pulsing around her. When she breathes in, all the other children coalesce, pale and shivering shadows with blank eyes.

"We'll be fine," Kitty says in the interviewer's voice. "Because they're still out there, listening. Waiting to watch again. We'll find new friends. We always do. We'll send out our lures, flashing and bright with hope, and we'll find a new Mister Magic. A better Mister Magic. And then—"

"Stop it." Val's voice cuts through the darkness. The lost children around Kitty tremble, their edges blurry.

Kitty scowls ferociously. But at least it's her again. For now. "It's not *my* fault. I can't help it. Someone has to hold the magic, shape the hum. Make deals with those boring people who want the show back. So the darkness uses me. And now I'll have to do it *again,* and once there's a new Mister Magic, I'll be gobbled the rest of the way up. I barely taste like anything anymore. It tells me all the time. It's rude." She tilts her head to the side, nodding as though listening. "I'll taste like the color black, and then I'll be nothing, forever."

Her eyes are no longer electric blue. They're bled of color, bled of life. "I'd rather taste like sparkles," she whispers.

The pathetic shadows flutter around Kitty. Val wonders who those children were, who they could have been. "I can't leave any of them," Val says, even though she knows they can't get out. This place devoured them, but it's also all that's sustaining them. Out there, they'd be ghosts. Memories. A flash of static and then nothing. Kitty's already almost destroyed, so little left of the girl they had known.

"Val," Isaac says. She holds up a hand to cut off whatever he's about to offer. Isaac worries about what he passed to Charlotte, but she knows who he is. Kind, compassionate, and generous to a fault.

They would be happy together. She can feel it just beyond her fingertips. Waiting to be asked for, waiting to be called into reality: her future.

*A future.*

Kitty doesn't have one anymore. There will always be this power, this place, and there will always be the people of Bliss, using it to remake children in their own image.

It isn't Val's fault. None of it is.

She puts a hand on Isaac's cheek and turns his face away from Kitty. Val presses her lips to his, reminding him of the joy and the desire and the companionship that they're allowed to want. Reminding herself, too.

She pulls back and looks into his beautiful eyes, forever magnified in her heart. His eyes that always saw her, and found her when no one else could.

"I would have loved you so well," she says, smiling. Then she pushes Isaac through her door and closes all the doors to this place so firmly that *no one* will ever be able to open them again.

She's good at that.

By the time the mayor realizes she "fixed" it but locked everyone else out, the others will be safely away, safe with their kids. Sometimes *safe* really is the best way parents can offer their children love. And it's the best way she can offer the same to her friends.

Val sits next to Kitty, pulling her close. She opens her arms and the other lost children crowd in, something a little brighter in their eyes, a little more solid in their movements. Infinite vessels of hope, like all kids.

"You stayed," Kitty says.

"I stayed." Val reaches into herself, certain at last of who she is and what she wants. She finds the pool of magic and possibility deep inside, where it's always been waiting for her to tug it free. Her future is infinite, just like her love for Kitty. She'll never burn through either.

*If you can't beat a small, petty god . . .*

*Become one.*

"It's magic time," Val says, and throws the cape over her own shoulders.

# EPILOGUE

It's springtime on the ranch. If you could taste colors, you would know spring green, tender and so bright it's nearly gold, tastes like spinning in circles on a tire swing, as a perfect breeze kisses your temples.

Spring green is a delicious color. A color the town of Bliss, bankrupt, with abandoned businesses and homes being reclaimed by the desert, can no longer afford to be. They never could have tasted it, anyway.

In fact, the only people who know what spring green tastes like are all here, inside the big house, gathered in the kitchen. Marcus and Javi are laughing, fingers entwined, telling Gloria how Javi's daughter was so mad no one at their marriage ceremony would be in a wedding dress that she insisted on wearing one. Marcus's son sneaks three cookies, one for himself and two for the new siblings he never asked for and wouldn't trade for anything, before hurrying back to the other room.

Isaac is worried about how picky Charlotte is, so Jenny's telling him about having lots of food available but not pressuring her to eat any of it. And then offering to send him a dozen recipes for sneakily working vegetables into things, just as soon as she's finished her term paper. She's thriving, even considering going past her bachelor's straight for a PhD. One of her daughters shouts from the other room that she's thirsty, and Jenny shouts back, *I'll bet there's something you can do to fix that.*

They're all learning, and it's a struggle, and it's beautiful. If this scene were a color, it would be the sky right along the horizon on a brilliantly sunny day, blue washed almost to white. None of them ever tasted that color, but they are now, even if they don't realize it. You can taste it, too, if you close your eyes and try. Go on. I believe in you.

Isaac slips out of the kitchen to the porch swing. He sits there for a while, remembering. Watching the road as though he might see her there, walking up with her long, confident strides, that thick braid swinging behind her back.

He knows he has to stop waiting for her, but he doesn't know how to.

Back inside, he stops at the entrance to the den. All the kids—a veritable riot of them, his, Jenny's, Marcus and Javi's, and even a few of Gloria's grandkids—are piled onto the couch. Some are sitting on the arms, some are sitting on each other. Charlotte perches on the back of the couch like it's a pony. She's braiding Jenny's youngest daughter's hair, but they're both distracted. Their eyes are glued to the screen like everyone else's.

*Mister Magic* is online now, accessible everywhere, to anyone, anytime. There are no ads, and episodes cut off neatly after twenty minutes with no autoplay. But there are infinite episodes, more than any child could ever watch, which is good because they watch and they watch.

The show is filled with worlds built by children so it seems absurd to adults, but that's because they've stopped being able to see the absurdity of the world they've built for themselves.

Children accept absurdity because *everything* is absurd, everything made up of complex rules and systems that they don't understand. Arbitrary rules that are arbitrarily enforced.

You know what that's like, if you let yourself remember. Maybe, in addition to regular rules, you were given a god who watched everything from an easy, safe distance. A god you poured love into, who gave you rules and condemnation in exchange. A magic man demanding perfect obedience and the performance of a life instead of the living of one.

Regardless of who gave them to you, the rules you had to navigate this biting, lonely, absurd reality changed you. Told you that you deserved to be broken, you should be grateful to be broken, and you should be ashamed of it, too.

Mister Magic doesn't think you're broken at all. You're just changed, and that's okay.

On today's episode, Kitty and her friends find a toy that doesn't work anymore. They're sad, because they loved that toy. But now they're finding new ways to use it, making something beautiful out of what's still there.

Isaac can't tell what it will be yet, but that's not really the point.

"Why is it called Mister Magic when she's a girl?" Charlotte frowns, popping her thumb in her mouth. Isaac's been patiently ignoring it, on the advice of the therapist they've been seeing since Javi helped him get custody.

You would be proud of him, if you knew how hard he was trying. It's not perfect, but it doesn't need to be.

"Girls can be anything they want," Marcus's son says.

"How do you know that's a girl?" One of Jenny's girls leans closer to the screen.

"Because Mister Magic has a long braid," Javi's daughter says, poking a finger at the screen where a swish of darkness down the cape implies the existence of a thick braid.

Isaac resists the impulse to pull her back, to drag them all away. But this isn't the show he was on, the rules and lessons that chipped away at him, the rules and lessons that might have infected you, too.

This new circle has so many friends who come and go as they please, all led by Kitty. Kitty has such wonderful adventures with them. There are no more rules, only silly songs they make up themselves. Mister Magic is always there, and always listens. When someone's sad, Mister Magic lets them be sad, and sits with them in their sadness. When someone's happy, Mister Magic lets them be happy, however loudly and brightly it comes out. When someone's shy, Mister Magic lets them engage however and whenever they want to. When someone's angry—usually Kitty, because Kitty has a lot of strong feelings now—Mister Magic lets her be angry, and helps her find ways to express why she's angry so she can understand it and not be overwhelmed by it.

Mister Magic doesn't talk, but somehow everyone watching understands the message: What matters to you matters to Mister Magic. The good feelings and the bad, because in that space, there's no distinction. No qualifiers. They're all just *feelings,* and they're yours, and Mister Magic loves everything that makes up the wonder that is you.

"Oh, is it that magic show again?" Gloria leans next to Isaac, arms folded as she watches the screen. "I don't know why they like it so much. They should have cast someone as handsome as that magician, at least."

"Their first choice was much less attractive," Isaac says with half a smile. His hand drifts over the back of Charlotte's head and he strokes her hair. She's so used to affection, so accustomed to being loved, she doesn't even notice. It's beautiful.

Gloria sighs wistfully, softening as she watches Mister Magic, some hint of recognition there. Then she shakes it off and turns back to the kitchen. "I'm glad you suggested this memorial. We all miss Val so much." She drifts away, not worried about what the kids are watching, not questioning what it is about this show that's so mesmerizing.

Isaac, too, is mesmerized, wanting to look away, unable to. He hates this show and he loves it, and he hopes— Well, he always *hopes*. He doesn't know what he's hoping for.

"Kids!" Jenny shouts from the kitchen. "The cookies are ready!"

"I'm eating them all!" Javi shouts. All the kids turn at once, outraged, their connection to the television briefly severed. And in that moment, Mister Magic turns and looks directly at the camera.

Directly at Isaac.

For the space of a single breath, there's a face where none has ever been seen. Isaac braces himself. He could always find her, and, at last, he's found her again.

But he doesn't find pleading terror, the desperate look of a prisoner. Instead I smile and wink. And then the moment is broken. The kids turn back to the screen as Mister Magic's cape swirls, unknowable once more, a thought and a feeling and an idea in place of a person.

Isaac lets his tears fall, nodding, at last able to stop looking. Because I'm still *his* Val. Your Val now, too, sending my own most powerful want into the magic that seeps into little minds watching everywhere:

Open the doors.

# ACKNOWLEDGMENTS

I'll save you the work of trying to decipher the Google results:

Yes, I was Mormon. No, I am not anymore.

There's a whole world of pain and trauma and anger and loss but also hope and strength and happiness and peace between those two sentences.

Fun fact: Brigham Young really did hate some of my great-great-etc.-whatevers, and sent them to Monticello, Utah, and Colonia Juárez, Mexico, to get them far away from his seat of power. But none of them found a mysterious, terrifying magic in the desert.

That I know of.

It's interesting coming from such a long line of belief ranging from quiet to fanatical, though. My ancestors traversed oceans, walked across countries, endured the abuse of polygamy, and accepted losing their families, all in the name of faith.

The choices of my childhood and young adulthood were informed by that same faith, and it's a strange place to be in—happy with my life and many of the results of those choices (hi, beloved spouse I married as a teen! hi, beloved children we had way too young but wouldn't trade for anything!), while also acknowledging the terrible swath of destruction cut by that religion, both through my internal landscape and through the wider world.

In the end, though, it was faith that let me walk away. Faith in myself, faith in my spouse, faith that we were doing what all parents should: making the best choices we could to protect our children while they grew into themselves. It's been a years-long process, dismantling the structure of toxic belief, and I suspect I'll be confronting and grappling with it for the rest of my life. And that's okay.

So, thank you to the friends who patiently waited for me and supported me at every stage. Thank you to my family who listened and loved. Thank you to my in-laws who have been so graceful and accepting of our decisions.

Thank you to my spouse, Noah, for walking every step of this path with me.

Thank you to my children, and also, you're welcome.

(Hey, you know what's awesome, though? Having actual weekends. Saturday *is* a special day when it's not spent running errands and cleaning and prepping so you can church all day on Sunday. And Sunday? Sunday is the *best*. So thanks, Saturdays and Sundays. Sorry I work on you so often. I have a lot of stories to tell.)

And thank you to everyone who reads this deeply personal book. I've talked about this stuff sideways for a long time, and it means more to me than you'll ever know to engage directly with it. (Though still fictionally, because that's what I do.)

Tremendous gratitude to the team who helped me figure out the story and get it to you. My stalwart agent, Michelle Wolfson. My brilliant editor, Tricia Narwani, and her assistant, Bree Gary. My publisher, Del Rey, with special shout-outs to my publicist, David Moench, and the publisher, Scott Shannon. Craig Adams, thank you for patiently dealing with my fundamental misunderstanding of when to use hyphens. You will never be out of a job.

Special thanks to Stephanie Perkins, the first non-Mormon friend I ever had, who not only helped me see how much hope and light and goodness existed outside the narrow confines I'd been given, but *also* helped me fix this book (and every other book of mine anyone has ever read). I'm so glad you're in my life, Steph. And to Natalie Whipple, whose responses to my earth-shattering texts are usually, "That sounds right. Good for you." I'm glad I have you, and I'm glad your family has you, too. And huge thanks to Eliza Brazier, who saved me from starting another panicked rewrite when I was afraid I could never get this story right. I'm so glad you're legally obligated to be my friend and sister.

It took me too long to settle on the song for this book. Depeche Mode, Silversun Pickups, Joywave, and Foxing helped along the way, but Crows and their song "Healing" delivered the actual perfect soundtrack.

Regarding my dedication, to those who have looked at me and asked, and to those who may look at me and wonder: Yes, it's hard to leave. Yes, it will unmoor you and break your heart and reorder the entire world around you. And yes, it's worth it.

And finally, to those in any religion or community telling you that who you are will never be good / will never be pure / will never be enough in the eyes of the god they made in their own petty, bigoted images: Fuck that. The new Mister Magic believes in you, and so do I.

## ABOUT THE AUTHOR

Kiersten White is the #1 *New York Times* bestselling, Bram Stoker Award–winning, and critically acclaimed author of many books, including *The Dark Descent of Elizabeth Frankenstein,* the And I Darken trilogy, the Slayer series, the Camelot Rising trilogy, and her adult debut, *Hide.* White lives with her family in San Diego, where they obsessively care for their deeply ambivalent tortoise, Kimberly.

kierstenwhite.com
Twitter: @kierstenwhite
Instagram: @authorkierstenwhite